MORGAN

Rebirth of the
HUMAN RACE
BOOK 1

CONRAD A. FJETLAND

ISBN 978-1-64471-492-8 (Paperback)
ISBN 978-1-64471-493-5 (Hardcover)
ISBN 978-1-64471-494-2 (Digital)

Covenant Books, Inc.
11661 Hwy 707
Murrells Inlet, SC 29576
www.covenantbooks.com

For my wife Judy for her continuous faith and support

PREFACE

In 1975 I was participating in a Department of Interior training program in Washington, DC that included a section on creative writing. I had recently read Poul Anderson's classic novel *Tau Zero* and always liked hard-science fiction. Doing some research in the Interior Library, I stumbled on a little report from 1964 by Stephen Doyle titled *Habitable Planets for Man*. These two books gave me the inspiration for this book and those that will follow in the series. The first pages herein and the calculations used throughout this series were completed for that writing assignment. I carried those handwritten pages and notes around for years as my family and career moved through life. While I always wanted to turn that little exercise into a realistic, near-future science fiction novel with a moral basis, life's challenges kept it on the back burner. Finally, after my third retirement in 2013, I began to seriously write this series. I have tried to be as accurate as possible with the scientific calculations, environmental issues, and genetic information contained herein. Any errors or misinformation are solely my responsibility.

Of course, a lot of help from many people went into the writing of this book. First and foremost is my wife of over fifty years, Judy. I have always had her full support as this work developed. She has edited numerous drafts, helped me with character development, and talked me through sections of dialogue. She never doubted that I would complete what I had started. But most important is Judy's faith and understanding of the Bible.

Over the course of our marriage, Judy has led me to a closer walk with the Lord and the principles I have tried to emphasize in this book.

Next, I want to thank my three children, Kristin, Conrad, and Laura. Laura and Kristin, both teachers, have also read numerous drafts and provided important content and editorial feedback. Conrad provided helpful information concerning genetics and biochemistry. They have also provided the encouragement and help I needed when things were going slow. Several other people, too many to mention by name, have read early portions of this series and provided valuable feedback as the final version emerged.

Finally, I want to thank those who brought this work from a manuscript to a published novel. An agent Jim Hart, although he couldn't take on the project because of other commitments, provided valuable guidance in how to improve an earlier draft. Kolleen Taylor, my cousin and a librarian in Iowa, provided valuable insight in how to make the book more readable for its intended audience. Finally, all the folks at Covenant Books who agreed to make this project a reality.

I hope all who read this will enjoy it as much as I did in writing it. Thank you for reading my fictional story of a possible future.

CHAPTER 1

It is not often that a species of life plummets to the very brink of extinction only to rise and flourish once again, but then the species known as man is no ordinary species. I am old now, and my duties, which I once thought were indispensable, have been assumed by others. And so I find that I have the time to reflect on the events that have given man his second chance.

Where does one begin the story of the rebirth of the human race? The reporting of history, unfortunately, does not lend itself to neat packages with convenient beginnings and endings. Any historical record must begin by breaking into a sequential course of events at some point and end without ever having a final chapter. This story could logically begin when the first primitive ancestor of man began to reason. The birth of Christ is another possible starting point as that event clearly forms a historical break in the history of the human race. The decade of the 1960s when man first physically left the planet Earth could also serve as the beginning of this work because the events that happened then set the stage for man's second chance, although nobody knew it at the time. Other events that ultimately became major factors in man's second chance (and in man's reasons for needing a second chance) include the Great Famine of the twenty-first century, the development and use of nuclear weapons by terrorists, and the development of the Perry-Warner interstellar drive in 2051. All of these events are important, but they all have been reported by authors from the past.

Rather than duplicate the work of previous authors, I have decided to begin this record with an event that no historian could possibly have known had any of them still existed. The event was a decision, and the decision was made more than ten light-years away from Earth near the star Epsilon Eridani. No one knows what would have happened to man if that decision had been made differently. Indeed, there might very well be no humans left alive today to tell this story and thus no story to tell. Of course, while we knew that the possible outcomes associated with the choices facing us in that decision were critical to us, as with most decisions we had no idea of the real importance of what we were deciding. For what was at stake was not the lives of the people aboard the starship *Mayflower*; it was the continued survival of the human race itself. Before I get further ahead of myself, let's go back to that beginning.

At the time, we were orbiting Ararat, our name for the second planet of Epsilon Eridani. We had been there for over a year studying the planet's physical characteristics, geology, climate, and biology. Our purpose was simple—could Ararat support human life on a permanent basis without external support? If it could, we intended to colonize the planet. Ararat would replace the *Mayflower* as our permanent home. If it could not, we intended to move on in accordance with our long-range flight plan.

Our first impression of Ararat while we were still decelerating into the Epsilon Eridani system was positive. The planet was quite similar to Earth in both positional and intrinsic properties. However, as we neared orbit around Ararat, differences in the planet became apparent, particularly the amount of surface water available. Thus, we embarked on our study to determine if we could modify Ararat's ecosystems to fulfill the requirements of human life.

Morgan Parker paused.

All that remained was to give the command to Purple to complete the analysis. Yet Morgan paused. This was one of those questions he didn't want answered, but in his heart, he already knew the answer. In one last attempt to avoid the inevitable, he asked the computer, "Purple, is there any other information we can give you or that you need that could possibly modify your answer to the question I am about to pose regarding the suitability of Ararat for human habitation?"

"No," replied the computer. "Based on the charter of the *Mayflower* and the data and studies you and the other crew members have provided to me, I am prepared to respond to the question you are about to ask."

Laura, strapped into her workstation next to Morgan's, looked at Morgan and asked, "You already know the answer, don't you?"

"I do," replied Morgan. "Call it a gut feeling if you will. I've been studying human environmental requirements for over twenty years, including the last twelve years we have been on this ship, and I don't need all these sophisticated calculations to tell me what's obvious. We simply cannot make Ararat support our people with the technology we have on this ship. And we can't depend on support ships and supplies arriving from Earth to supplement what we have. As chief ecologist in charge of *Mayflower*'s habitat evaluation team, I should have let my feelings be known a long time ago when we first entered orbit."

"If you had, you probably would have been charged with heresy," said Laura. "The crew wants to get their feet back on solid ground. When Nels first announced that Epsilon Eridani had a planet much like Earth, the crew's spirits rose to a level not seen since we departed on this odyssey. No one was in the mood for a bucket of cold water at that time."

Morgan looked at Laura. Barely a teenager when the *Mayflower* had left Earth, Laura Simmons had developed into an attractive young woman of twenty-five. Unlike many of the crew on the *Mayflower*, Laura worked out every day in the ship's gym to keep trim and fit even when in zero gravity. Laura also took advantage of the ship's tanning facilities to keep her skin tone from becoming pallid. She had selected human-habitat evaluation as her specialty early into the journey. Studying continuously, she quickly developed into an expert in the field. Although technically she served as Morgan's assistant, they worked as partners on the Ararat evaluation.

"Do you think I'm wrong, Laura?"

"As much as I want to call Ararat home, no, I don't think you're wrong. I think about all the pioneers of the old American west and how they carved a country out of the wilderness. My wishful thinking is that we can do the same thing here. But those pioneers were starting with an environment in which humans had evolved. All the components for existence were already there. All they had to do was rearrange the components. The situation is different here. Too many of the things we need are missing, and I don't see any way we can modify the planet enough to suit our requirements. It's been my opinion for a long time that Ararat just won't do the trick for us."

"Well," sighed Morgan. "Let's get the suspense over with and make it official."

Before he could formulate his question to the computer, Ben stuck his head into the compartment. "Hey, Dad," he said, "how is the Ararat study going?"

"We're just about done, Ben. What are you up to?"

"Just finished a dodgeball game in the gym. I got whacked just before I was going to take out Anne. But I'll get her next time. I'm off to the galley for a snack before my math class. See you later," he said as he drifted back out of the compartment and disappeared down the companionway.

"He's sure growing up fast, isn't he?" observed Laura.

"That's right. I think he has a crush on Anne. Wanting to *take her out* is how fifteen-year-old boys think. At least that's how I remember it."

Morgan turned his attention back to the computer. "Purple, based on the data and information you have, will Ararat support human life on a permanent basis?"

Morgan was surprised when the computer didn't immediately respond. He had become used to the instant calculating capabilities of the *Mayflower*'s main computer. But the computer was silent for over ten seconds, a short time in human terms but an eternity in the nanosecond world of computers.

Finally, Purple spoke, "Morgan, based on the information you have given me and the data the ship's sensors have collected, the statistical probability that Ararat will support human life without external support is near zero."

"Purple, you said *near zero*. What is the statistical probability that Ararat will support the crew of the *Mayflower*?" asked Morgan.

After another brief pause, the computer responded, "The probability that Ararat will support the crew of the *Mayflower* without external support is zero, and you have not provided me with any information that would indicate such support would ever be available."

Morgan was puzzled by this answer. The computer was not known for responses that did not directly address the questions posed to it. "Purple, you said Ararat would not support the crew of the *Mayflower*. Will it support some smaller contingent of humans?"

Again, the computer hesitated for more than two seconds. "That is why I took so long to respond to your first questions. In the past, you have always presented this question in relation to the crew of the *Mayflower*. But the first calculation you asked for today was 'Will Ararat support human life on a permanent basis?' As a result, I examined a variety of scenarios for populations smaller than that aboard the *Mayflower*. Based on this analysis, I found that there is a small chance a limited group could survive for an extended period of time."

"Purple, give me the details on this smaller group," Morgan asked.

"A small group of up to forty humans can survive for an extended period in the base camp established on Ararat. However, the oxygen deficiencies in Ararat's atmosphere would likely prevent most members of this group from expanding beyond the supplemental atmospheric conditions of the base camp for a long time. Without external support, there is more than a 95 percent probability that this group would die out before they could adapt to the environment existing on Ararat."

Morgan leaned back in his Velcro chair and thought about the exchange he had just had with the computer. Now he knew why the computer had hesitated before giving him his first response. While there was a small possibility that Ararat could support *some* human life, the planet could not support the entire crew of the *Mayflower*. Further, there was nothing in the *Mayflower*'s charter that contemplated splitting the crew into more than one colony or establishing outposts. Morgan was upset that he had not phrased his question more precisely. Purple had taken his slip of the tongue literally, and now he had some information he would rather not have.

Morgan looked at Laura who had unstrapped form her chair and was floating quietly a few feet away. "What do you think of that?" he asked.

"I don't see where it makes any difference," she responded. "Ararat will not support us, so it's time to move on to our next destination, Tau Ceti."

"You're probably right," Morgan mumbled but without a great deal of confidence. Morgan activated his personal communicator and hailed the captain.

Captain Howard Larson responded immediately, "I expected to hear from you this morning, Morgan. What's the verdict?"

"Not good," replied Morgan. "The computer's analysis indicates—"

"Spare the details, Morgan. Come up to the operations-center conference room. I will assemble the other division chiefs. We need to discuss our future."

"That's strange," argued Laura. "What is there to discuss about our future? We all know that if Epsilon Eridani is not suitable, we will set course for Tau Ceti. That has been our plan ever since we left Earth twelve years ago. In fact, it's been part of the fundamental mission goal since this pilgrimage was conceived more than thirty years ago."

Morgan looked at Laura, noting how upset she was becoming as she spoke. "I don't know. But I'd better get up to the conference room and find out." With that, Morgan detached from his workstation and pushed his 180-pound frame toward the ecology center's doorway.

"I'll stop back and let you know what the captain was referring to," he said over his shoulder as he exited the ecology center.

As Morgan drifted toward *Mayflower*'s central companionway, he pondered Laura's concern about Captain Larson's statement. All the captain wanted to do, he thought, was discuss the logistics of getting the *Mayflower* under way again. There were a lot of preparations to be made before the ship accelerated out of the Epsilon Eridani system. When they had departed Alpha Centauri, most of the crew was in good shape physically. However, when the ship began deceleration into the Epsilon Eridani system after the long period of weightlessness, several crew members had been injured. Even though the weightless time around Ararat had been much shorter, it made sense that the captain would want to discuss the departure with each division head before they got under way. Morgan was convinced this was the purpose of the meeting as he entered the conference room.

John Malcolm, the ship's communications officer, and Sandra Sanchez, the chief medical officer, were already seated at the table. Planetologist Nels Brunken was also there, drifting to his chair at the far end of the room. Judy Polachek, the ship's agronomist, was right behind Morgan, followed by Randy Edwards, chief engineer.

Morgan was fastening himself into his seat as Captain Larson entered the room. Morgan noticed that the captain's demeanor was reserved. He said nothing as he took his place at the head of the conference table.

Sandra said to the captain, "You are looking tired, Captain. I would like you to come to my office for a scan. You are past fifty years old, and it's time for a checkup anyway."

"Actually, I'm fifty-one," he murmured. "But there's nothing wrong with me that you need to worry about."

"I don't agree," answered Sandra. "But it's your choice." Sandra knew the captain had previously been in excellent physical condition. During the weightless periods of flight to Alpha Centauri and Epsilon Eridani, he had rigorously worked out to maintain his muscle tone and weight. He resumed his daily workouts when we went into orbit around Ararat. But he stopped about six months ago as concerns about the suitability of Ararat mounted. Now he looked pale and run-down.

A few seconds behind the captain, Sarah Parker, the chief of the Nutrition Department, pushed herself into the room. Sarah glanced at her husband, Morgan, and immediately knew the Ararat results. The look of concern on Morgan's face was unmistakable. There was bad news written all over it.

About thirty seconds later, Graysun Williams, the ship's systems officer, arrived. When Graysun completed attaching the fasteners at his position, only one spot remained vacant, that of Melissa Grant, the head of the education and morale functions on *Mayflower*. Captain Larson sat quietly, saying nothing while he waited for Melissa. No one else felt the need to break the silence.

About ten minutes later, Melissa arrived and quickly pushed herself into her seat. "My apologies, Captain. I was gathering the figures you asked for."

Captain Larson nodded but did not respond directly as Melissa took her position at the table. "I called this meeting," he started, "because Morgan and Purple have completed their analysis of Ararat. Morgan, if you please, we would like to hear your report. Take the time to summarize the problems we have with Ararat and what your conclusions are."

Morgan briefly mulled over how best to say what he needed to before he announced the computer's final analysis. "As you all know, we have been studying Ararat ever since we entered orbit here nearly a year ago. I need not go into all the differences between Ararat and our home planet. Suffice it to say, it all boiled down to whether we could bring the oxygen content of Ararat's atmosphere up to levels where our population could grow and flourish. Ararat's atmosphere is technically breathable, but the partial pressure of the oxygen content is so low that any attempt to do work without supplemental breathing equipment would bring on immediate symptoms of hypoxia. Most of us could not adapt to these conditions. So we looked at a wide range of possibilities to increase the content of oxygen in the atmosphere. Nels, would you please comment on your investigations in the geological area?"

Nels, usually quiet at these meetings, gave Morgan an icy look before slowly saying, "I'm not sure why it's necessary to repeat what you already know, but since I have been asked, here goes. I examined the possibility of increasing volcanic activity to release trapped gases such as water vapor, carbon dioxide, and sulfur dioxide, all of which obviously contain oxygen. Unfortunately, the planners of this mission didn't anticipate our need to activate volcanoes. They didn't include the tools or weapons, if you prefer, in our supplies. The core of Ararat is too stable for us to stimulate volcanic activity with what we have. I also looked at reduction of metallic oxides to release oxygen, but we don't have the equipment with us to do that either on a scale that would make any difference. I think the time has come to abandon this planet and move on to Tau Ceti."

"Not now, Nels," said Captain Larson. "We will be discussing our future plans in a few minutes. Morgan, please continue."

"Judy, you investigated whether we could establish a large-scale irrigation project and use plants to convert the high levels of carbon dioxide in Ararat's atmosphere to oxygen and stored carbon. Will this work?"

"Technically, yes, but not to the level we need," she responded. "We have farming equipment including several miles of irrigation pipe in our lockers but not near enough for the size of project that would significantly change the makeup of the planet's air."

"Sandra, you studied the adaptability of the human body to the atmospheric conditions now existing on Ararat. Is that a possibility?"

"For some, yes," answered Sandra. "As you said, the air is technically breathable, and some could adapt to those conditions similar to very high altitudes on Earth. But they would be the exception, not the norm. I agree with your statement that many of our crew would succumb without assisted breathing. In the long run, I believe future generations could adapt, but we don't have the luxury of time to go through that evolutionary process. From a respiratory standpoint, Ararat is not currently suitable for the bulk of our population."

"Thanks, Sandra," continued Morgan. "All of this information and much more that we collected has been fed into our main computer. I asked Purple if there was any other information we could gather that might modify its analysis, but Purple said no." Morgan paused before he went on, choosing his words carefully. "The computer provided the following analysis of our studies—the probability that Ararat will support the crew of the *Mayflower* without external support is zero, and you have not provided me with any data that would indicate such support would ever be available."

Morgan looked around the table, noting that nobody seemed surprised by the results. After a short pause, Captain Larson asked, "Does anyone have any questions or comments?"

Judy Polachek asked, "What would the probability be if we received some support from Earth?"

"We have not heard from Earth since before the Perry-Warner drive was started for deceleration into the Alpha Centauri system more than nine years ago," John Malcolm responded. "I don't know why, but the base camp is no longer sending us any data or information. I still send monthly status reports in the hopes that someone is listening, but I really don't expect to hear from Earth again."

The captain said, "The last message we received from Brad Johnson at the base camp was very bleak. With us gone, his financial support dried up. He indicated that there was a lot of unrest in the area and didn't know how much longer he would be able to operate the communications station. The base camp may very well no longer exist. I think it is fair to say that we are completely on our own. We can't depend on Earth for anything. I directed Morgan to conduct all evaluations under the assumption that there would be no outside support from Earth."

"Well then, Captain," Nels blurted, "can I now say that it's time to quit hanging around this star and get under way to Tau Ceti? That is what our charter says we should do."

"It's not that simple, Nels. Randy, will you please share the results of your analysis of the *Mayflower's* integrity?"

Randy looked uncomfortably at the captain. He had briefed Captain Larson two weeks ago on his concerns. Captain Larson had asked him to hold off on saying anything to anybody else until the analysis of Ararat was completed. Clearly, now was the time to speak up. "I have been reviewing the *Mayflower's* overall fitness for farther travel while the Ararat studies were being completed," he began. "The Perry-Warner drive system is in good shape and should cover many more journeys. Judy and Graysun have informed me that the food production and life-support systems are stable. However, I have found some problems with the ship's hull."

"What kind of problems?" asked Graysun.

"My measurements of the *Mayflower's* hull indicated that hull erosion is greater than anticipated. The cosmic dust we encountered while traveling to Alpha Centauri and then to Epsilon Eridani has resulted in a 35 percent decline in hull strength in the most exposed sections of the hull. I now calculate an additional 10 to 15 percent erosion during the four-and-a-half-year journey to reached Tau Ceti. I also calculated that at the current rate of erosion, we can travel a total of about nine years under the Perry-Warner drive before the most sensitive sections of the hull reach critical stage. Obviously, if we have a hull failure, all will be lost."

Randy paused before continuing. "The bottom line is if we do not find a habitable planet at Tau Ceti, it would not be safe to try and go anywhere else. Since Nels predicts the statistical probability of finding a habitable planet orbiting Tau Ceti at less than 10 percent, our future looks grim."

Several tried to speak, but before anyone got the floor, Captain Larson held up his hand. "There is more. Melissa, please share your findings."

Melissa cleared her throat and said, "I told the captain a few weeks ago that I was concerned about the morale of the crew. I was seeing a decline in morale as the studies of Epsilon Eridani and Ararat looked increasingly discouraging. Captain Larson asked me to determine whether the situation would get worse if we had to leave here and head for Tau Ceti. After interviewing numerous members of the crew and in particular the younger members, I have concluded that there will be some severe psychological problems by the time we get to Tau Ceti, and the situation will become intolerable if we don't find a habitable planet there. Simply put, the euphoria we all felt when we left Earth has long since disappeared, and the brief lift we received when we first saw Ararat is now working against us."

Captain Larson looked to Dr. Sanchez. "Sandra, do you agree?"

"I do," she responded. "I have seen a number of patients whose problems can be traced to underlying depression. In at least four cases, my conclusion is that depression directly contributed to death. I don't think we, as a group, can take many more disappointments."

There was silence around the table. Finally, Nels said, "What difference does all this make? We can't stay here. We need to get under way for Tau Ceti. While the odds there aren't that great, they aren't zero either. Unlike Epsilon Eridani's K spectral class, Tau Ceti is a class-G star similar to the sun. Evidence is that there are several planets around Tau Ceti, and one of them is probably within the zone of habitability. We need to investigate this planet and see whether it will provide a home for us. We all agreed when we left Earth that this was a risky undertaking. If we don't find a habitable planet at Tau Ceti, we'll address these ship and crew concerns at that time."

Nels's statement was true to his character. He was born an adventurer and explorer. On Earth, Nels was frustrated because there were not any places left to explore. He took up the study of planetology where he excelled and begged his way onto the crew of the *Mayflower*. The journey for Nels is as important, if not more important, than the destination. Five years before the *Mayflower* departed Earth, Nels and his wife, Ida, sailed around the world nonstop. Emblematic of his pioneer spirit, they accomplished this feat in an old single-hulled engineless sloop. Nels had told Morgan years ago that the trip was a rush and his arrival back at his port of departure was a tremendous letdown. Prior to marrying Ida, Nels had also accomplished the Seven Summits challenge, climbing the tallest mountains of the seven continents on Earth and doing all of them except Mount Everest without supplemental breathing equipment. Nels maintained himself in excellent physical condition, always ready for the next challenge.

Graysun joined Nels, interjecting brashly. "Forget the odds. We need to keep going. We have no other choice." Graysun frequently acted impulsively, probably a remnant of his upbringing as a smart kid in a tough neighborhood. His nature was to forge forward no matter the obstacles in front of him.

There was a general murmur of agreement around the table. Then captain waived everyone to silence. "There is another choice," he said. "We can return to Earth."

For a moment, there was a stunned silence in the room. Then everyone tried to speak at once. Captain Larson held up his hand in an attempt to restore order. Finally, he shouted, "Silence." In all the time he had been commander of the *Mayflower*, he had never had to raise his voice to maintain order. The captain's unusual command quickly regained control.

Once everyone was quiet again, he continued. "Thank you. Now I know what I just said was a shock to most of you. But this is a matter I have been considering for some time. I was concerned that the Ararat results would be as Morgan announced today. That is why I asked Randy to examine the status of the ship and Melissa to evaluate the morale of the crew if we had to leave Epsilon Eridani and Ararat. When Randy told me the results of his study, I had to carefully consider the implications of any decision to move on. With the information provided by Nels about the likelihood of finding a suitable planet at Tau Ceti and the concerns about the crew expressed by Melissa and Sandra, I was faced with a choice between the lesser of two evils. Either we proceed to Tau Ceti and have a greater than 90 percent probability of failure and loss of the entire crew, or we return to Earth in defeat. There is one additional piece of information I need before I make my final decision. I asked Melissa earlier today to evaluate what would happen to the morale of the crew if I made the decision to return to Earth. That is why she was a few minutes late to this meeting. Melissa?"

"Yes, Captain, I was somewhat hampered in this evaluation because I couldn't directly broach the subject," Melissa responded. "But I was able to get a reasonable feeling as to how the crew would react to such a decision. The reaction breaks down into three distinct groups. The first group is those members of the crew, about three hundred including all of us, that were adults when we embarked on this journey twelve years ago. For these people, a return to Earth would be very demoralizing. We are well aware of the deplorable conditions on Earth when we left and had no intention of ever returning. We can't imagine that conditions would be any better and are probably correct in assuming it will be much worse. We do not believe we can reassimilate into a society that rejects the tenants of the moral code that is so fundamental to the daily life of all of us.

"The second group, about one hundred, is composed of those who were between the ages of about eight and sixteen when we left Earth. As I said earlier, this group is demoralized now. These members of the crew were the idealistic ones when we departed and, like typical youth, are impatient that we haven't found their Garden of Eden already, so to speak. Using an old euphemism from Earth transportation, they are the ones in the backseat crying, 'Are we there yet?' They are no longer satisfied to pursue a twelve-year-old dream. For this group, I believe they would actually react better to a decision to return to Earth. They want the journey to be over wherever it is.

"The third group consists of the 100 members of the crew that were too young when we departed to have formed any strong ties to earth and the 152 that have been born along the way. For this group, they know nothing about living on land. This ship and the frequent periods of weightlessness they experience is all they know. They know nothing more about life on Earth than they do about possible life on a planet around Tau Ceti. Therefore, I don't see how your decision will have much impact on them psychologically one way or the other."

"Thank you, Melissa, for your comments," Captain Larson responded. "I tend to agree with your assessment, and I appreciate your breaking the 652 souls on this ship into the three groups. Group one, which includes all of us, entered into this odyssey fully aware of the risks and rewards involved. A few members of group two also volunteered for this crew. But most of group two along with all of those in the third group did not choose to be here. They are here because we put them here. Obviously, I need to consider their future as I decide what future course of action we take. Does anyone have anything further to add?"

Morgan looked around the conference room to see if anyone was going to speak. He had been wondering how to share Purple's analysis that a small contingent of humans might survive in Ararat's base camp for an extended period. He had doubted this was important if the *Mayflower* departed for Tau Ceti. There had never been any discussion about dividing the crew to plant outpost stations. The charter of the *Mayflower* was clear when it departed Earth—find a planet that could support human life and colonize it. Since Purple's analysis was that there was zero probability that Ararat would support those aboard the *Mayflower*, Morgan had concluded, just as Laura had when Purple announced its findings, that those findings didn't make any difference. Now, however, the situation was changing. If the captain made the decision to return to Earth, he was in effect abandoning the mission charter. Could it be that Purple's analytical capabilities had anticipated this possibility? Morgan decided it was time to let everyone know about Purple's analysis of alternative scenarios.

Before Morgan could speak, his wife Sarah responded to the captain's invitation. "Captain, I am certainly one of those in the first group that Melissa described. When Morgan and I volunteered for this mission, we did so with a hope that we could establish a new colony somewhere in the universe. I feel we were like those who boarded the first *Mayflower* in the 1600s. We were trying to escape the depressing conditions in our homeland. The fact that we are pioneers is a by-product of those conditions, not our primary motivation. Morgan and I want to find a better life for our son who was three when we left and our two daughters that have been born during the journey.

But that hope for a better life is premised on the basis that we will find a place where they can survive. My first instinct is to make sure they do live. Based on Nels's and Randy's findings, I think the risk of going to Tau Ceti is too great. I, for one, do not wish to risk the lives of my children when going to Tau Ceti leaves no alternatives. If we return to Earth, at least they will have a future. Who knows, maybe a better star drive than the Perry-Warner engine has been developed since we left, and we can set out again."

"Sarah is right," said Sandra. "Miguel and I have always wanted what is best for our four children. We have raised them with a strong commitment to our moral code and the word of God. Regardless of how decadent Earth has become since we left, if we have to go back, we will find a way to live according to our principles within that society. If Earth is the only way to guarantee them a future, then that's where we will want to go."

Judy and Melissa nodded agreement with Sarah. They, like every adult family on board the *Mayflower*, had children of their own. The crew of the *Mayflower* was based on ensuring it would have a genetically viable population that could survive indefinitely at whatever location it colonized. Since the twentieth century, biologists had been concerned about the concept known as *minimum viable population*. A minimum viable population is defined as the smallest possible number of a species necessary to ensure between 90 and 95 percent probability of survival generations into the future. This population is one that can sustain itself from natural disasters, environmental changes, and inbreeding concerns indefinitely without importation of genetic material from individuals outside the population. There must be sufficient genetic material in the population to balance mutation against genetic drift. The actual number required for a minimum viable population depends on a number of factors including a balanced sex ratio, reproductive capability of those in the population, inbreeding characteristics of the members of the population, and the vitality of the environment where the population lives.

The *Mayflower*'s charter included a strong moral code based on family values and a respect for human life. The breakdown of these values on Earth was a significant factor in the overall decline of society in the years before the *Mayflower* departed. Much of the Earth's population thought the *Mayflower*'s moral code was centuries out of date, but the founders saw no reason to attempt the mission if those on the mission didn't establish a new civilization rejecting what had become the norm in most of the world.

With this limitation in mind, the planners for the *Mayflower* project took all the scientific evidence on the subject into account and determined that a population of five hundred would be sufficient from a genetic standpoint with certain qualifications built into the initial population. First, every member of the crew had to be willing and able to reproduce. The three hundred adults over the age of twenty-five selected for the crew were composed of 150 married couples, all with at least one child. The two hundred additional young adults and children were equally balanced between males and females, and all were tested to ensure they were fertile and had no genetic disease. Further, family histories of all crew members were examined to ensure that there were no relationships between crew members closer than third cousins to eliminate concerns about inbreeding. With these factors in place, computer models predicted a 99 percent probability that the *Mayflower* would flourish in any ecosystem similar to Earth's.

"Captain," Morgan said before anyone else could join into the debate, "there is something else I think you should know before you close this discussion."

"Go ahead, Morgan. What is it?" Everyone else in the room, including Sarah, looked at Morgan curiously. What else could there be?

"When I told you the results earlier, I quoted Purple's analysis as 'the probability that Ararat will support the crew of the *Mayflower* without external support is zero, and you have not provided me with any data that would indicate such support would ever be available.' That is word for word what Purple said to me. But it is not the first response to the question I posed to the computer. I had asked Purple, 'Will Ararat support human life on a permanent basis?' After pausing for a moment, Purple answered that the probability was near zero, not zero. So when I asked for a clarification, Purple added the word the *crew* of the *Mayflower* to his answer. That led me to inquire whether the answer was different for some smaller group. Purple responded that a group of up to forty humans could be maintained for an extended period in Ararat's base camp, but there was a 95 percent probability it would die out before it could adapt to Ararat's atmospheric conditions. Neither Laura nor I thought this was important at the time, but now I think it is something to be considered."

"Why would we consider that?" Graysun Williams said. "This mission has never been about establishing outposts. We left Earth permanently. Returning there is not an option. I agree with Nels. Our only choice is to head to Tau Ceti. If we can't colonize there, we can live on this ship indefinitely. The life-support systems on *Mayflower* have proven to be self-sustaining. We will eventually be able to solve the hull erosion problems and move on."

"Have you all forgotten the reason we left Earth?" Nels declared. "I will not go back. I would rather see my two children die than put them back in that hellhole. I would rather see them with a less than 5 percent survival probability in an outpost here on Ararat than returning to Earth. If you decide to go back, leave my family here."

"Personally, I agree with you, Nels," the captain said. "But I cannot let my personal ambitions and desires override my responsibilities for everyone under my command. I will not make any decisions based on the personal preferences of any member of this crew. And what is best for the safety of this crew is that we return to Earth. I have made my decision. We will begin preparations for our departure. In the meantime, Morgan, evaluate Purple's revelation of a possible smaller colony further. If it really looks feasible, I will consider establishing an outpost on Ararat before we leave."

CHAPTER 2

W hen the charter for the *Mayflower* was written by the mission's sponsors in 2062, absolute authority of the captain was clearly established. The captain was given an advisory board of his division chiefs, but the decisions of the captain were final and not subject to review. The planners for the mission knew that if there was any opportunity for disagreement with a decision made by the captain, ultimately that would lead to chaos and mission failure. Thus, the charter mandated that when there was a decision to be made, the captain could assemble the division chiefs to give him input, but when the captain announced his course of action, the debate was over. That was how it had worked for the twelve years since the *Mayflower* had left Earth's orbit. Once the captain announced a course of action, discussion was over, and everyone quickly left the conference room to carry out their respective duties.

This time, it was different. Nels threw his arms in the air so violently that his Velcro ties pulled loose, and he began to drift out of his seat. As he grappled to grab the edge of the table to avoid floating to the ceiling, he yelled, "Never! I will not return to Earth. There must be another way! Leave me here on Ararat." Nobody else dared to make such an outburst, but Graysun Williams muttered in agreement.

Morgan was not sure whether he was more concerned by the decision of the captain or Nels's outburst. No one had ever challenged the authority of the captain before. Morgan knew that the captain could have Nels confined to his quarters for his dissention. Instead, the captain looked at Nels and said, almost tearfully, "Nels, I understand your frustration with my decision. Earth offers you nothing. I have no desire to return there either. But one of the reasons Earth and particularly the North American continent became such a disappointing place to live is that the people came to think only of what was best for themselves. Personal greed destroyed what was best for society. I will not let that happen here. My decision is what is best for those I am responsible for, not me and not you. This meeting is adjourned. Everyone please return to your duties and begin preparations for departure. We will meet tomorrow at 10:00 a.m. to discuss the schedule for departure. Morgan, please report back to me before tomorrow's meeting with any further analysis of a potential outpost on Ararat."

With that, everyone unstrapped and began to leave. As Morgan pushed out of his chair and headed toward the central companionway to the lower decks, he looked back over his shoulder and saw Captain Larson still slumped in his chair. Morgan had never seen the captain look so pale and defeated. Clearly, he had made a decision that was best for the ship but contrary to his personal ambitions.

Morgan paused and asked, "Captain, are you all right? Is there anything I can do?"

"Not really, but thanks," Captain Larson mumbled.

Morgan said nothing further. As Morgan drifted through the passageway, he reflected on the amazing events that had just occurred. Never in his wildest dreams did he think that returning to Earth was an option. He was so preoccupied that he forgot to duck as he entered the central companionway hatch between the operations center and the *Mayflower*'s office and laboratory space decks.

"Ouch!" he uttered softly to himself. "You would think by now I would know how to automatically navigate through this ship weightlessly."

The nasty bump on his head brought him back from his musings. He decided the first thing he needed to do was discuss the situation with his wife, Sarah. Laura would have to wait.

"Sarah," he called on his personal communicator, "where are you going?"

"I'm heading back to our quarters," she replied.

"I'll join you in a couple minutes," Morgan said. He was surprised at how quickly Sarah had processed the idea of returning to Earth. It was something they had never discussed, and Morgan had never even thought about it.

He quickly pushed his way past the main corridor of the office space decks and this time ducked as he entered the companionway for the deck where their quarters were located. Morgan turned left at the first branch corridor and arrived at the hatch to his and Sarah's living space. Relatively speaking, they had a large cabin. It consisted of a living space of about eighty square feet and two small sleeping rooms. Morgan and Sarah's sleeping room was nine feet by six feet, and the three children shared a triple-bunk room of nine feet by four feet. These two rooms opened off the back bulkhead of the living room. Since all meals were taken in the galley, there was no kitchen. The Parkers shared separate lavatory spaces for males and females with three other families. The cabins, like all living and working space on the *Mayflower*, were designed for use under either weightless conditions or normal gravity.

Sarah was loosely strapped into the double lounger when Morgan entered through the quarter's hatch. Morgan mentally reminisced about their life and family together as he joined Sarah on the lounger. They were married eighteen years before in 2066 when Morgan was working on his PhD in ecology at the University of Texas, and Sarah was completing a PhD program in food and nutrition at Saint Edwards University in Austin. Both twenty-two on their wedding day, they quickly completed their studies. Two years later, when the private Space Colonization Consortium announced it was receiving applications for its journey to the stars, Sarah was pregnant with their son Ben. Like about ten thousand other young scientists, engineers, and other people looking for an interstellar adventure, Morgan and Sarah applied for the program. After an extensive battery of intellectual, genetic, behavioral, psychological, and physical tests, they were selected for the crew. Ben was born in 2069 while they were training for the mission in the California desert. Their oldest daughter, Emily, a precocious eleven-year old, was born under normal gravity during the acceleration phase of the journey to Alpha Centauri, and sweet Jessica, almost eleven, was born soon after the *Mayflower* entered the weightless phase of the trip from Alpha Centauri to Epsilon Eridani.

"Wow, that was something we never talked about," Sarah said as Morgan settled in. "What was your initial reaction?"

"Confusion. I had never considered returning to Earth. I don't know what to think right now."

"Tell me, Morgan, what was the reason we volunteered for this mission?"

"As I recall, we were young and loved the opportunity to do something no one else had done—travel to the stars."

"No, Morgan, that was part of the excitement of the moment. Look deeper. What was driving us?"

"Well, we were unhappy with the direction society was taking and wanted an opportunity to start our family in a new place. We were like the pilgrims of the seventeenth century. We were unhappy with the world we lived in. We were willing to take the risks of this journey to find a new world where we and our fellow travelers could live according to our beliefs and values. That's why we named our ship the *Mayflower*."

"There is one difference, Morgan. The pilgrims knew the new world was there. We didn't. We were betting on a statistical probability that we would find a suitable new world."

Morgan paused for a moment. "I agree, Sarah. We were betting our lives on a one-way ticket to the unknown."

"Exactly, but do we have the right to bet the lives of our children? As the discussion developed a few minutes ago, I began to think about them. What would happen to them if we failed again at Tau Ceti? Our girls would never see a sunrise. They would never walk barefoot on a beach. They would never feel the wind in their face or experience rain. I am a mother first before a scientist, explorer, or pioneer. And as a mother, I surprisingly felt relief when the captain made the decision to go home. Yes, Morgan, it is home, and I am glad my children will have the opportunity to see it."

Morgan looked at his wife and reflected again on how blessed he was. "I am always amazed at how you can think outside the box, Sarah. I was just beginning to think about the implications for us and our children when I entered the cabin, and you have already analyzed the situation. You are right. But remember, it's not all that nice back home. By the time we get back, there might not be any clean beaches to walk on. We need to talk more tonight. But right now, I need to get back to my office to complete the additional analysis of a possible outpost that Captain Larson asked for. Laura is there, and I promised her I would fill her in on our meeting."

"Go ahead, Morgan. I'll pick up the girls from the gymnasium and tell them what has happened," Sarah said. "They are playing weightless dodgeball with some of the other girls their age. My guess is that Ben already knows. He always seems to know the scuttlebutt as soon as something happens. We will wait for you for dinner."

Morgan looked at Sarah as he unstrapped from the lounger and headed toward the central companionway. She had an upbeat look he hadn't seen for some time. Clearly, Sarah was becoming comfortable with the captain's decision. Morgan wondered how long it would be before he accepted the fact he was going to return to Earth. There would be more time to reflect on the day's developments later. Right now, there was work to do. As he headed back to the ecology center, he hoped that Laura would not be upset that he had forgotten her. It had been almost three hours since he had left the office for the conference room.

The corridors were much busier than usual as he passed through the office and laboratory spaces. The word was quickly spreading that Ararat would not work and they were not heading to Tau Ceti. There was a heated argument going on in Graysun William's office as Morgan drifted past. Across the corridor, Nels Brunken was huddled with his wife and family in the planetology center. He met Judy Polachek as she headed toward the officer's living quarters. She didn't even seem to notice he was there as she drifted past.

Laura was seated at her workstation as he floated into the office. Before he could say anything, she said, "First of all, don't say anything about not coming back here right away. I just talked to Sarah, and she said you were on your way. You were right to go to her first. I have had a dozen or more people stick their heads in here to tell me we were going back to Earth. Word is spreading like wildfire."

Before Morgan could respond, their personal communicators crackled to life. "Crew of the *Mayflower*, this is Captain Larson speaking. As many of you are hearing through the grapevine, we have determined that Ararat will not be our new home.

After considering a number of factors, I have decided that we are going to abandon our charter and return to Earth. So that there is no misunderstanding of the facts that went into this decision, I am posting in Purple a summary of the information that led up to this decision. This summary will be available at the conclusion of this broadcast. I will announce the schedule for departure in three days."

The *Mayflower* charter established that a twenty-four-hour day, seven-day week, and 365-day year, Earth-style clock and calendar would be used until a habitable planet was colonized. While some discussion took place of changing to a twenty-two-hour day to coincide with Ararat's rotational rate, Captain Larson had made it clear that no such change would occur until a decision was made to colonize the planet. The bulk of the crew was assigned to an eight-hour work day, five days a week. Weekends were for rest and exercise, with optional church services on Sundays. Those members of the crew responsible for operation of the ship's systems were assigned to an eight-hours-on, sixteen-hours-off watch schedule that rotated each Sunday with a dogwatch to shift the schedule. The term *dogwatch* originated in early seamen terminology and is believed to have referred to the Dog Star, Sirius, which was often the first star visible in the evening sky when the watch schedule shifted.

Almost immediately after the captain completed his remarks, Laura's screen flashed with the captain's summary message. Morgan decided to let her read it before he said anything. He climbed into his seat next to her and contemplated what he needed to ask Purple while she read the message. After a few minutes, Laura said in her typical youthful exuberance, "Wow, I never saw that one coming! And you know what? I agree with Mrs. Grant's evaluation. I'm at the lower end of group two, and I do want to find a place to plant roots. I don't remember that much about Earth, but it's nice to know there is a defined end to this journey. I want to get married and have children that will have open spaces to walk in."

"Married?" Morgan said. "Do you have anyone in mind?"

"Henry Brunken," Laura responded. "We have been seeing each other for about two years now but agreed that we would not get serious until we could get off the *Mayflower*. That's been the decision of many of the crew members around our age."

Morgan thought about Laura's comments. He had not had any idea the younger crew members thought this way. Earlier, Laura had sounded like she was ready to set out for Tau Ceti. Melissa had uncovered something that he had completely missed. It was in the best interest of the younger crew members to find a permanent home, and the *Mayflower* was not suited for that purpose. He could only hope that Earth would not be too big a letdown to them.

"Did you say anything to the captain about Purple's report that Ararat might be able to support a small outpost?" Laura asked.

"I did. He asked me to look further into the outpost scenario and let him know what we find before we meet again tomorrow. Let's get to work."

Morgan and Laura spent the next hour discussing what additional information and questions they needed to feed into Purple. Why did Purple analyze smaller groups? Why did Purple suggest the number of forty humans? What were the factors in Purple's determination that there was a 95 percent probability the base-camp group would die out before it could adapt? Could anything be done to improve the chances of survival? In addition to these questions, Purple would now have to consider the conference-room discussion and the decision made to return the *Mayflower* to Earth. Purple, of course, recorded all conversations on the *Mayflower* but did not analyze those conversations or discussions unless specifically directed to do so. Otherwise, the computer would be overwhelmed by trivial and often-conflicting information.

The *Mayflower's* main computer had been named *Purple* to take advantage of its ability to communicate in natural language. Purple, orange, silver, and month are four words in the English language that do not have other words sounding the same. Of the four, purple was the least likely to be used in any context other than intended as a communication with the computer. Thus *Purple* was the name selected to initiate verbal communications with the computer. All crew members could talk to Purple though their personal communicators to ask questions and retrieve information. They could receive verbal responses or displayed information as they wished. However, to prevent the possibility of Purple receiving direction not in the best interest of the crew, only the captain, Morgan, John Malcolm, and Randy Edwards had the authority to speak directly to the computer to give commands and discuss information that affected the functions or mission of the *Mayflower*.

Morgan wanted Purple to consider everything that had been said in the conference room earlier that day as well as the captain's statement to the crew. In addition, Morgan wanted the computer to consider the implications for those returning to Earth on the *Mayflower* if forty or so members of the crew were left behind in a base camp on Ararat. Morgan and Laura worked for some time to carefully structure the questions to ask the computer. Once that was done, Morgan directed Purple to provide its analysis of the questions posed and given the new information from the decision to return to Earth, a refined analysis of the feasibility and survival of an outpost on Ararat.

The computer responded immediately, "Morgan, I will answer your questions in the order you submitted them. First, you asked why I analyzed smaller groups. You will recall that your question was whether Ararat would support human life on a permanent basis. I answered the question as a near-zero probability because I considered all numbers of humans between 1 and 652, the population currently on the *Mayflower*, as the starting point. Within that range, there were certain numbers that had a probability above zero.

"That leads to the answer to your second question. I had already told you that Ararat would not support the crew of the *Mayflower*. When you asked me about smaller groups, I analyzed the decreasing probability of survival from a minimum viable population standpoint within the constraints of the *Mayflower* charter as the size of the group decreased against the increasing probability of survival from an environmental standpoint as the size decreased to find the highest chances of survival for any given group. The environmental side of this analysis considered three competing factors—how many people could the base camp support, how quickly could the people in the base camp adapt to conditions outside the base camp, and how long would it take before the people at the base camp could completely replace any supplies they had on hand. In other words, would they run out of food and supplies before they developed a self-sustaining infrastructure? In addition, I factored in the variations in the physical fitness of the individual members of the crew and weighted my analysis toward those crew members in the best condition to survive the harsh conditions existing on the surface. This number turned out to be forty.

"As to your third question, while forty was the best number, survival chances were still below 5 percent for two reasons. First, this number is well below what is considered ideal from a genetic standpoint. Second, since at that time the *Mayflower* was to leave for Tau Ceti and an outpost camp had not been considered in the planning process for this ship, the amount of materials and supplies that could be left without jeopardizing the primary mission was limited. Considering these factors, there was no number that rose above a 5 percent survival probability.

"Next, you asked me how the establishment of a base camp would affect the crew of the *Mayflower* as they returned to Earth. I incorporated all of the information provided by Melissa Grant and Sandra Sanchez at the conference. My analysis indicates that leaving an outpost would have a positive impact on Melissa's group one. This would give those members of the crew some feeling of accomplishment as they returned home. I see little impact on groups two and three other than some minor family disruptions depending on who might be selected for remaining at the base camp.

"Finally, you asked me to refine my analysis of the feasibility and survival of an outpost on Ararat based on the captain's decision to return to Earth and look for ways to improve the survival probabilities. I now find that an outpost is feasible but risky with a 35 percent probability that it could survive indefinitely into the future. Three significant factors contributed to this increased chance of survival.

"First and most important is the announcement by the captain that the charter was being abandoned. With this revelation, I was able to ignore the moral code that constrained my analysis from a viable population standpoint. This significantly altered the genetic side of the equation. I assumed that an outpost colony would use a managed reproductive program to maximize genetic variability. In addition, I assumed the frozen human sperm and female eggs currently stored on board would be left at the outpost, and the outpost members would use the sperm and eggs as necessary to inject additional genes into the population as environmental factors allowed their numbers to grow. By adding the availability of frozen human sperm and eggs to the genetic variability of the outpost, the limiting factor imposed by the genetic side of the analysis was largely eliminated. While there are no frozen human embryos available and presumably no time to develop a significant supply of them, the outpost population will have adequate time to maximize genetic variability through use of the frozen material. In effect, the population base genetically will be near 350 and not the few humans that actually compose the founding population.

"Second, with the decision that the mission plan is cancelled and the crew will return to Earth, there is no need to keep the large store of supplies on board that were destined for a permanent colony. I assumed that all equipment and supplies not necessary for the return flight will be left at the base camp. This significantly changes the survival chances on the habitat side of the analysis. The initial base-camp members would have all the materials necessary to expand its physical plant and living space over time as they slowly adapt to Ararat's atmospheric conditions.

"The third factor may not appear significant on the surface, but I found that it will have considerable motivational impact. If the *Mayflower* leaves an outpost behind when you leave for Earth, those occupying the outpost will no longer consider it to be an outpost. They will be the colony, the only one established by man in the stars. They will take every measure conceivable to survive and flourish. Included in this motivation will be significant planning as to reproduction, population growth, and adaptation to Ararat's environmental conditions. This will significantly reduce the risks of failure. Further, if the outpost does survive, it will provide invaluable scientific information for any future space-colonization efforts. My analysis concludes the outpost is worth the risk.

"Finally, I recalculated the number of crew members that would have the greatest probability of survival. The elimination of the genetic concerns leaves only the environmental side of the matter to consider. Any initial population above forty results in decreasing survival chances because of the limited initial habitat conditions in the base camp. Between forty and thirty-two, the probability remains fairly constant at about 35 percent. Below this number, the loss of diversity in skill groups begins to take effect, and survival chances begin to quickly decline. While I assumed that the outpost colonists will use advanced reproductive techniques and the frozen human sperm and eggs, there is no equipment on the *Mayflower* that could be used to reproduce humans outside the womb. Therefore, the initial population should be between thirty-two and forty and dominated by women in at least a two-to-one ratio or better."

Morgan looked at his communicator; it was a little after 5:00 p.m. "Well, this certainly puts a new light on everything," he said to Laura. "Here I was, looking for a refinement of Purple's earlier pronouncement, and I got a completely new scenario. I'd better tell the captain right away." Laura didn't say anything as Morgan activated his personal communicator. "Captain, I have new information on the outpost possibilities. I think you need to hear this."

"Stay there, Morgan. I'm passing through the office-deck companionway now. I'll be there in less than a minute."

Morgan settled back in his chair to wait. He looked around the cramped office that had been his primary place of work since leaving Earth twelve years before. It was called the ecology center, but it wasn't equipped like a traditional laboratory at any college campus on Earth. The eight-by-ten-foot space had two desks for use by Morgan and Laura. There was a third chair adjacent to the compartment entrance. Each desk had a terminal for access to Purple. There were no bookshelves or file cabinets. All information on the *Mayflower* was stored electronically to save space. There was no need for books, printers, or paper. Morgan's one concession to his academic background was a large electronic whiteboard he had installed on the back bulkhead of the compartment. He liked to draw out scenarios on the whiteboard as part of his thought-formulation process. The whiteboard allowed him to lay out ideas in a larger format than the computer screens did. He could then stand back (or float back) and analyze the problem he had presented. In recent years, Laura had begun to use the whiteboard herself as she worked through analytical questions.

Laura still said nothing as they waited. Morgan looked toward her and wondered what she was going through her mind. Could Laura possibly be considering volunteering for the outpost? Finally, she glanced up at Morgan. He could see in her expression that she was deeply disturbed by the computer's revelation. Before either could speak, Captain Larson entered the compartment and strapped into the spare chair.

"Purple has upped the outpost ante," Morgan said. "The computer now puts the survival chances of an outpost as high as 35 percent and concludes that while risky, it is worth the risk. Purple identified three factors leading to its revised estimate—abandonment of the charter would give the outpost population the ability to resolve genetic concerns, cancellation of the mission allows us to leave significantly more supplies for the outpost, and knowing they are the only human colony planted in the stars gives additional motivation of those populating the outpost to survive. If we go in this direction, I suggest we drop the term *outpost* and call it the *Ararat colony*."

"What do you mean by the charter being abandoned?" Captain Larson asked.

"In your statement earlier today to the crew, you said, 'We are going to abandon our charter and return to Earth.' I asked Purple to consider the conference-room discussion and the decision to return to Earth in its revised analysis. Purple included your statement and eliminated any constraints the charter had previously imposed. This included ignoring our moral code. Without the restrictions of the code, Purple was able to eliminate genetic constraints and focus on environmental considerations. The computer assumed that the colony would have frozen sperm and eggs from all of the crew and use them when feasible to obtain the desired genetic diversity. Thus, a small group could survive in the base camp until adaptation to Ararat's environment is achieved."

"I certainly did not mean that we were abandoning the entire charter. As smart as our computer is, it still sometimes takes things too literally. Our moral code is fundamental to this crew. I am not sure how many would be willing to abandon it. Did the proposed initial population of the colony change?"

"Yes. The computer's analysis now proposes a range of between forty and thirty-two as ideal. In addition, since the analysis assumed advanced human-reproductive techniques, Purple determined the majority of the initial population should be female in at least a two-to-one ratio. In effect, the initial population would be agreeing to an artificial-breeding program."

Captain Larson pondered this information for a few moments, trying to decide whether he wanted to go down the road of suggesting to the *Mayflower's* crew the possibility of leaving some members behind in an outpost. It was clear that if a colony were established, it would require abandonment of one of the fundamental principles of the *Mayflower's* mission. Would it be worth it to completely disregard the moral standards of the mission in an effort to establish an outpost with only a 35 percent probability of survival? Finally, he looked directly into Morgan's eyes. "I have to offer this as an option. There are many people aboard, including me, who have no desire to return to Earth. I believe there will be some who are willing to accept anything as a better alternative than going home. To deny them the option of staying here is not fair. Please refine what additional factors should be considered if enough people volunteer for this colony. But don't say anything about what you learn before we meet tomorrow. I don't want the rumor mill to get ahead of the decision-making process." Without waiting for a response, he spun himself around and pushed his way out of the ecology center.

Laura said nervously, "It looks like the captain is amenable to establishing a colony on Ararat. Boy, what a day! A few hours ago, I was preparing myself to go on to Tau Ceti. Then it was back to Earth. Now the door is opening for some people to stay here. It's enough to make my head spin."

"Are you thinking about staying?" Morgan asked.

"I don't know. All of this is too sudden. I want to think about it. I also want to talk to Henry. But right now, we need to work with Purple to determine what additional selection factors need to be considered when the captain discusses the Ararat colony at your meeting tomorrow."

Two hours later, Morgan and Laura had enough information to present at the next morning's meeting. As Laura turned left toward the women's bachelor quarters, she said, "I hope Henry has finished his work in the hydroponic gardens. I need to find out what he is thinking. As the captain requested, I won't mention the colony possibilities, but I want to know how he feels about returning to Earth."

"I'll stop by in the morning to chat before going to the conference room," said Morgan as Laura headed toward her compartment.

It was well past normal supper time, so Morgan headed toward the galley for a bite to eat. He called Sarah to see if she was still waiting for him, but she said she had eaten earlier with the children. She was back at their cabin, and the girls were getting ready for bed. Morgan ate a quick meal of synthetic vegetables, fruit, and meat substitutes before setting out to join his family.

Almost half of the space aboard the *Mayflower* was devoted to food production. It was essential from the start of the mission that the *Mayflower* had to produce a self-sustaining environment for the crew. Thus, while an emergency supply of rations was included in the cargo enough to feed the entire crew for over a year, those rations had not been used. Almost all nutrition on the *Mayflower* was produced in hydroponic gardens. Space limitations did not allow the production of a wide range of agricultural products. Instead, quinoa, a grain-like plant originally from the Andes of South America, had been adapted for growth hydroponically under either weightless or normal gravity conditions. Quinoa is an excellent source of protein and was fashioned into many products that simulated fruits, vegetables, and meat products. Meals on the *Mayflower* had the appearance of coming from a wide range of animal and vegetable products but in reality, were almost exclusively made from quinoa.

The *Mayflower*'s diet was not entirely vegetarian however. Shrimp-farming techniques were adapted to conditions on the starship, and a large-enough population of shrimp was maintained that each member of the crew could have twenty-one shrimp per week. Shrimp assisted in maintaining healthy circulatory systems because they have high levels of cholesterol but insignificant amounts of saturated fat. Thus, shrimp consumption helps the crew members improve LDL-to-HDL ratios and also help to lower triglycerides. This is particularly important to crew health during the long periods of weightlessness.

The builders of the *Mayflower* had originally considered adding a stem cell–meat production unit to give the crew an additional source of protein. However, because the process provided no real benefit over that received from the various quinoa recipes available and the additional space required was deemed excessive, the use of artificially produced meat was not included on the *Mayflower*. There was a supply of frozen farm-animal embryos on board for development upon settlement of a new world, but there was no room on the ship to raise these animals for food. Other than the shrimp, all food on the *Mayflower* came from the quinoa gardens.

All crew members were required to eat in the galley. Since the *Mayflower* was a closed ecosystem, it was important that nothing be wasted. If food was allowed to be taken outside the galley, it was inevitable that some would be lost to the nutrient system. The galley had an air lock that every crew member passed through on departure that captured any crumbs on a person's body. All leftovers were also recycled. In addition, all human waste products were recycled back to the hydroponic gardens. In spite of these efforts, Judy Polachek estimated that about one percent of the organic content of the *Mayflower* had been lost from the nutrient cycle by the time they entered the Epsilon Eridani star system.

Morgan pondered how he would discuss the events of the day with Sarah when he got to their cabin. They had signed on to the *Mayflower* crew as a team, and he knew neither of them would consider staying in the Epsilon Eridani system without the other. Further, even if they decided to stay together, the genetic requirements of an Ararat colony would not let any child, much less three, stay with their parents, and there was no way they would abandon their children. It was clear that the only option for Morgan and Sarah was the return to Earth, but that option was not something he was looking forward to.

The Space Colonization Consortium was formed by a small group of highly successful entrepreneurs in the mid-twenty-first century. The five founding members responded to a growing concern that mankind, in general, and government, in particular, had lost its spirit to take on new challenges. When physicists Rolf Perry and Bernhart Warner produced a working model of a drive system that could take man to the stars, there was no government in the world that was interested in putting man back into space, much less financing a one-way journey to another solar system. The United States, China, and Russia had all abandoned space exploration by 2030s. No government could see any return on an investment in interstellar space travel, and governments weren't interested in anything that didn't produce revenue. By the time the Perry-Warner drive was developed, governments were so overburdened with debt and social commitments that they had abandoned funding virtually all research and development programs and concentrated their limited resources on the declining condition of mankind throughout the world. The international space station had been vacant since the Great Famine of the 2020s.

Not all activity in space had ceased however. Private corporations continued to launch communications satellites as necessary to maintain data communications. In addition, a private shuttle program had been in operation since 2030. This program was used to maintain satellites, conduct medical research in space, and produce certain valuable chemicals and metal alloys under zero-gravity conditions. In addition, there was a small market for the very wealthy to take tourist trips into space. By 2051, there were twenty private operating shuttles making routine flights into space.

Soon after development of the Perry-Warner drive was announced, John Chu, owner of the world's largest telecommunications company, decided to invest in a possible use of the system for a manned interstellar mission to the stars. He put up twenty billion American credits as an initial investment and sought other investors. Four others matched his initial investment, one from the pharmaceutical industry, two from energy backgrounds, and one from the data-management business, and the Space Colonization Consortium was formed. By making the consortium a separate nonprofit corporation dedicated to space research and exploration, investments in the venture were protected from the onerous tax burdens being placed on the wealthy. Within two years, over twenty-five additional investors were attracted to the consortium, giving it a capital base of over two hundred billion American credits. In addition, the three corporations that owned private shuttles donated all their resources to be used as necessary by the consortium. All of these founding partners in the consortium knew that they were too old to partake in the mission they were planning. Three of the five founding partners had died before the mission departed Earth's orbit twenty years later on August 1, 2072. But their vision was not for themselves; it was for the future of mankind. The consortium was convinced that mankind on Earth was on an irreversible downward spiral. By planting an additional population in another solar system, man's chances of long-term achievement of excellence would be enhanced. This new population would have the opportunity of establishing a system of government and society with the full knowledge of why such ventures in the past had been short-lived regardless of the form of government chosen.

The consortium's mission plan was simple. They would send an expedition to the stars in search for a new home for man. The mission would first travel to the star Alpha Centauri, 4.3 light-years from Earth, in search of a suitable planet. If no such planet was found, the expedition would then go to Epsilon Eridani, 8.8 light-years from Alpha Centauri and 10.8 light-years from Earth. If Epsilon Eridani also proved to have no suitable planet, the plan then called for the group to go to the star Tau Ceti, 5.2 light-years from Epsilon Eridani and 12.2 light-years from Earth. These three stars were selected as those close to Earth having the highest probability of containing a suitable planet in their system based on all information on Earth in the mid-twenty-first century. Beyond that, no definite plans had been made.

The Alpha Centauri system was found to contain only large gaseous planets, three in orbit around Alpha Centauri A and two around Alpha Centauri B. They only stayed in the system for a month before departing for Epsilon Eridani.

Morgan first became aware of the consortium's plans when it bought the abandoned international space station in 2055. He remembered the news releases about the event and the outcry from the public about all the money that the wealthy were wasting on a pie-in-the-sky plan. The consortium's news release of the purchase stated the space station would be used as a base camp for the initial stages of construction of an interstellar space ship. Morgan, like most eleven-year-old boys, had little interest in the project at the time. His family was still somewhat insulated from the needs and problems of most of society. His father, a medical doctor, had managed to keep his family out of public housing and send his children to private schools. It was only after Morgan entered college that he began to understand why the consortium plans were relevant. Soon after he first met Sarah in 2063, he learned that she also could see the importance of the consortium's goals. Before they were married in 2066, they agreed to dedicate their lives to the mission. Ever since they were selected for the crew in 2068, Morgan had been focused on nothing other than being a pioneer on a new planet. Until today. Now he was looking at returning to a planet and its problems he had all but forgotten. He wondered how he would adapt to once again being one of ten billion souls instead of being one of six hundred.

When Morgan finished his meal, he returned to his quarters. Emily and Jessica were in their sleeping containment bags fast asleep. Ben was still awake reviewing his calculus assignment for the day. Sarah was reviewing weekly reports from the galley when Morgan drifted through the entryway. Ben looked up at his father and asked nervously, "Dad, what's Earth going to be like when we get back?"

Morgan thought carefully about Ben's question. Ben was only three when the *Mayflower* departed. He had never made a trip to Ararat's surface, so for all practical purposes, his only life experiences were aboard the *Mayflower*. Most of that experience was under weightless conditions. Morgan and Sarah were very strict about the children maintaining their strength and body tone during the weightless periods, but they realized it was not the same as living under normal gravity on a planet's surface.

"Well," Morgan answered, "first of all, it's big. It's not like what you have seen in the videos we have on board. News videos and video productions tend to focus on the sensational, not the normal. What you have seen focuses on the urban areas. Many areas on Earth are virtually unpopulated. Not all animals are domestic or held in zoos. There are wild, free-roaming creatures in many places. Not all fish are raised in farms. Some species still thrive in the oceans. Not all the atmosphere is polluted. The sky is still blue in some places. Not all people on Earth were living in poverty and squalor when we left. There were places and people where personal responsibility and hard work were still considered important. I expect we will find many people that continue to adhere to the same Christian values that we have emphasized here on the *Mayflower*.

"Who knows, Ben, it could be that someone or some group has risen to the challenge, and we will find conditions are better when we get back than they were when we left. In a way, the decision to return is a good one. At least we are going to be headed to a planet that we know is capable of supporting human life. You and all those aboard the *Mayflower* will have a fantastic story to tell and a wealth of knowledge to contribute to society. I suspect we will be warmly greeted upon our arrival.

Remember, we will have been gone for a long time, and nobody thought we would ever come back. It will be the news of the century when they learn we are coming back."

Sarah smiled at Morgan as Ben absorbed what his father had said but said nothing. Later that evening as they lay quietly fastened into bed, she softly whispered to Morgan, "Those were wonderful uplifting comments to Ben. He had been talking with the other kids his age when they heard the captain's announcement. He was very worried about going back to Earth earlier this evening. For the last twelve years, all these kids have heard is the reasons we left Earth. Now we are telling them it's the best choice we have."

"I suppose there will be a lot of reeducation for everyone, including us, on the journey back. At least we have several years to prepare." With that, Morgan drifted into a restless sleep.

CHAPTER 3

Morgan woke early the next morning along with Sarah. They didn't say much other than normal morning platitudes as they gathered their clothes for the day. They were able to get to the lavatory cabin before any of the families they shared the space with arrived to use the facilities. After a brief shower, they dressed and went to the galley for a morning breakfast of synthetic coffee, quinoa porridge, and something that tasted a little like grapefruit.

"Well, at least I know of one benefit to returning to Earth," Sarah said. "We won't have to eat this quinoa stuff anymore."

"Amen to that," Morgan responded. "Quinoa porridge, quinoa patties, quinoa soup, quinoa bread. I'm ready for a dietary change. I swear, if the cooks knew how to make quinoa ice cream, they would."

Morgan was glad that Sarah had diverted his thoughts from the weighty issues he would be facing that day. They spent the next fifteen minutes in trivial conversation about the children and how their studies were going. When they finished eating, Morgan told Sarah he was heading directly for the fitness center for his daily workout. Sarah said she would go and get the children moving for the day and would see him later at the conference room. As she unstrapped from her place at the galley table, she said, "Morgan, I know you and Laura learned more about the possibility of leaving an outpost here at Ararat. I could tell by your restless sleep last night. I assume you will be making an announcement at this morning's meeting. Don't worry about it. Whatever happens, happens. Captain Larson will make the best decision for all of us just as he always has."

"Thanks, dear," Morgan replied. "I can always count on you for putting things into proper perspective."

After recycling the scraps from breakfast, Morgan headed to the gym and fitness center. He remained very disciplined about his daily workouts, spending at least an hour a day on the exercise bikes and resistance-stretching machines. Many of the crew had become lax about fitness over the last few months as the *Mayflower* remained in orbit around Ararat. It was becoming obvious that those crew members would have a difficult time when they returned to normal gravity. Morgan hoped they would begin working out again before acceleration commenced. The distance back to Earth was longer than either the distance from Earth to Alpha Centauri or the distance from Alpha Centauri to Epsilon Eridani. They would be in weightless flight for over six years on the return flight. If people did not maintain muscle strength and body tone during that period, he doubted they would be able to function when deceleration to Earth began. He assumed this would be a major subject of discussion in the departure-planning meeting in a few hours.

Morgan finished his routine at 9:30 a.m. On his way to the captain's conference room, he checked in at the ecology center. Laura was there at her desk reading a report. "Anything interesting?" Morgan asked.

"I've begun reviewing environmental issues on Earth. I haven't looked at any of this stuff for years, figuring I would never need the information. Guess I was wrong."

"Did you talk to Henry?"

"Not about the outpost scenario. I did not want to violate the captain's request to keep the matter confidential. But we did talk about returning to Earth. Henry is very depressed about the matter. He has his father's genes. I am worried that when he learns about the outpost possibility, he will want to stay. Also he told me that Nels was very angry last night. Henry is concerned about his father."

"I can understand how the possibility of splitting up the crew could cause some major rifts in relationships. I hope you and Henry will be able to work everything out."

"Me too," mumbled Laura. "I really love Henry and hope he feels strong enough about me."

"I'm heading to the conference room now," Morgan said. "I want to get there a few minutes early to collect my thoughts. It's important that the risks are properly understood when Captain Larson brings up the outpost. As soon as the meeting is over, I will stop back and fill you in."

"Thanks," Laura said. "I'm really nervous about how all of this will turn out."

Morgan considered this as he drifted to the conference room. Laura was as levelheaded as anyone on the *Mayflower*. If she was concerned, what would the general reaction be?

Morgan arrived first, about twenty minutes before ten. As he strapped in to his seat, he pondered the analysis that Purple had provided and how he would discuss the outpost option. He knew, of course, that all calculations of survival probabilities are just that—calculations. There were many examples back on Earth where statistically a population was doomed to extinction yet had recovered and survived. An excellent example was the whooping crane, a large crane found in North America. In the 1940s, there were as few as eleven whooping cranes left in the population, and the genetic base for the population was as little as four breeding pairs. Through extensive management, habitat protection, and breeding programs, the number of whooping cranes increased to about four hundred by the beginning of the twenty-first century and numbered over 1,500 when the *Mayflower* left Earth. In the case of the whooping crane, the species had overcome the high statistical probability that it would be extinct before the year 2000. Other examples include several of the large cats in Africa and Pacific salmon populations in western North America.

Morgan was concerned that the Ararat colony would need to take extreme measures to minimize mortality until they could adapt to the Ararat environment. Further, could an outpost population agree to a managed breeding program that would approach the theoretical level assumed by Purple? If it did, what would happen to the moral beliefs of those left behind at the colony? Assuming the colony did survive, would future generations resemble in any way what was envisioned by the founding partners? If they survived but abandoned all of the moral principles so fundamental to the *Mayflower*'s mission, would the outpost be a success or a failure? Morgan knew that how he presented the colony option would have a great deal of influence on the discussion that followed and the ultimate decision made.

Morgan's thought process was interrupted shortly as Melissa and John Malcolm arrived. Judy Polachek and Sarah entered together a few minutes later. Morgan assumed they had been discussing food production and consumption at the hydroponic gardens. Randy Edwards and Graysun Williams also arrived together. Sandra Sanchez floated in just before Nels. Morgan noted that Nels looked particularly glum. Captain Larson arrived precisely at 10:00 a.m. He looked more chipper than he had the day before. Morgan wondered if it was because the decision regarding Ararat had finally been made and he was ready to take the *Mayflower* back to Earth or if he was considering staying at the outpost.

The captain skipped any preliminary comments and dove into the business at hand. "The first order of business is to discuss the return flight plan. Randy?"

"As you all know," Randy began, "the distance to Earth from Epsilon Eridani is 10.8 light-years. After the acceleration phase, we will be weightless for over six years before deceleration begins. In ship's time, it will take us just under eight years to achieve Earth's orbit from the time we depart."

The concept behind the Perry-Warner interstellar drive was not how fast one accelerated but how long one accelerated. The developers of the system found a way to adapt common elements for use in a fission engine that would allow acceleration for a long period of time. As the *Mayflower* leaves orbit, it accelerates at 980 cm/sec^2 or at one gravity. This is maintained for three hundred days at which time the speed is 2.5402×10^{10} cm/sec or 0.8473 the speed of light. When the ship reaches this speed, it is 0.3482 light-years from its departure point. The ship then drifts at that speed until it is the same distance from its target destination at which time the engine is used to decelerate at the same rate until it arrives at its destination. New material can be found at the destination to repeat the process on the next leg of the journey if necessary.

The Perry-Warner drive is not capable of faster-than-light travel, but the physics of relativity and time dilation result in time moving relatively slower on the moving ship in relation to a stationary object. The principle is known as the tau concept and is represented by the formula $T = \sqrt{1 - \frac{v^2}{c^2}}$ where v is the velocity of the *Mayflower* and c is the speed of light. To obtain the time that is experienced on the *Mayflower*, time on Earth is multiplied by the tau value. After accelerating at one gravity for three hundred days, tau equals 0.5310. Thus, for the return journey to Earth, the acceleration and deceleration phases cover about seven tenths of a light-year, leaving 10.1 light-years coasting. By applying the tau factor, the *Mayflower* will cover these 10.1 light-years in 6.33 years ship's time (10.1 ÷ 0.8473 × 0.5310 = 6.3296 years). In the meantime, the 10.1 light-years will take 11.92 years to a person on Earth. An additional thirty-one days of time distortion is added for each acceleration and deceleration phase of the trip. To a person on the *Mayflower*, it does not appear as if time is slowing down; instead the universe around them is slowing down. Thus, while the stationary person sees the ship traveling slower than the speed of light, a person on the *Mayflower* sees the distance being covered faster than light speed. Only after they stop do they see the effect of the time dilation.

"What about the hull erosion problem you mentioned yesterday?" Captain Larson asked. "Should we alter our normal operational flight plan to improve the life expectancy of the *Mayflower*?"

"I asked Nels to look at the star charts and all available interstellar data between Epsilon Eridani and the solar system. He did not see any unusual densities of interstellar gases along our route beyond what we have encountered to date. The margin of error in the calculations I reported yesterday are more than adequate to allow us to return to Earth safely.

"Even so, I ran a variety of scenarios to see if any change in our standard flight plan is recommended," Randy continued. "For example, we could accelerate for two hundred days at one gravity instead of three hundred. This would give us a drifting speed of 0.5648 the speed of light. The tau factor under this scenario would be 0.825, and we would be weightless for 14.75 years. I also looked at lower rates of acceleration, but they all result in a much lower speed. While there are some benefits to a lower speed, in my opinion, they are outweighed by the extended time we would be drifting under zero-gravity conditions."

"I agree," said Sandra. "We were weightless for a little over five years on the trip from Alpha Centauri to Epsilon Eridani, and the physical implications of that have been serious. Several children were injured when we began deceleration into this system. Many of the crew members have let their conditioning decline during the year in orbit here, and I expect we will see some injuries as a result. Six-plus years of weightlessness will be extremely difficult to prepare for. In my opinion, fourteen years or more would be catastrophic."

"Does anyone have anything further to add on this issue?" the captain asked. He looked directly at Nels, but Nels stared at the table and said nothing. "All right, we need to discuss a number of details regarding crew and ship preparations, but before we do that, as I requested yesterday, Morgan revised his analysis of an outpost here on Ararat. Last evening, he told me that new data associated with the decision to return to Earth resulted in a substantial increase in the likelihood that the outpost could survive. Morgan, please bring us up to date on your analysis."

Morgan looked to Sarah as he prepared to speak. She gave him an almost imperceptible vote of confidence with her eyes. Morgan also noticed that Nels was now paying attention. "Yesterday I mentioned that Purple had identified the possibility of an outpost being left at Ararat's base camp, but the probability of long-term survival of such a camp was less than 5 percent. After yesterday's decision to return to Earth was made, Laura and I asked Purple to reevaluate an outpost scenario using the new information that we would not be going on to Tau Ceti. Purple found three significant new factors that increased the probability that an outpost could survive to about thirty-five percent. While still risky, an outpost appears statistically to be worth the risk."

Nels interrupted before Morgan could go into the details Purple had identified. "This is outstanding news! I, for one, will take that risk."

"Nels, please let Morgan finish," Captain Larson said. "There is much more before we consider this as an option.

Morgan, please tell us what would need to be done if we decided to establish a permanent base camp on Ararat."

Nels reluctantly complied, but from his body language, it was clear he wanted to stay on Ararat regardless of the dangers it might pose.

"As we all know," Morgan continued, "our original plan was that once we found a planet to colonize, we would use the construction materials on board to build a camp big enough to house the entire crew. Then we would cannibalize the *Mayflower* to establish facilities to produce food and energy resources until the colony became self-sustaining. When Purple first considered leaving an outpost on Ararat, it was under the assumption that the *Mayflower* would need everything on board at Tau Ceti. Thus, the base camp would be all that was left on Ararat. The facility now on the planet's surface is small. It will only house forty people under the most cramped conditions. Our surveys indicate there is little in the way of natural resources in the area around the base camp that could be used to expand the base. Without the construction materials and equipment on the *Mayflower*, it would be extremely difficult for the initial population to expand.

"Further, the computer assumed neither the animal embryos nor the equipment necessary to raise those embryos would be available to the outpost. Since our surveys have found little in the way of native animal life on Ararat, the prospect for the establishment of a viable ecosystem and diversified food supply friendly to humans was virtually zero. The base-camp population would be forced to survive under the extremely harsh conditions of Ararat until they could adapt to the planet's existing conditions. Purple determined there was a 95 percent probability they would die out before that happened."

Morgan decided he would leave the enhanced reproductive issue to be the last one discussed. "The first new factor that the computer identified in its revised analysis," Morgan said, "is that we no longer need the supplies for establishment of a base camp for the entire *Mayflower* population. Under the assumption the *Mayflower* is returning to Earth, all equipment and materials not required for the return flight can be left on Ararat. This includes all the building materials, agricultural equipment, environmental machinery, and seed stock. The computer also included a proportionate amount of our hydroponic garden system and medical laboratory to be off-loaded for the colonists. Basically, if it's not needed for the return flight or to off-load once the *Mayflower* reaches Earth, Purple assumed it would be left for the colony's use. Purple also included a proportionate supply of our emergency rations be allocated to the outpost population. As you know, we have a one-year supply of stored rations on board that to date we have not touched. By leaving a year's supply for the outpost population, they will have time to bring their hydroponic equipment on line and begin the establishment of crop production in Ararat's environment."

"I am concerned about giving up any of our emergency supplies," Sarah interrupted. "While it's true we left Earth with a year's supply and we haven't used any," she continued, "that year's supply was based on our initial population of five hundred. There are over 650 souls on the *Mayflower* now. If we had a total failure of our hydroponic system, we could only live off the rations for about nine months. As Randy just pointed out, the return flight will take about eight years. I don't think we should reduce that safety margin further."

"We haven't decided to establish the outpost yet," Captain Larson said. "Let's get through that discussion before we get into the details of what we do and do not commit to any colony we may found. Morgan, please continue."

"The second new factor Purple considered," Morgan went on, "is the psychological impact on those occupying an outpost

59

on Ararat. Purple determined that knowing they are the only human colony outside the solar system would provide additional motivation to survive. I was surprised that Purple considered this in its analysis, but the computer found this to be fairly significant. With the rest of the crew returning to Earth, those who choose to stay on Ararat will know they are going to be the ultimate measure of success or failure for this entire adventure. The entire responsibility of the mission of the Space Colonization Consortium will be on their shoulders. The net result is a significantly enhanced desire to succeed."

Morgan looked around the group to see if anyone was going to comment, but no one spoke up.

"The third factor," Morgan continued, "is the most significant and requires some background. As you all know, a strong moral code based on traditional family values was a fundamental building block of the consortium's plan for this journey. The founding partners were convinced that society was on an irreversible downward spiral on Earth. What had originally been man's desire for freedom and liberty was turned into a license for moral depravity. Thus, when the partners decided to sponsor an attempt to establish a new population of mankind outside the solar system, they wanted to make sure that new population would not repeat the same errors as it grew and prospered. The partners knew that strict laws and regulations were not the answer. Instead, they built a moral code into the *Mayflower*'s charter and carefully screened all prospective applicants for the crew to make sure their core beliefs were consistent with that code. All of us passed that screening process and agreed to abide by the standards it established. Those standards included, among other things, a commitment to traditional family values and rejection of available artificial-reproduction techniques. We have all lived by that code since we were selected for the crew. Further, the constraints of the moral code were a significant factor in determining that the crew had to have a minimum population of five hundred to ensure genetic viability."

"We all know this," Nels interrupted. "Why are you wasting our time? Get to the bottom line."

"I am," Morgan responded. "But this background is important in understanding the computer's revised analysis. You will recall yesterday when the captain announced the decision to return to Earth, he said, 'I have decided that we are going to abandon our charter and return to Earth.' Captain Larson, of course, was referring to the charter's flight plan to continue on to Tau Ceti if Epsilon Eridani did not have a suitable habitable planet. Purple, however, took the statement literally. When I asked the computer to revise its analysis of an outpost's survival chances based on our discussion and decision, it included the captain's statement and eliminated any constraints imposed by the charter."

"What are you saying?" Dr. Sanchez asked.

"What I am saying is the computer ignored the moral code in revising the outpost survival chances to as high as thirty-five percent."

"Is this what you intended?" Sandra asked Captain Larson.

"Absolutely not," he responded. "My statement yesterday was simply that we had to return to Earth. Let me state unequivocally that nothing in our charter has changed except our next destination. I expect every member of this crew will continue to abide by the moral code we all agreed to as long as we are part of this crew.

"On the other hand," he continued, "I know that the decision that we return to Earth is devastating to many of us. When Morgan told me that Purple had given an Ararat outpost a reasonable chance of survival if not constrained by our moral code, I decided we had to consider the option. If enough people want to accept the requirements identified by the computer as a condition of staying here, I believe they should be given that opportunity. Once we depart, they will be completely on their own and can adopt any standards they wish. They will no longer be a part of the *Mayflower* complement."

Several people tried to ask questions, but Captain Larson cut them off. "There is much more to consider before any decision is made on this. There are significant issues regarding the size and makeup of a colony we might plant on Ararat. After Morgan told me about the new survival chances for a colony on Ararat, I asked him to refine the analysis for today's meeting. Incidentally, I propose we now use the term *Ararat colony* instead of base camp or outpost. Now, Morgan, before we get further afield, please tell us what additional details you garnered from Purple's revision."

"The initial proposed population of the Ararat colony is still no more than forty," Morgan continued. "However, the number could be as low as thirty-two. Purple determined that the colony has to start small in order to give it time to develop the needed infrastructure. But certain skill sets are required in the initial population, and when the number drops below thirty-two, the absence of all required skills causes the survival chances to quickly decline.

"Forty, of course, is well below what is considered a minimum viable population of five hundred. However, there are many examples of endangered species dropping well below the minimum viable population number but avoiding extinction and recovering.

"Two elements are common for those species that have been able to recover. First, habitat protection and restoration reduce environmental conditions as a limiting factor and allow populations to expand. Second, breeding programs can dramatically increase the number of individuals available to occupy that habitat. Consider, for example, the California condor, a large vulture originally found in the Western United States. In the wild, the California condor does not reach breeding age until age six and lays only one egg every two years. Because of a variety of factors including poaching, poisoning, and a loss of native habitat, natural reproduction did not keep up with mortality. By the 1980s, only twenty-two were left in the world. In 1987, all these birds were captured and placed in a captive breeding program. From one egg every two years, production increased to over two eggs every year. In addition, mortality dramatically decreased in captivity. Late in the twentieth century, efforts began to reintroduce condors in the wild in California and Arizona. By 2010, there were nearly four hundred living California condors, including about two hundred in the wild. There were over one thousand California condors in the wild when the captive breeding program was terminated for budgetary reasons in 2035.

"These same principles apply to the Ararat colony. By leaving everything not needed for the return to Earth, the colony will have an abundance of materials in which to expand the artificial habitat of the base camp in the short run and time to adapt to Ararat conditions and habitat in future generations. Having ample habitat is not enough however. The colony will also have to use methods similar to captive breeding programs to reduce the dangers of genetic problems within the population. As you may remember, we have on board frozen sperm-and-egg samples of most of the adults that embarked on this adventure when we left Earth. Purple has incorporated this genetic material into its calculations."

Morgan paused to see what reaction there might be to the use of the frozen sperm and eggs. Before the *Mayflower* left Earth, there was some concern that years in space exposed to zero gravity and interstellar radiation might result in reduced reproductive capability and sterility. To guard against this possibility, samples were placed in storage cases where it was protected from harmful radiation. The material was then available to be used if necessary when a new planet was colonized. As it turned out, there had been no fertility problems on the *Mayflower*. None of the material had been used and, for the most part, had been forgotten.

"That is not why I placed some of my eggs in storage," Melissa said. "It was for my personal use if I became sterile during the voyage. Those eggs are my personal property. I can't imagine them being used by someone else." Several others nodded agreement with Melissa's comment.

"I understand your concern, Melissa," Morgan responded. "Nevertheless, the computer determined that the initial colonists will have to use the frozen genetic material to maximize the genetic diversity of the population as it expands. This will require the use of artificial insemination and *in-vitro* fertilization techniques to supplement the natural reproductive capabilities of the initial colony population. Further, the need to maximize the reproductive capability of the initial population impacts the desired sexual makeup of that population. We do not have the capability on the *Mayflower* to reproduce humans outside the womb. Therefore, the founding population will have to be dominantly female, about two to one. All of these individuals should be of reproductive age. The maximum age for males recommended by Purple is forty-five, and the maximum age for females is thirty-five. Both sexes need a uniform age distribution up from the age of sixteen."

Graysun Williams interrupted Morgan. "Wait a minute. Those upper age limitations, particularly for the women, will eliminate virtually every adult couple that joined this mission. My wife is thirty-seven now, but she was just twenty-one when we were selected for the crew in 2068. Why did the computer set the maximum age limit so low?"

"Purple was looking at ideal survival chances," Morgan replied. "For women, Purple considered the number of reproductive years in a woman's life span and the need to grow and expand the small core population. Every deviation from those ideal conditions will change the probability of survival. But other factors will also impact the bottom line such as the skill sets of the core members." Morgan glanced at Nels to see if he was going to say anything, but Nels had assumed a sulking demeanor and remained silent. "If we decide on leaving a colony, I will ask the computer to recalculate everything once all the information is entered. For now, there are several other things I want to discuss."

No one objected, so Morgan continued, "While currently married couples could theoretically be considered for the colonists, the breeding requirements of the colony would result in substantial deviation from the moral standards adopted by this crew. Crossbreeding would be a requirement. I will yield to Melissa's opinion on this, but I believe the tension between colony breeding requirements and a marriage bond would be unhealthy for the colony."

Morgan paused to let this sink in. He knew this would cause a great deal of concern for the crew. The founding partners of the Space Colonization Consortium believed that the moral fiber of mankind had declined to decadent levels by the mid-twenty-first century. They believed that there was little point in establishing a new population of man in the universe without core values that rejected the lifestyles of the majority of mid-twenty-first-century humanity. Thus, they included moral standards in the psychological testing of applicants for the crew. Among the characteristics they screened for were a belief in family values, commitment to marriage between man and woman, rejection of sexual relations outside of wedlock, recognition of the value of life, truthfulness, and a standard of self-reliance.

Many candidates for the crew were not selected without knowing that they were rejected because they did not have these basic values required by the founding partners. The final step for all prospective crew members was adoption of the *Mayflower*'s charter. Every candidate for the crew was required to sign the charter before they were accepted as members. When knowledge of this final step in crew selection leaked out shortly before departure, the vicious pulp press labeled the *Mayflower*'s crew as *the twenty-first-century edition of the seventeenth century Puritans*. To the surprise of these muckrakers, the crew reveled in this title.

As Morgan looked at those around the table, it was obvious that this information was very troubling to most of those present. Nels who had been alert at the beginning of the discussion had drawn back and looked defeated. Nels was forty-eight years old, beyond the maximum age recommended by Purple. Further, his specialty as a planetologist would likely not be a highly desirable skill set for an Ararat colony. No one spoke for a couple of minutes. Finally, Captain Larson asked if there were any other factors regarding the makeup of an ideal population for the Ararat colony. Morgan described some additional matters to consider such as the physical condition of the colonists but emphasized that the importance of the genetic and psychological characteristics of the colonists in combination with representation of all the required skill sets overwhelmed any other considerations.

"Well, Melissa," the captain asked, "what are your thoughts about this?"

"Quite frankly, I don't know what to think," Melissa responded. "The entire purpose of this mission has been to establish a new population of humanity based on core values that had been largely lost on Earth. What's the point of establishing a colony if it violates the very purpose we set out to achieve? Every one of the adult members was screened to ensure that they believed in marriage and family values. In the twelve years since we left Earth, I know of no examples of marital infidelity. Further, these values have been so ingrained into the younger crew members that premarital sex is unknown as far as I know. We haven't even had to talk about it. It's simply something everyone has accepted as a standard to live by. Sandra, have you seen any evidence that our code of conduct is being violated?"

"No," Dr. Sanchez responded. "The health and sex education classes taught by the clinic include a strong emphasis on abstinence for both moral and health reasons. If managed crossbreeding for the Ararat colony is required, it would mean a dramatic shift in the belief patterns of the members of the colony. I don't know how many would be willing to do that."

Graysun Williams spoke up. "That's ridiculous! We can manage whatever reproductive program is necessary if the survival of the colony is at stake. Natural reproduction is only one way to reproduce. I don't see why the colony couldn't implement an artificial insemination program and use *in-vitro* fertilization as necessary. If married couples agreed to these techniques, they could be included in the Ararat population and still maintain their moral standards. I, for one, would agree to such a program if it meant I didn't have to return to Earth. I have no doubts that my wife, Kayane, will agree with me."

"Well," Sandra responded, "the use of artificial insemination represents a substantial deviation from our moral code. Melissa, do you think an Ararat colony could maintain a standard of family values with the implementation of a managed and artificial breeding program?"

"I doubt it," Melissa said. "I think that within a few years, certainly within a few generations, reproduction would become a matter of group survival and not a matter of personal family choice. Under such a program, the principles of our charter would become meaningless."

"Screw the charter," Nels blurted out. "The charter doesn't contemplate returning to Earth either. Captain Larson has already abandoned the charter."

Captain Larson bristled at Nels's outburst. "That's enough, Nels. I made the decision to return to Earth, and I will make the decision what criteria will be used to select volunteers for an Ararat colony, if there is one. That decision has not been made yet. Morgan, are there any concerns about the supplies for an Ararat colony that Purple identified as either unnecessary for the return to Earth or necessary for the colony?"

"Food production is the major area of concern. Purple calculated that only a proportional amount of hydroponic equipment could stay with the colony. With only about six percent of the growing capacity, the colony would not be able to produce the variety we have on the *Mayflower*. Quinoa would be the main staple for the colony. Further, the computer did not indicate any of the shrimp-production facilities could be separated from the *Mayflower*. Thus, the colony would be vegetarian until they developed the capacity to bring some of the animal embryos into production. Purple calculated it would be about two generations before there was sufficient infrastructure for this to happen." Morgan hesitated before he stated one factor Purple included in his calculation of a thirty-five percent survival probability. "Purple initially addressed this concern about the food supply by including all the emergency rations in the supplies left for the colony. For forty people, the *Mayflower's* one-year supply could maintain the colony for fifteen years. If they used the emergency rations to supplement what their hydroponic capabilities were, they could survive much longer."

"Absolutely not," Sarah said. "If we had any failure in the hydroponic gardens, we would be doomed. Captain, you must not allow our safety net to be left on Ararat."

Before the captain could respond, Morgan said, "I agree. I asked the computer to look at how a proportional amount of the emergency rations would affect the colony's survival chances. Purple determined that a one-year supply of emergency rations would only reduce survival chances by two percent. Further, the loss of that amount of emergency rations would have a negligible effect on the *Mayflower*."

Morgan looked at Sarah to see if she was satisfied with that result. "As I said before," she said, "I am concerned about any reduction in our emergency rations. While I agree that a proportional amount will only result in a small reduction in our safety margin, that reduction is not zero. If we decide to leave supplies for the colony that could be needed for the return to Earth, we need to understand the potential risk of that decision."

"Anything else, Morgan?" the captain asked.

"Yes. I don't want anyone to lose focus on the risks involved to an Ararat colony. Under the ideal conditions projected by Purple, the chances of success are still only one in three. Remember, these are just statistical projections. In the real world, unknowns can enter any equation and drastically alter the outcome. I talked earlier about success stories in species recovery. There have also been many failures. Consider what happened to the mountain gorilla, one of the most closely genetically related species to man. Highly endangered because of habitat destruction, poaching, and population fragmentation, efforts were begun in the twentieth century to protect and recover the species in the mountainous regions of Africa. Early in the twenty-first century the outlook was very optimistic with the population growing to over eight hundred individuals in two populations. Then the *Ebola* virus entered the populations. In spite of all the efforts on man to protect the species, numbers decreased dramatically, and by 2030, there was no longer a viable breeding population in the wild, and by 2050, the mountain gorilla was extinct. Something unknown in the Ararat environment could easily have the same impact on the colony.

"Conditions will be very difficult on Ararat, both from an environmental standpoint and from a psychological standpoint. If a decision is made to establish the Ararat colony, every effort must be made to give them the best chance to survive possible. Captain, if you decide to offer this opportunity to the crew, I suggest we establish a selection committee to screen potential volunteers and follow the computer's recommendations as closely as possible. Assuming there are sufficient numbers of qualified volunteers, I suggest we ask Purple to recalculate the survival chances again based on exactly who is going to remain and what supplies and materials they will have. Let them know how they stand before they make the final commitment to stay."

"Those are good words of caution, Morgan," Captain Larson said. He paused and contemplated what he was going to say next. "Okay, there are obviously lots of details to work out, but I have decided we need to offer the Ararat colony as an option. I will prepare remarks for the crew and make an announcement this afternoon. Nels is right in one way. We have abandoned our charter, but that doesn't mean we have all given up on our moral standards. I don't know how many crew members are willing to abandon those standards, but it is their decision to make, not mine. The volunteers will have to agree among themselves to accept a managed breeding program and understand their survival chances are only one in three. As to the stored sperm and eggs, I agree with Melissa that they belong to the donor and are not the property of the crew. Each individual that has genetic material in storage will have to make his or her own decision as to whether the Ararat colony will have access to it. The standards for selection will be as outlined by Morgan. But I will not constrain potential applicants by focusing on the ideal age factors and skill-set requirements. I will appoint a committee to review potential volunteers and incorporate those considerations into their recommendations. Do I have any volunteers? If you are considering volunteering, I will assume you are not interested in staying yourself."

Morgan looked at Sarah. He knew neither of them would be willing to risk their family and life together to stay on Ararat. But Morgan did not want to be on the selection committee, and he suspected Sarah felt the same. After a brief pause, Melissa spoke up, "I will serve on the selection committee if you want me to. I know I could not participate in the Ararat colony under the conditions you have described."

"I can also do it," Randy said. "My wife and I talked about returning to Earth last night, and we actually found we were looking forward to it." Randy's wife, Samantha, was a natal nurse working in the shop's nursery. They had three children, all born on Earth before the *Mayflower* departed for Alpha Centauri.

"Anybody else?" Captain Larson asked. When nobody else spoke up, he said, "All right, I will consider you two as part of the committee. I would like to have one more participant, preferably someone younger. Morgan, do you think your assistant, Laura Simmons, would be interested?"

"Perhaps, I will ask her," Morgan responded.

"Now let's get back to the business of preparing for departure," the captain said. The next hour was spent discussing details of the review of potential volunteers and what was needed to make the *Mayflower* and the crew shipshape for acceleration at one gravity. It was agreed that the crew members would be given three days to decide whether or not to volunteer for the Ararat colony. The selection committee would develop any additional criteria for Purple to consider and provide the names of any volunteers to the computer for evaluation. Using the information concerning these volunteers, Purple would then prepare a report on the revised calculation of a colony's chances of success. This report would be available almost instantaneously after entry of the volunteers' names. Assuming there would be a sufficiently reasonable probability of success to go forward with the colony, the logistical details of off-loading supplies and materials were discussed. Everyone agreed that it was fair to give the colony a proportionate share of the emergency rations. Sandra again expressed concerns about the physical condition of the crew and suggested that they needed at least ninety days of exercise to adequately prepare for acceleration. Melissa pointed out that anyone that was selected to stay in the colony would need the same preparation for the return to gravity. Further, she expressed concern that the psychological pressure of the selection process on anyone who volunteered made it imperative that they know their future as quickly as possible. Captain Larson agreed that there was no reason to delay once the computer had completed its analysis. The final determination on the colony was to be completed within twenty-four hours after completion of Purple's report. When the meeting broke up, the group had agreed on a tentative departure date—one hundred days in the future. Captain Larson closed the discussions by setting a follow-up meeting for the same time the next morning.

CHAPTER 4

Morgan motioned to Sarah to wait a moment as the rest of the staff unstrapped and left the conference room. Normally there was a lot of chitchat between at the conclusion of a staff meeting. Not this time. Captain Larson appeared pensive as he retreated to his cabin without saying another word. Nels Brunken was obviously upset as he quickly headed down the main corridor. Morgan assumed he was going to find his wife, Ida, who worked in the ship's recycling facilities, or Henry in the hydroponic gardens.

John Malcolm had not said anything during the discussion, something not unusual for John. As the ship's communications officer, John's usual demeanor was very quiet and laid back. Now he was muttering to himself nervously as he left the conference room. Morgan could not tell what John thought about the Ararat colony or the return to Earth. As far as Morgan knew, John and his wife Rebecca were happy with each other. Rebecca had been teaching advanced agricultural science to the teenage members of the crew. They had two young boys that were friends of Emily and Jessica.

Randy Edwards and Melissa Grant left together, talking about the responsibility they faced. As they drifted around the companionway corner, Morgan heard Melissa say, "I'll join you in the break room in a few minutes. I want to stop and tell my husband Antonio what is going on." Antonio was a shuttle pilot and one of the few crew members that had actually been on the surface of Ararat. By all appearances, he and Melissa had a very happy, stable relationship. They had one son who was seventeen years old and had shown a great deal of interest in terraforming science.

Judy Polachek looked concerned as she departed. She had joined with Sarah, Sandra, and Melissa in expressing agreement that returning to Earth seemed the best alternative. Judy had a boy and a girl with her husband, Mark. Mark was an assistant engineer for the *Mayflower's* mechanical systems. Morgan was aware that Mark and Judy had drifted apart over the years of the flight. Judy had previously talked to Sarah about it, and Sarah confided in Morgan that they might eventually split up once they settled on a planet's surface.

Graysun Williams, on the other hand, seemed to have a new purpose in life as he left. He had certainly discussed the decision to return to Earth with his wife, Kayane, after yesterday's meeting. He did not like that decision but undoubtedly felt there was no choice with the computer originally putting chances of survival in an Ararat colony at less than five percent. Now with the chances of survival rising to an acceptable level, he was clearly considering volunteering for the Ararat colony and seemed confident his wife would want to stay as well. Whether both he and Kayane would meet the selection criteria was another matter, something Morgan thought Graysun was considering. Since Kayane's expertise was in genetics, she had a skill set that would undoubtedly be of high value to the colony. Their three children were also an issue. Graysun was a lot like Nels. Morgan doubted he would have a problem leaving his children in favor of the opportunity to stay on Ararat. But Kayane was a good mother. If it came down to a choice between her children and a return to Earth or her husband and the chance to be a pioneer on Ararat, Morgan was not sure which path she would choose.

There was little doubt that Sandra was committed to returning to Earth. She and her husband Miguel had four children and were a devout and committed family. They would stay together, period. Miguel was an engineer responsible for the *Mayflower*'s air-purification system and served on Sundays as one of the ship's church leaders.

Morgan looked at his watch; it was a little after noon. "I'm going to stop by the lab and see if Laura is willing to be a part of the selection committee," he said to Sarah as she drifted up to him. "I will meet you in the galley in half an hour."

"Sounds good. The kids will be done with their morning school classes by then. I will round them up, and we will have lunch as a family. According to the selection criteria you laid out, none of them are old enough to stay. Quite frankly, I am glad of that. I can't imagine Ben having that choice to make."

Morgan quickly pushed through the corridors to his laboratory. Laura was still there, obviously waiting to hear what had happened. She looked at Morgan apprehensively. Morgan proceeded to slowly review everything that had been discussed. As he laid out the selection criteria for the outpost that had been agreed upon, he noticed that Laura was nodding her approval of the decision. Before he relayed the captain's request for Laura to be a part of the selection team, he asked, "There is one thing I would like to know, Laura. Are you considering volunteering to stay on Ararat?"

"No," Laura responded. "I was just nine years old when my parents were selected for the mission. They discussed it with me before they volunteered, and I thought it would be a great adventure. What did I know about life at that age? The last couple of hours, I have been evaluating my purpose in life. Now I know what I want, or at least I think I do. One thing I know for sure is that I don't want to be a breeding machine, and that is what I think any female who stays will become. Besides, I am not that big a risk taker. The odds may be up to a 35 percent survival rate, but that is still way too low for me. I don't remember that much about the conditions on Earth when we left, but I do know they were not good. Maybe in some small way I can do something when I get back to make them better. Assuming everything goes as scheduled, I will be just thirty-four when we arrive back at Earth. On the return trip, I intend to digest all the information Purple has on Earth and the status of its ecosystems. Who knows where I will fit in to Earth's population, but I want it to be where I can use my knowledge, skills, and ability in the best way possible."

"I understand your reasoning, Laura. Sarah and I feel the same way. As to your concerns about how you will fit in, I have no doubt you will be able to make significant contributions to finding solutions to Earth's problems. I will work with you on the return trip to Earth to understand Earth's ecosystem, the impacts man has had on the environment, and whether we can do anything about those impacts. Quite frankly, I need to retrain myself as well. Ever since Sarah and I applied for the *Mayflower* crew, we have focused our energies on how to colonize an uninhabited planet. Now we need to learn how to contribute to a planet with too many people. If nothing else, we will have a new area of focus during the return trip.

"There is a reason I asked whether or not you were considering staying, Laura. The captain has decided to appoint a selection committee to review potential volunteers for the Ararat colony. Randy Edwards and Mellissa Grant both agreed to serve on the committee. Captain Larson wants a third person, someone to represent the younger members of the *Mayflower* crew. He suggested you, Laura. Would you be willing to do that?"

Laura looked stunned. Finally, she stammered, "Why me? There must be someone better qualified."

"Don't sell yourself short, Laura. You are a brilliant young scientist. You know more than anyone else about the criteria for survival on Ararat. It will be a huge responsibility, but the captain and I both know you are up to the task. My only concern is whether you may be conflicted because of your relationship with Henry Brunken."

Laura was quickly over her initial shock and was in deep thought. After a few moments of silence, she said, "How soon do I need to decide?"

"He said he would make an announcement this afternoon. That announcement should contain details about the survival chances for an Ararat colony and what will be required of anyone who volunteers to stay. Our overall schedule for departure is in one hundred days. We agreed that we would allow three days for anyone who was interested to volunteer. I know that's not much time, but there is a tremendous amount of work to do to prepare the *Mayflower*, the crew, and set up the facilities for those who choose to stay. I asked Captain Larson how soon he needed your response, and he said by the end of the day. If you decide not to do it, he needs time to find someone else. Now that decisions have been made, things are moving quickly. Can you decide that fast?"

"It's enough time," Laura said with conviction. "I have already pretty much decided, but I want to talk to my parents and Henry before I announce my decision."

"That should work. I'm glad you are returning to Earth and have already started working on environmental problems there that we know about. Of course, who knows how conditions might have changed by the time we get back. I'll see you later this afternoon."

Morgan departed the ecology center and joined Sarah and their children in the galley. Morgan and Sarah explained to the children what was going to be announced by the captain.

Ben eased any concerns Sarah might have had by saying he was looking forward to seeing the Earth as Morgan had described it. After finishing the noon meal, they went back to their cabin to await the captain's presentation.

At one thirty that Monday afternoon, the captain opened an all-hands channel to say he was going to make a major announcement in fifteen minutes. Every member of the crew that was not involved in critical work should cease what they were doing by then so that they could listen to what he had to say. Fifteen minutes later, he began by explaining that unlike his brief comments the day before followed by a written summary, he was going to personally discuss in detail the latest developments and the decision to return to Earth. He urged everyone to devote complete attention to his remarks as each member of the crew will be faced with a potential life-changing decision in the next three days.

"I know that many of you are aware of the reasons I announced yesterday that we were returning to Earth," he began. "In addition, I posted more details in the computer for you to see. Now we have additional information that will require many of you to make a very difficult and irreversible decision. So I want to review the facts leading up to the position we now find ourselves in.

"As we all know, Epsilon Eridani's planetary system is much like Sol's. Ararat, the second planet from Epsilon Eridani, has a mass of 0.92 in relation to Earth and an orbit with a mean radius of 0.65 astronomical units. Since Epsilon Eridani is in spectral class K2, it is somewhat cooler than Sol, and therefore Ararat is well within the region of space where a habitable planet could exist.

"However, there are significant differences in Ararat's properties that raised questions as to whether its ecosystem will support human life. First, the inclination of Ararat's equator is only

3.2 degrees, and the orbital eccentricity is 0.09. Ararat's sidereal year is 191 Earth days. With these characteristics, Ararat's seasonal variations will be negligible. Absent a significant axial inclination and without sufficient time for the slight orbital eccentricity to allow thermal variations to develop, temperatures are pretty much controlled solely by distance from the equator.

"This problem in itself is not serious however. There are many places on Earth where climatic conditions are fairly constant throughout the year. The main problem is the atmosphere. You will also recall that Nels first calculated Ararat's rotational rate to be about fifteen hours. Even without a moon, Ararat's closer position to Epsilon Eridani should have resulted in tidal braking in the planet's oceans to about this level. Ararat, however, turned out to have an actual rate of rotation of just over twenty-two hours, nearly 50 percent more than Nels's original calculations.

"The reason, of course, is the lack of large areas of surface water on Ararat. While Earth's surface is over 75 percent water, Ararat has less than 10 percent surface water. Without the seas, tidal braking effects are less significant, resulting in the faster than anticipated spin of Ararat. The one shallow sea straddling the planet's equator is not a significant factor. Nels has reported to you that the reason for the lack of water on Ararat can be traced to the formation of Epsilon Eridani's solar system. Evidence such as the smaller and cooler star and the smaller and more numerous planets indicates that this system formed more slowly than Earth's. Slow development of the planets means that they have more stable cores. Stable cores mean less volcanic activity, and volcanoes are the primary source of surface water on a planet with the characteristics of Earth and Ararat. Absent volcanoes, it is not surprising that Ararat is a relatively arid planet without expansive oceans.

"In itself, the lack of major oceans would not be a problem. We have the technology and the resources to irrigate more than enough land to support a population many times that contained on the *Mayflower*. The real problem lies in the lack of a significant natural ecosystem on Ararat. While a simple biological community has developed in the sea and short distances inland, most of the planet is a virtual sterile desert. As you know, the major source of oxygen in Earth's atmosphere is from plant photosynthesis of carbon dioxide and water. On Ararat, this source of oxygen has been missing for the entire life of the planet. The result is low levels of oxygen and high levels of carbon dioxide in the atmosphere. As a side note, there is virtually no carbon stored on the planet as fossil fuel.

"Ararat's atmosphere is technically breathable, but the partial pressure due to oxygen is so low that any attempt to do work would bring on immediate symptoms of hypoxia. While humans could exist on Ararat, under these conditions a population of humans could never grow and flourish. This concern has led to the studies we have undertaken for the last six months. Since all the ingredients—water, oxygen, carbon dioxide, and nitrogen—are present for an acceptable ecosystem, what could we do to improve the mix and make Ararat suitable for our new home? The result has been a concentrated series of studies in the areas of biology, geology, and medicine.

"Morgan Parker was charged with coordinating these studies and making sure our computer had all the data it needed to analyze the probabilities. The computer's task was to not only evaluate each proposal individually but also to look at every conceivable combination of the ideas proposed. Some of the principal studies in the biological realm included widespread irrigation of the planet's surface to improve the rate of photosynthesis and fertilization of the shallow sea to dramatically increase its biological productivity. In the medical arena, Sandra led studies in long-range adaptation to the environment and genetic enhancement of future generations to improve the body's oxygen efficiency. In the geological arena, Nels headed studies into the possibility of increasing Ararat's volcanic activity, reducing metallic oxides in the planet's surface material to free up oxygen, and artificial conversion of carbon dioxide in Ararat's atmosphere to free carbon and oxygen. These and many other more exotic ideas were considered, evaluated, and fed into the computer.

"Yesterday, Purple informed Morgan that it had all the information it needed to evaluate the suitability of Ararat for occupation by our crew. After Morgan posed the question to the computer, Purple responded that there was zero probability that Ararat would support the crew of this ship.

"We then discussed our original plan to continue on to Tau Ceti. Because of the low probability of finding a habitable planet there and growing concerns that the *Mayflower* was aging and it would not be safe to travel farther if we were unsuccessful at Tau Ceti, I made the difficult decision that for the safety of the people for which I am responsible, our only option was to return to Earth.

"However, because computers by their design always take questions literally, we learned that there might be a chance for a small outpost on Ararat. First, Purple revealed to Morgan that a smaller contingent of people, about forty, had a very small chance, less than five percent, of surviving on Ararat long enough to adapt to the harsh atmospheric conditions. This did not seem very important at the time, but I asked Morgan to look into it further because I knew there was considerable dissatisfaction among some people about the decision to go back to Earth. I wanted to make sure that there was no feasible alternative for anyone on board. Morgan asked Purple to reanalyze the possibility of an outpost's survival chances. Purple took all of the discussions we had yesterday into account, along with my announcement that we were returning to Earth. A key factor in this announcement was my statement, 'We are going to abandon our charter and return to Earth.' Of course, I was only referring to that portion of the charter calling for us to go on to Tau Ceti, but Purple did not hear anything in my statement that would limit the scope of my statement. In its new calculations, the computer took my statement at face value and disregarded all elements of the charter that might limit the survival chances of a colony on Ararat. In addition, the computer assumed that with the *Mayflower* returning to Earth, there was no need to keep the store of supplies that were to be used for a permanent colony. By applying all of the alternative scenarios that were now available in the absence of those limitations, the chances of survival of a small base camp population rose significantly to as high as thirty-five percent.

"Now I want everyone to listen carefully to what this means," the captain continued. "I have decided that assuming there are enough volunteers who want to stay here, we will establish a colony on Ararat. But each one of you needs to know what it will mean to volunteer. Before I even get to the implications of the computer's interpretation of my statement, you need to know that conditions will be very harsh, and once we leave, you will be entirely on your own. The atmosphere on Ararat does not contain enough oxygen to allow one to avoid hypoxia. You will need to live in an artificial environment or use supplemental breathing equipment. Once we depart for Earth, there will be no turning back. So the earliest you could see any outside help from Earth would be in twenty-seven years Earth time, even assuming there is another interstellar ship available to make the journey. The *Mayflower* is wearing out, and the return trip to Earth is in all probability the last trip the *Mayflower* will make. So for all practical purposes, any Ararat colony will be entirely on its own. There are still two chances in three that the colony will perish. For the colony to even reach that level of survivability, each and every colony volunteer will have to commit to all of the factors Purple considered in its revised analysis.

"Critical to this commitment will be a life-choice decision each volunteer must make. That choice will not be easy. You all know how important the moral code is to the sponsors of this mission. They believed there was little point in establishing a new population of mankind if that population was destined to repeat the mistakes being made on Earth. They believed mankind as a whole had lost any sense of decency and personal responsibility by the mid-twenty-first century. They believed Earth's population had achieved its greatest level of civilization and had entered into a downward spiral toward a repeat of Earth's dark ages. They had seen how all efforts of mankind over the ages from religion to law failed to maintain a morally responsible population over the long haul. Greed, moral depravity, and laziness eventually led every rising civilization back into decline.

"The founding partners of this mission were determined to select a crew that could break the chain of the rise and fall of civilizations. Every adult member of this crew was carefully screened to find applicants who maintained high standards of moral behavior, family values, and personal responsibility. You were not selected because you agreed to the moral code of the *Mayflower* charter. You were selected because the standards of that code were a fundamental core belief you held. In effect, you being a part of this crew is the result of a careful process of elimination of anyone from the applicants who did not have these core values. To date, the founders' plan appears successful, as we have had no known violations of the moral code since we left Earth. Every indication we have is that you all have been living according to the standards of the moral code, not because you are being told to but because you truly believe that is the standards by which you should live.

"Therein lays the dilemma each of you must face should you be considering volunteering for the colony. When Purple eliminated the charter from its calculations, it also eliminated the moral code. The computer assumed there would be no moral constraints on the colony population. To achieve maximum genetic diversity and a survival chance of up to thirty-five percent, the population would need to utilize all available reproductive techniques including crossbreeding, artificial insemination, and *in-vitro* fertilization. To volunteer, you must be willing to subject yourself to these techniques as dictated by the population's needs. If enough of you are willing to do this, you will have a reasonable chance to survive for generations to come. If not, there is no point in leaving anyone here."

The captain then went on to describe other factors that would be considered in the selection of a potential Ararat-colony population including sex ratios, minimum and maximum numbers, age parameters, and skill sets. He, however, refrained from putting any specific limitations on those factors as had been identified by the computer. He also discussed the genetic material in storage, how it was incorporated into Purple's analysis and the option each member will have as to the availability of that material.

"There is something else I want you to consider as you weigh the options you have," he continued. "It has been twelve years ship's time since we left Earth, and we haven't heard anything from our sponsors for years. On Earth, over eighteen years have elapsed. By the time we get back, Earth and its population will have aged over thirty years. Conditions were definitely deteriorating prior to our departure, and it is unlikely that pattern has reversed. You should expect living conditions on Earth to be much different than on this ship and what we were planning for as a colony. In particular, those of you in your midtwenties and younger have no real understanding of what was happening to society on Earth. We will change our education program to prepare everyone for what to expect, but that will take time and will not happen until after you have decided whether or not to volunteer for the Ararat colony. For those of you who meet the minimum criteria, you are in a sense faced with a choice between the lesser of two evils. Do you volunteer for the radically altered lifestyle required by the Ararat colony knowing the odds of survival are low, or do you accept the fact that you are returning to everything you and your parents so desperately wanted to leave when you signed on to this mission?

"I know this is a lot for many of you to digest," he concluded. "But I need to make a decision quickly so we can get on with the preparations for our return to Earth. I have appointed a selection committee to review any crew members expressing a desire to stay. They will determine whether there are enough volunteers that meet the criteria and if so, which ones should be offered the opportunity to stay. Assuming there is a viable set of volunteers, we will meet with that group to discuss in detail what they will face and give each one an opportunity to change his or her mind. If you want to stay, you need to inform the committee of your decision by noon Thursday.

"In addition, I need a response from each of the adults on board that provided frozen sperm or eggs before we left Earth as to whether or not you will allow that material to be left on Ararat to increase the colony's genetic variability and thus chances of survival. If anyone has any questions regarding the colony decision, contact Morgan in the ecology center. If you have questions about your frozen sperm or eggs, contact Dr. Sandra Sanchez."

Morgan looked at Sarah as Captain Larson wrapped up his comments. "Sarah," he said, "I didn't anticipate that last comment. I'd better head back to the center. I expect there will be lots of inquiries."

Sarah nodded in agreement. "What a choice people are going to have to make, especially those younger crew members that have not yet formed strong marital relationships. I remember reading as a child about the pioneers in the early United States. They would leave family and friends behind to set out to the west, often never to reestablish contact with those they left behind. That's what we did when we boarded the *Mayflower*. Now some of us will choose to do that again. I am glad that there is no issue between us, Morgan. Whatever lies ahead, we will deal with it as partners in life.

"I will look for you at our quarters before our evening meal. Judy and I need to make plans for division of the hydroponic equipment and the emergency rations. The hydroponic system is dependent on complete recycling of organic matter to maintain an ecological balance. I want to make sure we can remove a part of that system without upsetting that balance."

Morgan left their quarters and worked his way through the corridors toward his office. He knew Sarah was concerned about the food supply; that was her job. But he also knew that Sarah would come up with a plan that gave the Ararat colony a fair share of the hydroponic system without jeopardizing the *Mayflower*'s food supply.

Laura was at her workstation when Morgan arrived at the ecology center. From the look on her face, Morgan knew her conversation with Henry did not go well. "Henry said he would rather die than return to Earth," she said. "He asked me if I was going to volunteer, and when I said no, it didn't faze him a bit. It was like our relationship didn't mean anything. He also said his dad was very angry and was going to volunteer even though he knew he was over the recommended age limit."

"I'm sorry Henry hurt you," Morgan said awkwardly.

"I'm not hurt. I'm mad at him. Here I thought he was as serious about me as I was about him. But he didn't even want to discuss my concerns about volunteering. When I said I didn't want to stay on Ararat, all he said was, 'That's your choice.' What a jerk. You know, I think we are not as committed to our moral code as we think we are. The captain said there have been no violations of the code. Maybe it's because we haven't faced any temptation on this ship before now. As soon as something like the colony comes up, people like Henry quickly forget about things like honor, commitment, and family. Here I thought I knew him."

"What about Ida?" Morgan asked, trying to divert her thoughts away from the letdown Henry had been to her.

"Henry didn't say anything about his mother. I don't think she's as down on returning to Earth as Nels is. I am sure Nels told her about the age issues, and since she is also over the age limit at forty-seven, I expect she won't have a problem having that fact make the decision for her. My parents feel like I do, and they were very proud that I had been asked to serve in the evaluation and selection process."

"What about your conflict of interest if Henry does volunteer?"

"What conflict? He's just another crew member to me now. I will deal with that when the time comes. If he objects to my being on the committee, I will recuse myself from any decision regarding Henry. But I am going to tell Captain Larson I will help with the selection process," Laura said. "I was just waiting for you to get back. I'm heading to his quarters now." Laura departed just as one of the hydroponics maintenance workers arrived with a question about the Ararat qualification factors.

Over the next two hours, fifteen crew members came to Morgan to ask questions. In most cases, they had not been listening closely enough to the captain's announcement and needed clarification as to what decision they had to make and when they had to make it. Most of them were younger members of the crew, and the questions were easily answered. Laura returned from her conversation with Captain Larson within fifteen minutes of her departure and sat in on the visits by those having questions. During a break between visitors, Laura told Morgan she had talked briefly with Randy and Melissa, and they were getting together the next morning to discuss how they would handle the selection process.

Sarah was in their cabin when Morgan arrived back from his laboratory at a little after six in the evening. "Where are the kids?" he asked.

"They went on ahead to eat. They said they wanted to go to the children's recreation center to meet with some of the other kids their age to find out what others were thinking."

"Probably a good idea," Morgan replied. "Besides I need some quiet time with you for a change. Let's go get something to eat."

"Quinoa, you mean," Sarah laughed. "It barely qualifies as *something to eat*."

They were surprised when they arrived at the galley by the number of people sitting around. Normally when a meal was finished, people left quickly. Unlike ships of old, everyone ate in the same space. There weren't separate facilities for officers and crew. In fact, there was no real distinction of rank on the *Mayflower* other than the designation of Howard Larson as captain, and even he and his family ate in the galley. The organization of the crew into various divisions and designation of certain crew members as leaders of a division was strictly for the purpose of efficiency and control and had nothing to do with rank or stature. Thus, while Morgan and Sarah could have normally found a table by themselves, the only places available were with a group of younger crew members that were discussing the Ararat-colony issue.

One of them, Josh Hernandez, a twenty-four-year-old medical technician, said to Morgan and Sarah as they strapped into the table, "This is crazy. How can we make a decision like this in less than three days? I was only twelve when we left Earth, and for the four years before that, I was at the flight-preparation base as my parents trained for this journey. I don't know anything about life on Earth. What should I do?"

"I can't advise you how to decide," Morgan replied. "Each of you must make your own decision. What I can tell you is that neither life on Ararat nor back on Earth will be anything like what you have experienced here on the *Mayflower* for the last twelve years. Further, life on Ararat will be about as opposite as life on Earth could be. Survival is only one thing you need to consider. Assuming the colony on Ararat makes it, will it be a way of life that would be acceptable to you? Or if you decide to return to Earth, could you learn to live amongst the many billions of people there and the conditions they have created that we so desperately wanted to leave? Also remember, whatever path you choose, your decision will be irreversible. If families choose to separate, it will be permanent, just as we thought it was when we left Earth. Have you talked it over with your family?"

"No, not yet," said Josh. Josh's parents, Mario and Sylvia Hernandez, were both agricultural-science experts and worked as a team in the hydroponic gardens. They had three children, Josh, his younger brother Colton, seventeen, and a daughter, Rose, who was born the same year as Emily. Morgan knew Mario and Sylvia well enough to believe they would not volunteer to stay and doubted they would want to see their family split up. They were regular attendees at Sunday worship ceremonies as were all their children.

"I know you didn't volunteer to leave Earth in the first place," Sarah said. "Your parents brought you along when you were a child because they wanted to find a better life for you and didn't want to leave you behind. It looks like whichever option you choose, that better life isn't in the cards. Now what you have to decide is whether you want to stay with most of your family and friends or want to venture into a truly untested and risky yet intriguing scientific experiment. If the Ararat colony is established and succeeds, it will have accomplished one of the goals of this entire mission. It will have planted the human race on another planet."

"Thanks, I think," Josh responded, "you've helped me focus." Several others at the table nodded in agreement. As they unstrapped from the table to leave, Morgan let them know he was available if any of them wanted to discuss the matter further.

"Can you imagine," Sarah said after they had left, "discussions like this are going on all over the *Mayflower*. After Ben heard the captain's announcement, he said he wanted to give it some further thought. He asked me for advice. I didn't want to squash his freedom of thought by telling him he was too young, so I discussed the matter much like we just did here. He appears to be evaluating the issue in a very mature manner."

"I know he will," Morgan said. Morgan and Sarah spent the next half hour in small talk about what they remembered and what they didn't about life on Earth. It was a pleasant escape from the weight of the process ahead of them and all the crew members for the next three days. After supper, they returned to their quarters. Emily and Jessica were there looking up Earth information on their monitors, but Ben was not. He returned an hour later. He said he had been talking with some of his friends, in particular a young girl in which he had recently taken an interest. Ben said none of his close friends wanted to stay, and he didn't either, a great relief to Morgan and Sarah.

CHAPTER 5

The next three days proved to be the most tumultuous on the *Mayflower* since their journey began. Morgan turned his office space over to Melissa Grant, Randy Edwards, and Laura for use in reviewing potential Ararat-colony volunteers and determining which, if any, would be a good fit for the colony. Captain Larson took the unusual step of authorizing the three of them to communicate directly with Purple during the review process to maximize the team's efficiency. They spent virtually the entire three days holed up in the ecology center discussing with each other and Purple various factors and how they would affect survival chances of an Ararat colony.

Captain Larson cancelled the follow-up meeting he had originally scheduled. He briefly announced to his staff that it would be fruitless to work on details for the departure until the colony matter was settled. Instead, he told everyone to report to the conference room on Thursday afternoon once the time frame for applying for the colony closed.

Without his office to escape to and, in reality, with nothing much to do anyway, Morgan spent the time wandering through the *Mayflower* talking to various members of the crew. He found that many of the young adults were very uncertain about what to do, just as Josh Hernandez and his friends had been. These people were in the group that Melissa Grant had described as wanting finality in the journey, whatever it was. Now faced with a choice as to which fork in the road to take and whatever choice they made the decision was going to be permanent and irreversible, they were struggling with the issue. For most of them, the most important decision they had ever made prior to this moment was choosing a career path in preparation for life as a pioneer on whatever planet was found to colonize. But most of that preparation was based on an expectation that the *Mayflower* would find a place like Earth. Perhaps it had never been realistic, but there was a hopeful belief throughout the crew that something like the North America of the 1600s would be found. Now the choice was between a cramped, hostile environment with an uncertain future on Ararat or what North America was expected to be like by early in the twenty-second century Earth time when they would complete the return voyage. It was one thing to want finality; it was quite another to have to choose between two very unattractive alternatives.

Unlike Morgan, Sarah was very busy determining how to best separate a portion of the hydroponic system without damaging what was left. Such a possibility had not been considered in the original design, but the system was simple enough that Sarah was sure it could be done safely. Late Wednesday afternoon, she called Morgan on the intercom and suggested they meet in the ship's lounge adjacent to the galley.

She was already fastened into a lounge chair sipping on a pouch of hot quinoa tea when Morgan arrived. Morgan floated over to the beverage machine, dispensed hot coffee into a weightless cup, and joined Sarah in the lounger. "Is everything going well in the hydroponic gardens," he asked.

"Yes, I worked it out," Sarah responded. "I'm glad that I have that worry off of my mind. We can remove a section of the system that will suit the colony's needs without jeopardizing food production here on the *Mayflower*. It's nice to be finally able to sit and relax for a few minutes. I have hardly had time to talk to you the last couple of days."

"That certainly hasn't been my problem. I really haven't had anything to do and no office to escape to either. So I've been playing the role the captain suggested for me," Morgan said. "I've been moving throughout the ship making myself available to anybody who has questions about Ararat or anything else."

"How is that going?" Sarah asked.

"Three crew members have already told me they are going to ask to stay. Several others are giving it serious consideration. When they ask for my advice, I tell them what I can, but I don't try and make the decision for them. If they are uncertain, I suggest they spend some quiet time to consider the decision. Two of them that indicated they wanted to stay said they are willing to accept the known environmental conditions they will face on Ararat no matter how difficult and alien in preference to the unknown environmental and social conditions that will exist on Earth when we get back in another eight years. They are just not sure about the reproductive requirements the captain described in order for the colony to survive."

"I'm glad I don't have to make that choice. It's hard to believe the conditions on Earth will be any better than it was when we left, but I wouldn't be surprised if they are much worse. Unfortunately, all indications at the time of our departure were that man's descent into moral corruption was accelerating. As to the environment, unless there was some cataclysmic event in the last twelve years or really in the last eighteen years Earth time, it shouldn't be that much different."

Morgan paused and thought about how the Earth's population had been evolving when they departed. Morgan and Sarah had been insulated from much of the chaos of the twenty-first century, first by their parents, and then by their university studies. Thinking he would never go back, Morgan had thought little about Earth since he and Sarah had boarded the *Mayflower* prior to departure. Now it was all coming back to him.

He remembered a sermon in a Sunday service when he was ten or eleven years old. Like most boys his age, he usually paid little attention during church services. He was there because his parents made him go. But this sermon was different. The minister called his sermon, "When We Allowed the Ten Commandments to Be Replaced by the Seven Deadly Sins," and Morgan listened. He didn't know what the seven deadly sins were, so he looked them up that evening when he got home and found they were wrath (anger), greed, sloth (apathy), pride, lust, envy, and gluttony. The minister focused his comments on the rise and decline of the United States, but his message accurately described the rise and fall of nations and civilizations worldwide throughout time.

The minister began by reminding his congregation as to why the people of the American colonies rose up against the king of England to win their freedom. They wanted a place where liberty was important, where a man could worship as he wished, where a man was free to say what he wanted, and where a man was protected from government intrusion into his life without due process. The founders of what became the United States wanted a limited government with checks and balances so that it was clear that the role of government was to serve the people and not rule them.

The government created by the founding fathers was not perfect, but through the next two centuries, most of the imperfections were fixed. A bloody civil war in the nineteenth century eliminated slavery, and by the early twentieth century, the women's suffrage movement had established women's equal role in the selection of the country's leaders. In two world wars in the first half of the twentieth century, the United States emerged as the dominant power in the world and a beacon for the liberties and freedom of its people. The years following the Second World War were an age of innocence and tremendous economic expansion for the country. Almost everyone who was able and willing found employment, and the country prospered. There was tremendous national pride and a sense of duty to spread the American dream throughout the world.

At his inauguration in 1961, President John F. Kennedy captured this spirit of America in his famous line, "Ask not what your country can do for you, ask what you can do for your country." The decade of the 1960s, however, ultimately marked the peak of America's greatness. By the end of that decade, John Kennedy and his brother Bobby had both been assassinated. The United States was embroiled in a bitter *no-win* war in Vietnam; the country had been wracked by race riots and homegrown terrorism. The traditional roles of the father and mother in the family unit were changing, and a new generation was more interested in *free love* and self-fulfillment than in honor, duty, and decency. By the end of the twentieth century, the religious freedom of the first amendment had been twisted into a concept of *freedom from religion*. God and biblical principles had been abandoned by the American education system, and the country was in moral decline. Under the guise of freedom of speech, pornography emerged from the shadows of dark alleyways to the living-room television and videos. Increasingly the American people were more interested in what they could get from the government than what they could do for their fellow man. By the first quarter of the twenty-first century, a majority of the population was willing to give up its liberty in exchange for cradle-to-grave government dependency. The founders' desire for a limited government and local rule had been supplanted by a burgeoning federal bureaucracy administering mountains of rules and regulations that stifled individual creativity and personal responsibility.

The minister concluded his sermon by stating that in less than one hundred years, the United States had been transformed from a God-loving, Christian country into a godless, self-centered society. Love of God had been replaced by idolization of celebrities and self. Respect for the name of God had been replaced by crude, vulgar language in everyday life. Honor of family had been replaced by self-indulgence and government interference in parental responsibilities. Respect for life had been cast aside under the guise of the rights of the individual. The sacred bond of marriage was diluted by changing the definition of it being a bond between man and woman and by openly accepting adultery from political and social leaders. Respect for the property of others gave way to a populace that increasingly found it easier to let the government redistribute wealth than earn it themselves. Honesty was no longer valued as a character trait. The entertainment and media industries created class envy that everyone should have what anyone else had based on fairness, not individual accomplishment. In less than one hundred years, the standards of the Ten Commandments were virtually gone in American society, having been replaced by the evils of the seven deadly sins.

There were, of course, exceptions. Some churches resisted the pressures to modernize their beliefs to conform to the changing societal standards. Private schools attempted to maintain high moral standards as well as giving a superior education. But these institutions found it increasingly difficult to maintain their standards in the face of oppressive government regulations to conform to national standards. The fact that the national standards set the bar well below what the private institutions required seemed to matter little to the bureaucrats; in their view, conformity was more important than individual achievement. If a religious group resisted complying with unacceptable government dictates such as refusing to conduct nontraditional marriages, the courts and the taxing power of the government were used to either force acquiescence or face financial ruin.

Morgan wondered if there was any chance the downward slide of society had been reversed since the *Mayflower* departed. He doubted it but wanted at least to hold out some hope that freedom was still possible on Earth. Morgan agreed with Sarah that returning to Earth gave their children the best chance of survival. The only question was whether they could find a meaningful place in Earth's twenty-second-century society and whether the family values established in the *Mayflower*'s charter would be lost in the pressures of the Earth's masses. Laura's earlier comment about how tenuous the moral standards of the *Mayflower* could be when confronted by temptation worried him. But he didn't want to let his concerns provide further fuel for any new doubts about the decision to return to Earth.

Sarah interrupted Morgan's thoughts. "Morgan, you look deep in thought. What are you thinking about?"

"I was considering what you said about how conditions on Earth are unlikely to be better than when we left. You are almost certainly right, but I am an eternal optimist. I am going to hold out hope that somehow a little common sense has arisen, and the downward spiral has been reversed or at least stopped."

"We shall see," Sarah said. "In the meantime, all we can do is prepare us and our children for the future that now awaits us."

"By the way," Morgan said, "have you thought about what you are going to do with your frozen eggs?"

"I have. As much as it concerns me morally, I think we need to give the colony every opportunity possible to survive. I am going to give the samples to the colony."

"I feel the same way," Morgan said. "It should be up to those who are selected to stay to decide when and how to enhance their genetic variability as much as they want."

Morgan and Sarah then called Purple and gave the computer their decision. Once that was done, they both felt good about their decision, knowing they had done what they could to maximize the colony's survival chances, if indeed there was a colony authorized by the captain.

Morgan looked up as Ben, Emily, and Jessica drifted into the galley. "This is special," Morgan proclaimed. "All of us together for the dinner hour." The family spent the next hour in quiet family time, talking about anything except the next day's activities. After dinner, they retired to their quarters and asked Purple to show them an old video of life on the nineteenth century American frontier. By the time the video was over, they were more than ready for a good night's sleep.

As Morgan and Sarah were tucking Jessica into her bunk, she asked, "Do you think anyone I know will want to stay?"

"Maybe some of the older people," answered Sarah, "but not any of your friends. They are all too young to be chosen for the Ararat colony."

"Why do they call that planet Ararat anyway?" Jessica asked.

"You were only five when the planet was named," answered Morgan, "and don't remember the discussions that went into the decision. Do you remember the Bible story of Noah and the ark?"

"I think so. It is about a big flood, isn't it?"

"Yes, it is. God was unhappy with people because most people had become sinful. So God decided to wipe out everyone with a big flood. But one person named Noah was still a good person and loved by God. So God told Noah to build a big boat, called an ark, and take his family and many animals on the boat to survive the flood that was coming. Noah did what God told him to do, and he and his family lived on the boat for a long time while the whole Earth was buried under rains and flood. When the rain eventually stopped and the earth began to dry out, the ark came to rest on a mountain called Ararat. This was the place where people could start over to try and live according to what God wanted. When we first saw the planet around Epsilon Eridani, we thought it was going to be our place to live the way God wanted us to. The planet reminded us of Noah's arrival on land, so we decided to name it after Noah's mountain, Ararat."

"I wish it was a nicer place so we could live there," said Jessica.

"So do I, so do I," whispered Morgan as Jessica drifted off to sleep.

Thursday morning activity was anything but normal on the *Mayflower*. Melissa, Randy, and Laura appeared briefly in the galley for breakfast but would only say that they were working on their task. At nine in the morning, Purple put out a general announcement that over one hundred crew members had not yet responded regarding the use of their genetic material. At 11:00 a.m., the captain notified the division chiefs that the selection committee would have their recommendations for consideration completed by 2:30 p.m., and all should assemble in the conference room at 3:00 p.m.

After briefly checking to ensure that everything was operating normally in the hydroponic gardens, Sarah joined Morgan in the galley. They spent the rest of the morning discussing the future of the *Mayflower* and its people with others as they came through for something to eat. Morgan had not seen such a high level of anticipation since the first announcement that Ararat appeared to be much like Earth. It was clear that many crew members were torn by the decision facing them and were waiting as long as possible before committing one way or another. It was not just the risk of survival that would be undertaken if they volunteered to stay; it was also the knowledge that volunteering would mean permanent separation from family and friends that chose to return to Earth. Alternately, there was a great deal of concern about returning to Earth and the environment the crew had so much desired to leave. Finally, there was also the troubling issue of abandoning their core beliefs if they chose to stay. These crew members were talking to everyone they could to weigh the pros and cons of either choice. As noon approached, several who remained on the fence quietly departed the galley to make their final decision.

Morgan and Sarah returned to their cabin for a couple hours of peace and quiet before heading to the conference room. Everyone, including Laura, was strapped in several minutes before three, waiting for the captain's arrival. There was virtually no conversation as they waited. As Morgan looked around the table, it was obvious that waiting for the results was weighing heavily on several while others appeared relaxed and comfortable. Nels Brunken was looking particularly grumpy as he knew the combination of his age along with his profession would likely keep him from being selected. Graysun Williams also looked concerned. Morgan wondered if his wife, Kayane, had chosen the same path as Graysun. Judy Polachek also looked apprehensive, probably because her husband had applied to stay. Finally, John Malcolm looked troubled. Morgan wondered if he or his wife had volunteered.

On the other hand, Morgan was glad to see that Melissa seemed relaxed. She had not mentioned her husband, Antonio, when she volunteered for the selection committee. Antonio's duties as a shuttle pilot had taken him to the surface of Ararat several times, and Morgan thought he might be interested in staying. Also their son Carlos had been studying terraforming and, at seventeen, was above the recommended minimum age limit. Terraforming would be an ideal skill set to have in the colony, but from the look on Melissa's face, Morgan was pretty sure their family was going to stay together.

Not surprisingly, Sandra Sanchez did not seem concerned about the impending discussion. She had told Sarah that she and her husband, Miguel, had talked with all their children, and they wanted to return to Earth.

Captain Larson arrived about five minutes early which was unusual for him. It was immediately apparent that he was not himself. Sandra said, "Captain, you look enervated. Is everything all right?"

"I was unprepared for how traumatic this process would be, both from a personal standpoint as well as from the responsibility I bear as leader of this mission," he responded. "But we are not here to talk about me. I see that Laura has joined the rest of us, so let's get started. Melissa, Randy, Laura, tell us what you have determined."

His attempt to brush off Sandra's concern generated several surprised looks around the table. Morgan was particularly concerned about his comment from a *personal standpoint*. The captain had been married to his wife, Deanna, for almost thirty years, and they had three children, all born before departure from Earth. Morgan wondered if there was discord in the Larson family and that at least one of his children was on the list of volunteers. His oldest daughter, Vickie, was twenty-seven and had completed training as a medical doctor and surgeon. She was currently in charge of the *Mayflower*'s nursery. He also had two sons Albert and Trevor who were educated to be skilled agronomists.

"We had forty-three people volunteering to stay, twenty-two men and twenty-one women," Melissa began. "Before I get into the details, I want to go over a couple of refinements we gave to Purple to consider. First, there were three married couples that volunteered. We told the computer that if one is selected, both should be, recognizing that this could have a negative impact on the overall survival probability. However, we did not want the computer to separate a couple that had chosen to stay together. Another issue we discussed and provided additional information to Purple about was exactly what training and skills would be immediately needed by the colony and what expertise could be developed over time. In view of the larger number of male volunteers, we asked Purple to balance these needs with the optimal sex ratio previously recommended by Purple of two to one or better. In this regard, we also told Purple to consider ages of volunteers in relation to their training and how anyone outside the recommended age limits would affect the overall survival chances."

"What about the stored human reproductive samples?" Sandra asked.

"That was a surprise," Melissa said. "Of the 320 adults that provided eggs or sperm, only 17 said they did not want to leave their genetic material for the colony. Purple incorporated this material into its calculations."

"What's the bottom line?" Captain Larson asked.

As the team had agreed, Melissa looked to Randy to pick up the discussion. He glanced around the table and said, "The bottom line is that the best survival chances are with an initial colony population of thirty-six. That includes all of the female applicants and fifteen of the males. With this initial population and all of the material support we have previously discussed, Purple computes the survival chances are 30.5 percent."

Before he could continue, Nels Brunken blurted out accusingly, "Did you leave me out?"

Captain Larson said, "Nels, you will find out soon enough. Be quiet so Randy can finish."

"Screw you, Captain," Nels shouted as he unstrapped from his place at the table. "I want to know now!"

Reluctantly Captain Larson nodded to Randy to go ahead and tell him.

Randy quietly said, "You are among the seven males that Purple calculated would reduce, not increase the survival chances. In your case, your area of expertise as a planetologist was not an immediate need for the colony. Your age also worked against you."

"What about my son?" Nels mumbled.

Randy looked to the captain to see whether he should answer. Receiving a positive nod, he continued, "Henry was selected."

"That's just great," Nels exclaimed. "You tell me I'm worthless to the colony and have to return to Earth. I will be worthless there too. Then if that's not enough, you tear my family apart. My wife wouldn't apply to stay no matter how much I pleaded with her. If she had, you would have taken me also, and we could have been together as a family. Between you, that stupid computer, and my wife, everything I have cherished has been destroyed." Without waiting for any response, he quickly pushed out of the conference room and disappeared down the companionway.

The captain said nothing for a few minutes, giving everyone time to collect their thoughts. "I know this process has been hard on everyone," he finally said, "particularly those who volunteered or had someone close volunteer. Perhaps it would be best, Randy, if you deviated from your intended presentation and told us the results for those in this room or connected to us. Once that is out of the way, we can get back to the larger issues."

"All right," Randy uncomfortably responded. "First of all, Captain, your daughter, Vickie, volunteered. As I already said, all the female applicants were selected."

Captain Larson slumped in his chair. "I was afraid she was going to do that. I can feel the pain Nels is feeling. My family will also be ripped apart. Like Nels, I have no future either. There won't be much demand for a sixty-year-old spaceship captain on Earth."

After a brief pause, Randy Edwards continued. Looking at John Malcolm, he said, "John, your wife, Rebecca, volunteered." It wasn't necessary to say again that all female applicants were selected.

"I knew she had," John said. "When you said all the females were selected, I knew our life together was over. But she felt someone with her expertise in agricultural science needed to stay if the colony was to have a chance. I will wish her well."

"Judy, your husband, Mark, also applied. He was selected to stay with the colony."

Judy almost looked relieved. "I think Mark will be happier here than if he had to return to Earth," was all she said.

Randy looked briefly at Graysun Williams before addressing the captain. "Graysun and Kayane Williams are one of the couples that applied and have been selected." Graysun looked pleased.

"Thank you," Graysun said. "I talked at great length with Kayane, and I am convinced we can accept the reproductive protocols the colony will demand while still maintaining our commitment to the basic philosophy of the charter."

"Anyone else directly affected?" the captain asked.

"Yes, one more." He looked at Dr. Sanchez. "Sandra, your son Luis volunteered and has been selected."

Sandra gasped. It was obvious she had no inkling that Luis had submitted his name for the colony. Luis was the Sanchez's oldest son at nineteen and was already trained to program and operate robotic machinery. Then Sandra spoke in a broken voice, "Captain, please excuse me. I have to go and talk to Miguel." Without waiting for a reply, she unstrapped and headed out of the conference room toward her quarters.

"Is there any flexibility in the recommended colony population once the list is announced in case anyone changes their mind and decides they don't want to stay?" the captain asked.

"That was the area I worked on," Laura responded. "First of all, I looked at the women volunteers. As you all recall, Purple determined the highest probability of survival was about thirty-five percent based on a total population of between thirty-two and forty dominated by women by at least two to one. That meant there needed to be at least twenty-two women volunteer to stay to reach proper ratio for the maximum survival level. With only twenty-one women submitting their names, Purple reduced the survival chances to thirty-two percent. Other factors such as job skills, the actual supply of reproductive material available to the colony, and the actual age of all the volunteers then further reduced it to under thirty-one percent. If any of those twenty-one women withdrew her application, the chances would fall below thirty percent.

"Then I asked the computer to run different scenarios for the male applicants. Based on reproductive needs only, Purple could have recommended as few as eleven males be included in the colony population. However, desirable skills, the marriage factors, and age issues raised the ideal number of males to fifteen. Once those fifteen were identified, I asked Purple to run analyses substituting the names of the other seven men for those fifteen. There were several possible situations where a substitution could be made with only a miniscule drop in the survival percentages," she concluded.

"Was that true for all seven of the men?" Morgan asked.

"No," Laura responded. "Only four of the men are close enough in qualifications to not cause a significant decrease in the survival chances. Since I am sure you are all concerned about Dr. Brunken, he is not among the four. Adding his name to the colony population under any scenario drops the survival chances to below thirty percent."

"Okay," the captain said. "We have identified seven of the selectees here plus one applicant that has been rejected. Melissa, will you and your group please personally notify all the applicants as to their status as soon as this meeting breaks up? In addition, please ask those selected and the four that could serve as alternates to assemble in the workout room tomorrow first thing in the morning. I want all of you there also. As I said when I announced the possibility of a colony, I want to brief them in detail regarding the atmospheric problems, the genetic requirements and give them a rough idea of what supplies and equipment we will leave for them. Morgan, I want you to take the lead on the oxygen issue. Dr. Sanchez will provide details regarding reproductive requirements and limitations. Randy, you will take the lead regarding supplies.

"Melissa, will you please pass this message on to Sandra? Also let Nels know he should be in the workout room at eight tomorrow morning. I don't want to make a general announcement to the crew before we discuss the implications of going forward with the colony volunteers. Are there any questions?"

Hearing none, Captain Larson adjourned the meeting.

Morgan and Sarah arrived at the workout room on deck three just before eight the next morning. The workout room was a rather large space, twenty by thirty feet, devoted to physical fitness. It was equipped with specialized machines designed to provide a variety of regimens for fitness in weightless conditions. It was one of the few places other than the galley where a group of more than forty could gather together. There were strap-in boots that could fasten people to the floor as well as benches for exercise activities where a person could hold himself in one position.

Most of the volunteers were already there as well as several of the division chiefs. As Morgan and Sarah fastened themselves to the floor, several more arrived. By the time the captain came in, all the selected volunteers and the four alternates were present as well as all of the primary staff with the exception of Nels. Morgan noted that the two other married couples present were both in their twenties. They had been married as the *Mayflower* approached Ararat during that euphoric time when everyone thought they had found a planet to colonize. Josh Hernandez, the young man Morgan and Sarah had talked to in the galley, was also present. By his demeanor, it was apparent that he was not one of the alternates. The atmosphere in the room was charged with anticipation as the volunteers prepared for the culmination of the process. Other than the four alternates who were gathered together in one corner of the room, only a couple appeared uncertain of their future course of action.

Captain Morgan briefly greeted each of the volunteers before beginning. "As each of you were informed by Melissa Grant and her team, there were sufficient volunteers to justify establishing an Ararat colony. The purpose of this meeting is twofold. First, I want to give each of you an opportunity to change your mind. There are four alternates here, all male, which could be substituted for any of the fifteen males that were selected. However, if any of the twenty-one women decides she does not want to stay, it would drop the survival chances for the colony below thirty percent. At that point, I would recommend you all give serious consideration to abandoning the colony idea and return to Earth with the *Mayflower*. However, I will leave that decision up to you.

"Second, for those of you that have not been involved in the detailed analyses of the Ararat environment or in discussions of colony requirements to give the best chances of survival, I want you to be fully aware of what you will face. Before you consider those factors, however, is there anyone who wants to change their mind and withdraw?"

After a brief pause, a young man in the back called out, "Captain, I no longer want to be a volunteer."

The captain, who knew everybody on the *Mayflower*, responded, "Nicholas Lachinski, are you sure?"

"Yes, Captain. When I volunteered, I thought my girl-friend, Laila, was also volunteering. She told me last night that she had changed her mind at the last minute. She said that after considerable prayer, she could not accept the so-called breeding requirements. She begged me not to stay either. Even though I have no desire to return to Earth, I want to spend my life with her. So I thank you for the opportunity to withdraw my name."

"Done," Captain Larson said. "You are excused. Laura, which of the alternates should replace Nicholas?"

"Nicholas's training is in the construction area," Laura responded. "Purple determined that if Nicholas withdrew his name, the best alternate is Richard Rundquist. He also is trained in construction, and replacing Nicholas with Richard will change survival chances by only .03 percent."

"Richard, do you want to stay on Ararat?" the captain asked.

"You bet," he responded with a big smile on his face. "I was afraid I had lost my opportunity."

"Okay, you are now part of the colony crew. Now, is there anyone else?" He paused for a few moments. One of the other married couples Paul and Lisa Martini spoke softly to each other, but no one else spoke up as Nicholas left the workout room. Morgan noticed that Richard quietly drifted away from the corner where the three other alternates were gathered and joined in with the main group of selectees.

"I would like the other three alternates to stay for now," Captain Larson continued. "After we go over the colony details, you will have another chance to change your minds individually and as a group based on your final colony makeup. Morgan, please discuss the difficulties the colony with face with atmospheric conditions on Ararat."

"As the captain announced earlier and as I am sure all of you have heard, the atmosphere is the prime limiting factor on Ararat. It all comes down to oxygen content and what partial pressure of oxygen is required for man to survive without supplemental breathing equipment. On Earth, the atmospheric pressure at sea level is about 760 millimeters of mercury (mmHg). This pressure is created by the weight of the atmosphere, which, of course, decreases as altitude increases. Twenty-one percent of the Earth's atmosphere is oxygen, so the partial pressure of oxygen on Earth at sea level is about 159 mmHg. Those are the conditions we have been maintaining here on the *Mayflower*.

"The total pressure on Ararat near its sea is similar to Earth's, 745 mmHg. However, the percentage of oxygen in Ararat's atmosphere is only about 10 percent or 75 mmHg. This means the partial pressure of oxygen near the site of the colony is only 47 percent that of Earth's oxygen at sea level. This is equivalent to an altitude of about 20,500 feet on Earth. In general, at altitudes above 7,000 feet on Earth, humans begin to feel the effects of hypoxia. Above 20,000 feet, it is generally considered that humans cannot live indefinitely. While some mountain climbers have gone as far as the top of Mt. Everest, 29,000 feet without breathing equipment, they are the exception, and studies have shown that hypoxia effects have caused brain damage in most of them.

"There are a few high-altitude civilizations on Earth. On the Tibetan plateau, people live near 14,800 feet where the oxygen partial pressure is 93 mmHg or 59 percent that of sea level. On the Andean Altiplano in western South America, over two million people live in the Bolivian capital city of La Paz at an elevation of between 10,500 and 13,500 feet with an oxygen partial of 63 percent. There are several other communities above this elevation, the highest being the mining city of La Rinconada in the Peruvian Andes at 16,700 feet. At this altitude, the oxygen partial pressure is 55 percent of sea level or 87 mmHg. This gold-mining town once had a population of 30,000 but was abandoned about twenty years before we departed from Earth."

"Did the people living in these altitudes have any physiological adaptations?" Kayane Williams asked.

"Yes, but they are not all the same," Morgan continued. "The highlanders in the Andean Altiplano adapted to the thin air by developing red blood cells that can carry more oxygen. Their breathing rate is the same as humans at sea level, but having higher hemoglobin levels allows them to deliver oxygen throughout their bodies more efficiently, thus compensating for the thinner air. Tibetans, on the other hand, have two different adaptations. First, they have an increased respiratory rate when compared to low-altitude people. Second, their lungs synthesize larger amounts of nitric oxide from the air they breathe. The nitric oxide allows their blood vessels to expand. Thus, more blood flows, compensating for the lower oxygen content of the blood."

"What does that mean for us?" Kayane asked.

"Sandra, will you address what this could mean?" Morgan said.

"Sure," said Sandra. "It is potentially good news for the colony, but I must emphasize the word *potentially*. It does demonstrate that man has a number of ways to adapt physiologically to hypoxia conditions. It is not necessary to genetically modify the human body to adapt to low oxygen partial pressures. However, those populations had many generations to adapt to their environment. We know that mountain climbers can make short-term adaptations, but the evidence suggests no matter how well they are prepared, they do incur long-term damage. Further, the highest example, La Rinconada, still had a partial pressure 16 percent higher than what exists on Ararat. The bottom line is we don't know how long it will take or even if it is possible for the human body to adapt to the atmospheric conditions on Ararat."

"There is one other consideration regarding the atmosphere," Morgan continued. "Our original plan was to develop a supply of meat once a planet was colonized. There is a variety of food animal embryos on board. The plan was to construct the equipment necessary to raise these embryos once a settlement was built and establish breeding populations of cattle, sheep, pigs, chickens, and other domesticated animals. Theoretically, you will still be able to do that, but these animals were not selected for their adaptation to high altitudes. Thus, whether or not you will be able to move past the vegetarian diet you now have is problematic. The bottom line from the atmosphere perspective is that you will have to live in an artificial habitat for a long time and will face many difficulties in developing domestic animals that can survive on Ararat."

"Quite frankly, it doesn't sound much different than living on the *Mayflower*," Graysun Williams offered. "We've been doing that for the last twelve years, and you will be doing it for at least eight more."

"That is true," Captain Larson said. "The implications are farther in the future. Now, Sandra, what are the reproductive implications for the colony?"

"Since I knew that Kayane Williams had volunteered along with her husband, Graysun, and since Kayane is an expert in human genetics, I met with her last evening. We had a long discussion concerning what would need to be done from a reproductive standpoint to give the colony a reasonable chance of survival for many generations to come. Kayane will likely be the first person responsible for that program in the colony, so I would like to defer to her for further discussion on this issue."

Kayane glanced at the captain who nodded his head affirmatively.

"Thank you, Sandra," she began. "Let me first of all thank all of you that have volunteered for this adventure. In addition to my discussions with Sandra last evening, I had a long talk with Graysun about our future and the future of the colony. For many of you, the extent of your knowledge as to what to expect on Ararat is limited to the announcement the captain made and what rumors you have heard. Before I talk about what has generally been referred to as our *breeding program*, I would like to cover a more general topic."

Captain Larson looked uncomfortable that the discussion could be straying from his agenda, but he said nothing.

"First of all, I don't want any of you to think Graysun as the senior member of the *Mayflower* crew selected for the colony will automatically be placed in charge. Also, the same applies to me. That is why I asked Sandra to say only that I am *likely* to be responsible for the maintaining the genetic diversity of the colony. I don't know how we will eventually organize, but those decisions will be made by all of us, not any one individual."

"You are getting far astray of the topic at hand," the captain said. "I had assumed you would meet together after all the volunteers were given a better understanding of what colony living would entail."

"I am sure we will do that," Kayane responded. "But it is important that we do not get off on the wrong foot. That is why someone other than Graysun had to start the discussion. Neither of us wanted to give any impression that Graysun was going to assume command of the colony. In fact, we are not sure how the colony will be organized and whether any one person will be *in command*, so to speak. I want to stress to all of my colony crewmates that these are just my thoughts on the reproductive issues facing us and not in any way policy decisions."

Kayane paused to see if any of her colony crewmates wanted to say anything. After a few seconds, Lisa Martini said, "I am glad you are bringing this up now. My husband and I both volunteered. We felt we could both adapt to a reasonable reproductive program, but we are concerned about the organizational structure of the colony. We don't want to get into a dictatorial situation where someone has all the power and we are forced to do things repugnant to us. After Kayane presents her thoughts and we get further details as to equipment and supplies we will have, I suggest we talk together alone before any final opportunity to change our minds is offered. We may find that one or more of us is simply not compatible with the group and how the colony plans to proceed."

"Fair enough," the captain responded. "You will have a reasonable amount of time to weigh your decisions, but I caution you that one person's decision could have dramatic impact on the others. So I urge you to be open with each other. Now, Kayane, go ahead with your thoughts."

"Thanks for speaking up, Lisa," Kayane said. "Your thoughts parallel what Graysun and I talked about. When the captain announced the colony option, he said we would need to use all available reproductive techniques including cross-breeding, artificial insemination, and *in-vitro* fertilization. He also said that we must be willing to subject ourselves to these techniques as dictated by the population's needs. That does not necessarily mean we have to totally abandon not only the moral code but also all sense of moral decency. What we decide should be up to us. I believe we can structure a growing population that promotes genetic variability without turning the women into breeding machines. We are fortunate that most of the adult crew members that had stored genetic material agreed to leave it for our use. We can keep sperm and eggs frozen indefinitely. Lisa's husband, Paul, is trained to build and operate the equipment needed to raise our farm animals from their current frozen embryo state. I talked with Paul early this morning, and he says he should be able to modify the medical equipment he plans to build to raise human embryos if it becomes necessary. In the meantime, we can grow the population slowly using whatever techniques we decide are compatible with our beliefs. I know we won't have Purple available to track our survival probabilities, but we will have other computers that can be set up to monitor our genetic health. Finally, we all know that Purple's statistical probabilities are just that—probabilities. I have faith in the human spirit that we can survive and will survive."

"Wow," said Vickie Larson. "That sure puts a different face on things. Any doubts I may have had just went out the air lock." Several others voiced agreement with Vickie.

"Good job," Sandra said. "You were able to put a difficult topic in a favorable light. I agree with your assessment of the human spirit. I also believe that the colony can grow and prosper without abandoning principles that have been instilled in humanity since the earliest biblical times."

"Randy, what supplies and equipment are you recommending we leave for the colony?" Captain Larson asked.

"We have already discussed giving the colony a proportional amount of the hydroponic gardens. Sarah, have you determined whether that can be done safely?"

"Yes," Sarah replied. "The main concern will be the variety of food that can be produced initially. However, the colony should be able to expand the growing capacity over time. They could then use some of the seed stock to bring other items into their diet. Josh Hernandez knows the hydroponic system very well. He should be able to keep it productive for the colony. I also looked at the shrimp-production facilities. There is no feasible way to give the colony a viable shrimp farm. They will have to be vegetarians until they can develop a farm-animal population or find edible sources within the native life on Ararat."

"We also previously discussed the emergency rations," Randy continued, "and decided we could leave a proportional supply of them, about one year's worth. Sarah just mentioned the seed stock. That was originally stored for a time when we developed agriculture on a new planet. I see no need to take it back to Earth. I recommend we leave it all here for the colony to use as they see fit."

"I would like to keep a small amount of quinoa seed, just in case we have a major problem in the hydroponic gardens," Sarah said. "I do agree that the bulk of it will be unneeded on Earth."

"Judy, separate a reserve supply of quinoa seed from the stores for our safety and make the rest available for off-loading," Captain Larson said.

"All of the heavy construction equipment can be left," Randy continued, "along with the modular construction materials on board. This should provide, when fully assembled, enough space for about two hundred inhabitants. We can also leave some of the tools and robotic construction machines, but we need to keep enough to address any emergency the *Mayflower* might face on the return trip to Earth."

"Why is there only enough material for two hundred inhabitants?" Rebecca Malcolm asked. "I thought we could build enough space for all of us when we colonized a new planet."

"That was true," Randy responded. "But it depended on cannibalizing the *Mayflower* when it was no longer needed. Obviously, we can't do that now."

"What about a shuttle?" Graysun Williams asked.

"We will leave one of the small shuttles that transports you to the surface, but you will have to cannibalize it for the power plant, computer capabilities, and air-purification equipment," Randy said. "We will need the rest of the shuttle fleet when we get back to Earth. Anyway, we could not leave enough fuel to make the shuttle functional for very long. It doesn't take much fuel to transport to the surface but a great deal to return to space. Further, the small shuttles are not designed for surface travel. You will have other equipment for that purpose."

"Do you have a schedule for preparation of the colony for permanent habitation?" Mark Polachek asked.

"Somewhat tentative but yes," said Randy. "We can begin dropping construction equipment and supplies to the surface at any time. The first shuttle trip should take place in about a month. That trip will be one way for the shuttle. It should transport the hydroponic system and a small crew to the surface. They will prepare the colony for permanent habitation. The main consideration will be for those who are going to be part of that first group to be prepared for gravity. They will need to begin a strenuous physical fitness regimen immediately."

"Who needs to be in that first group?" Graysun asked.

"Well, certainly somebody with mechanical skills to get the air systems and power plant out of the shuttle and operational needs to be in that first group. Also someone who can make sure the hydroponic system is functional and stable. I would also recommend a computer person that can take the shuttle's computer and modify it as necessary to serve the colony. Perhaps one or two more to help prepare the base camp for the remainder of the colony. It should take about a month to complete preparations for the rest of the colony inhabitants. Assuming they are prepared physically, they could be shuttled to the surface as soon as the base camp is ready to serve as a permanent home."

"Thank you," Captain Larson said. "Are there any questions or comments?" Hearing none, he continued, "I am sure there will be many details to work out as we go forward. Now, however, I think it's time for the volunteers that were selected to discuss their future as Kayane suggested. Those of us who are not part of the colony crew will leave you to discuss anything you want to discuss."

As Captain Larson unfastened his boots to leave, he said, "One thought I want to leave you with. The colony is yours. How you organize and what you decide to do is entirely up to you. We will provide you with whatever support that is within our capabilities, but we will not interfere with your decisions. I only ask that you let me know if there are any changes to your roster of volunteers. Until you depart for the surface, you are part of this crew and under my command. If something all or one of you decides changes your survival chances below what I determine to be an acceptable level, I am reserving my authority to cancel your mission."

Morgan saw that the captain's last comment did not sit well with several of the colony volunteers. Graysun Williams in particular was very agitated that the captain had thrown in that last statement. Morgan hoped that nothing would happen that would cause the captain to pull the plug on the colony. It is possible that something unthinkable, like a mutiny, could result.

With that, the captain left the workout room along with Morgan and the others that were not part of the colony population. Morgan noticed as he left that Mark Polachek signaled the three remaining alternates to stay, which they did.

CHAPTER 6

"It's really happening," whispered Sarah. "There is a part of me, albeit a small part, that wishes we were going with them." Morgan and Sarah were watching through one of the *Mayflower's* portholes as the shuttle *Explorer* maneuvered away from the loading dock on its way to the Ararat colony. The shuttle was carrying the first six members of the colony to the planet's surface.

Morgan wistfully nodded in response. After a few seconds, he said, "In one sense, it is what we dreamed of and what we planned for most of our lives—to colonize a new planet. But Ararat could not meet our dreams. We wanted to do it as a family, and this planet will not let that happen. I wish them well, but I do not envy the life they are facing."

Sarah put her arms around Morgan and hugged him closely as the *Explorer* drifted clear of the *Mayflower* and fired its engines to begin the descent. "Settling on a new planet was an aspiration, Morgan, but you are my life. We made the only decision our love for each other, our values, and our children would allow us to make. Think about Mark on that shuttle. He said goodbye to his wife and children for good this morning. I could never do that."

Morgan nestled into Sarah's arms as he reflected on the events of the past thirty-two days. The day after the work-out-room meeting, the colonists announced a number of decisions regarding the establishment of the colony. First, they asked that no further determinations be made by Purple regarding survival probabilities. They emphasized that the decision had been made to go forward, and worrying about any small change in the survival chances was counterproductive. "We are past how statistics could affect our decisions," they announced. "We want to focus on reality, not mathematical theory."

Captain Larson would not agree to this request, although he did tell the colony members that he would not advise them of changes in the probabilities unless they specifically requested the updated information. He, however, emphasized again that he reserved the right to cancel the colony mission.

The next decision was that they wanted all of the alternate volunteers to be a part of the colony. "We discussed whether anyone else had changed his or her mind, and no one has. It is our position that all who want to stay and are qualified are allowed to stay. We therefore decided that the three male alternates are also a part of the colony crew." Thus, the initial colony population increased to thirty-nine, twenty-one women and eighteen men.

Captain Larson asked Laura how letting the other three male alternates might change survival chances, and she reiterated that they would have minimal impact. "The key factor is women," she said. "As long as the total population starts out at forty or less, the three extra men do not significantly change the probabilities. However, if one of the women withdraws, things could change significantly."

The announcement regarding their organization left Morgan and most other crew members puzzled. "We have developed an organizational structure," the colonists said, "but will not announce or implement that structure until we are all on the surface of Ararat. Until that happens, we have selected two coleaders to coordinate decisions while still on the *Mayflower*. Those coleaders are Rebecca Malcolm and Paul Martini."

Two days later, Rebecca and Paul informed the captain of who would go to the surface as part of the initial crew. "After balancing current physical fitness with the needs on the surface, the following colony members will be on the first shuttle—Josh Hernandez, Lisa Martini, Mark Polachek, Richard Rundquist, Marlene Deveroe, and Eric O'Reilly."

These choices made sense to Morgan. Mark Polachek had told him the day before that they were going to start with a closed ecosystem in the habitat. They did not want to be dependent on any resources on Ararat for an extended period of time. Eric O'Reilly was familiar with the *Mayflower* atmospheric system and could adapt the shuttle equipment to the colony. Marlene Deveroe had earned her PhD in chemistry during the voyage to Epsilon Eridani, and her expertise was necessary to ensure that the hydroponics and waste-recycling systems were working in balance. Lisa would set up the habitat's computer operational system. Josh Hernandez knew how to establish and operate the hydroponic garden; and Richard Rundquist was qualified to operate the robotic machinery to begin expanding the colony space for the rest of the colonists. Mark was charged with overseeing the preparation of the colony.

Morgan did not see any major issues with the plan. The only advice he offered to Mark was that they start supplementing the colony atmospheric system with some of Ararat's air as soon as possible to begin to adapt to the different makeup of trace elements in Ararat's atmosphere. Mark agreed this was a good idea and said he would take the suggestion to Rebecca and Paul. Several days later, he mentioned to Morgan that they would start using the Ararat atmosphere in their system right away.

Sarah turned to Morgan, interrupting his musings about the previous month. "I just hate to see families broken up like this. At least for Mark's children, they will still have their mother.

And what about Rebecca Malcolm? She is leaving her two boys to stay here. Maybe I can understand a man doing that but a mother? The boys told Emily that their mother didn't love them. Also Graysun and Kayane are going to leave their three children parentless. Elizabeth was just born eighteen months ago. She will grow up without knowing her parents at all. How could they do that?"

"I don't know. Neither one has said anything to me. I'm not sure what plans, if any, they have made. None of the other volunteers has children, but one of the younger men is married. He knew his wife didn't want to stay, but he volunteered anyway. For some, I guess the colony challenge trumps loyalty to spouse and children. As Laura said to me a few weeks ago, that portion of our moral code is not as ingrained as we think it is."

Morgan and Sarah gazed at Ararat for about an hour before returning to their respective offices. Sarah had decided to try and expand the hydroponic gardens back to its original size. Now that the portion assigned to the colony had been removed, she was ready to begin the project. Morgan returned to the ecology lab where he and Laura were focusing on absorbing as much information as they could about the Earth's environment and how it was changing in response to the human-population explosion.

Captain Larson had asked each division to develop educational materials for use in teaching the youth on the *Mayflower* about Earth and its people. He wanted everyone returning to Earth to know as much as possible about the environment, the people, and the lifestyles they would face. Morgan was preparing teaching outlines on Earth's natural ecosystems and man's impact on those systems in the last three hundred years. Melissa Grant and Sandra Sanchez had agreed to prepare materials on Earth's cultural standards and how the children would have to live among people with entirely different moral values than those on the *Mayflower*. Dr. Sanchez also started a review of those diseases on Earth that had not been eradicated when the *Mayflower* departed. The children born on the *Mayflower* had never been exposed to any diseases other than the common cold which unfortunately was somehow brought on board when they left Earth. Dr. Sanchez planned to prepare inoculations as necessary to protect the crew when back on Earth.

Even Nels had agreed to help. For several days since storming out of the conference room, Nels had stayed in his quarters. He failed to attend several meetings, and as far as Morgan knew, nobody other than his wife and son had talked to him. Then one day, he seemed to come out of his shell. He informed the captain that he would prepare lesson plans on Earth's geology and weather patterns. Morgan and Sarah had talked to him a couple days before the *Explorer* departed, and he seemed back to his normal grumpy self. He didn't say much other than that he was working out again and wanted to maintain his physical fitness in preparation for his next adventure.

Melissa asked Sandra's husband, Miguel, to help prepare lesson plans on the various religions of Earth and how those religions did and did not accept the beliefs of the *Mayflower* population. The children born and raised on the *Mayflower* had no exposure to the many faiths on Earth other than Christianity.

It was not that the founders of the Space Colonization Consortium had a religious motive in their plans. In reality, they regarded religious conflict, particularly from the fundamentalists in the various religions, as a major factor driving the general decline of society. Their primary concern was the breakdown of the family unit, loss of moral values, decline in individual ingenuity, and abandonment of personal responsibility in favor of reliance on the government for cradle-to-grave dependency. So the founders added the moral code to the charter. The moral code was a blend of concepts from the Declaration of

Independence, the bill of rights, and the Ten Commandments. It emphasized life, liberty, pursuit of happiness, freedom, personal responsibility, respect for others, and strong family values.

The founders used these principles in developing the selection criteria for the *Mayflower* crew. The process was extensive and designed to eliminate anyone whose beliefs could later result in any departure from the primary mission of the consortium. It didn't really matter if one tried to answer questions as he thought they should be answered. The psychological evaluation was so complete that a person's basic nature could not be hidden. The unintended consequence of this process was the elimination of anyone whose moral and cultural background was not based on Christian principles such as monogamous relationships; equality of all, including women; sanctity of life; and respect for others. Not all of the initial crew members of the *Mayflower* were active Christians. More than one hundred expressed no particular denominational belief when the journey started. Several, as scientists, tended to be agnostics, asserting that the existence of God could not be proven. But none of those were of any religious background other than Christianity. Miguel's mission was to prepare the younger generation for the strange religious world they would see in a few years.

The *Mayflower* continued to drop supplies and construction equipment through the next two weeks after the *Explorer* departed. Graysun Williams used a process similar to early Mars missions around the turn of the twenty-first century. The drop was bundled under a parachute system and released as the *Mayflower* entered the right position in orbit over the colony. Attached to each bundle was a sled equipped with deceleration engines that would guide the sleds to a soft landing. More fragile materials were also encased in shock-absorbing airbags.

Just ten days after the preparation crew arrived on the surface, Mark reported back to the *Mayflower* that the colony quarters were pressurized, and the air system was functioning normally. They had established an initial oxygen partial pressure equivalent to about eight thousand feet on earth. The six members of the team had taken off their personalized breathing equipment and were breathing normally within the colony space. He also reported that Josh Hernandez had the hydroponic system started, and it should be producing enough quinoa to support the rest of the colonists by the time they arrived.

Five days later, Mark asked if the *Mayflower* could send another three-dimensional electronic replicator. Lisa was having trouble expanding the *Explorer's* computer to meet colony needs. The reproduction robot had received some damage during its drop and was not producing computer parts to exact specifications. She had identified the problem but would need another replicator to make additional components. There was some concern about the loss of additional rare earth materials, but John Malcolm said that since they were returning to Earth, he had enough for any anticipated needs on the return flight. After some discussion, it was decided to send another replicator on the second shuttle that would transport the rest of the colony crew. John Malcolm set about the task of building another replicator for the colony.

Another significant development involved the shuttles. Antonio Grant raised concerns about the amount of fuel that would be needed to bring a shuttle back to the *Mayflower* after the rest of the colony crew was off-loaded to the surface of Ararat. The captain called a meeting of his staff along with Rebecca Malcolm and Paul Martini to discuss alternatives.

When the decision to build the *Mayflower* was made, the twenty private shuttles on Earth were all committed to the mission. Of those, only seven were capable of liftoff from the Earth's surface without supplemental booster rockets. Those seven were designed for passenger use and were larger, capable of carrying up to seventy-five passengers. During construction of the *Mayflower,* nine of the smaller shuttles and two of the larger ones were incorporated into the *Mayflower's* hull. The remaining nine were stored for exploration of a future potentially suitable planet. Since the smaller shuttles required booster rockets to return to space, something the *Mayflower* did not have, they were considered only for one-way flights. Two had been used to establish the base camp when they had arrived in orbit around Ararat. A third, the *Explorer,* was now also on the surface.

Antonio said that he would rather have the fuel than the final one-way shuttle, the *Orion.* He was concerned that they could not get the right fuel when they arrived back at Earth. "Earth abandoned the use of shuttles when the commitments were made to the *Mayflower* project," he said. "They said they would go back to a rocket program to maintain satellites, but I saw no development of that before we left. I would not be surprised if there was no space program at all when we get back. I think we need to keep all the fuel we have in case we need it to off-load to Earth."

"It doesn't matter to us whether or not you leave the *Orion* on Ararat," said Paul Martini. "We already have enough machinery and equipment from the *Explorer* and the two earlier one-way shuttles used to build the base camp. Our main concern is whether the *Orion* will carry the remaining thirty-three colony inhabitants along with any supplies we don't want to drop."

"With a few modifications, yes," Antonio responded. "I can add additional deceleration chairs, enough to hold everyone. We kept several that we took out of the shuttles we used to build the base camp. The *Orion* has a large compartment that was originally used for satellites being transported to space. I'll use a portion of that space for the additional passengers and use the rest for storage. It will be a little cramped, but it will do."

"Did you consult Purple?" Captain Larson asked.

"Yes, and it said there would be no harm to the overall safety of the *Mayflower* with this change. It agreed that fuel could be an issue upon our arrival back at Earth if none was available there to supplement our on-board supply."

"Does anyone have any concerns about this?" the captain addressed to the other participants in the meeting.

After a moment, Nels asked, "If the colonists do not dismantle the *Orion*, what would have to be done for it to return to space?"

The captain, among others, looked at Nels questioningly. "An interesting question," he said, "but why do you ask?"

"Just a thought as a safety measure for the colony," Nels replied. "It would also allow them to place communications equipment or mapping satellites in space. It might help them as they expand."

"Well," Graysun Williams responded to Nels, "I suppose it's theoretically possible. We would have to build fuel plants and construct booster rockets. Quite frankly, I think it would be easier to build new shuttles that don't need boosters. But that is so far out in the future that I don't want to even think about it now. We need to focus on surviving as a viable subset of humanity. I think the *Orion* would be more valuable for its components than mothballing it for potential use. But it will be something for us to decide after we are all on Ararat."

"Okay, that's settled. Paul and Rebecca, you will use the *Orion* to transfer to the surface and then do whatever you want with it. Any concerns about the time schedule for taking down the rest of the colony members?" the captain asked.

"Yes," responded Sandra Sanchez. "Two of the six currently on Ararat are having physical problems. It's not the air pressure in the colony. It's the gravity. One of them is having considerable trouble walking. And remember, these six were in the best condition of any of the colony members when they left. They had vigorously worked out after being chosen as part of the construction crew. The situation here on the *Mayflower* is worse. The rest of the colony population is using the fitness facilities, but in my opinion, they are not ready to be functional in Ararat's gravity and will not be ready by their scheduled departure date in forty days.

"Of even more concern is the physical fitness of the rest of us. I anticipate over fifty people will have serious physical problems if we leave Ararat's orbit as scheduled. I think it will take us at least three more months to be ready, and quite frankly, some of the crew will never be physically ready to go back to normal gravity."

"I agree," chipped in Melissa Grant. "Morale is quite low, particularly among those over thirty. Going back to Earth is not a desirable outcome for most of us. So many are simply saying, 'Why bother?'"

"I haven't been much of a role model myself," the captain said. "I will try and do better. Please, all of you, do what you can to prepare us for acceleration. But let's get back to the colony. Rebecca or Paul, what do you think?"

"After I heard about Eric O'Reilly's leg problems, I talked with all of our members about getting ready for gravity. I agree with Dr. Sanchez. I think we should delay our departure by at least an additional thirty days. We do not have the morale problem Mrs. Grant described, but we will not be ready before then."

"We certainly are in no rush," the captain somewhat sardonically said. "Take whatever time you need to get yourselves ready, and let me know when you are."

As it turned out, the colony crew took three more months before they were physically fit and ready to go. The captain then announced that the *Orion* would depart in three days, and anyone who wanted to say goodbye should do it soon.

Graysun and Kayane Williams joined Morgan and Sarah at supper that evening. It was unusual as the colony crew had pretty much isolated themselves from the rest of the population over the last two months. They had said they needed to bond together and learn as much as possible about each other before they were forever placed in a world with nowhere else to go.

Kayane told Sarah that they had given their three children to a young married couple working in hydroponics. "They are devoted to each other, and she is seven months pregnant with a girl. It will give Elizabeth a little sister to take care of."

"Any regrets?" Sarah asked.

"Absolutely not!" Graysun said before Kayane could answer. "Kayane and I knew we would be miserable returning to Earth. When this opportunity came up, we both knew it would not only be the best option for us. It would also be better for our children. They will be living with a family that loves them and also loves the idea of returning to Earth. If we had stayed, our unhappiness would have rubbed off on them. We have left a message in Purple that will be available to each of them when they turn sixteen. Hopefully, they will understand why we chose to be pioneers on Ararat."

Kayane looked uncomfortable with Graysun's answer but said nothing.

"Would you have taken them with you if you had the chance?" Morgan asked.

"I don't know," Kayane responded. "That option was never discussed. But I don't think we would have wanted them to stay. Graysun and I are adults and know what it means to accept the risk of the colony. We were willing to accept that risk. But I don't think I could have imposed it on our children. Besides, on Earth, they will be able to carry on our family legacy. On

Ararat, we are not certain what *family* will mean within a few generations."

"Doesn't that bother you?" Sarah asked.

"Yes, it does," she responded. "But we won't be alive in a few generations. Graysun and I discussed this at great length before we volunteered. As I said before, we will do what is necessary to protect the viability of the colony. Hopefully, we can still maintain our personal relation with each other. The moral code was ingrained in our DNA, but I know we will have to give most of that up. We will try our best to make sure some of our original values survive in the colony."

"What about new children?"

"I should be able to have at least three or four more. Graysun and I will try and conceive the first one naturally as our combined genetics will not be represented in the colony population. After that, it will depend on the needs of the colony. If I'm lucky, the genetics needs will dictate I use sperm from the stored supply. Who knows, Morgan." Kayane laughed. "I may have your baby in a couple years." Graysun nodded his approval to Kayane's remark.

"Call him, Louie," Morgan offered. "I've always liked that name."

"If it's a girl, I vote for Esther," said Sarah. "She is one of my favorite women from the Old Testament. She never forgot the origins of her heritage."

"I like that," Kayane said somewhat wistfully. "I will name the first girl Esther, if the colony agrees."

Graysun gave Kayane a disapproving look at that last remark. "We'd better go," he said, terminating any further conversation. "There is a lot to do before we depart."

Knowing this was probably the last time they would talk with Graysun and Kayane, Morgan and Sarah hugged them for a long time and wished them the very best as they pushed away and moved down the passageway.

"That last comment by Kayane of *if the colony agrees* sure bothered Graysun," Sarah said as Graysun and Kayane disappeared around a corner. "As a matter of fact, I thought Kayane was choosing her words carefully all through supper. I wonder if she's really one hundred percent on board with what the colonists are planning."

"The colonists have been meeting together a lot the last few days. I expect there are many adjustments they are making to prepare for life on Ararat. They have wanted to keep these discussions among themselves so as to not be influenced by the rest of us. I think Kayane may have let something slip regarding how the colony will be making decisions. It seems strange to me that Graysun would be bothered by something as simple as naming a child, but he sure was." Morgan and Sarah then returned to their quarters for the evening.

One day before the scheduled departure of the *Orion*, Rebecca and Paul informed the captain that one of the female volunteers, a young woman named Erica Norquist, was expressing some doubts about her decision to stay on Ararat. They said the colony had determined that all volunteers needed to be 100 percent committed to their mission. Therefore, Erica was not going to be on the *Orion* when it departed the next day. Erica, nineteen years old, was trained in galley operations. Rebecca emphasized again that they did not want to know how this change might affect the colony's survival chances. "The decision has been made," she said. "We are staying on Ararat. We will survive regardless of what Purple says."

Laura asked the captain if he wanted to see how Erica's elimination from the colony was going to affect the colony's chances to make it, but he said, "Don't bother. It's too late.

They want to go, and all the preparations have been made. I'm not going to stop them now."

At 9:00 a.m. the next day, Captain Larson announced to the crew of the *Mayflower*, "Shipmates, this date, April 12, 2085, on the *Mayflower* calendar marks an epic date in mankind's history. We are officially establishing a human population on another planet today. All of you will remember this date as we return to Earth. While it is not the plan we had when we left Earth, all plans need to change as circumstances dictate. We are not returning to Earth in defeat. We have accomplished everything we could with the resources we had available to us in relation to the conditions here on Ararat. When we land on Earth, I want you to tell to all who will listen that humans now live in the stars.

"Now for the thirty-two colonists who are about to board the *Orion* for departure, I admire the courage you have to take on this adventure. I wish I could be there with you. This is the first day of the history of your adventure on Ararat. You will overcome all obstacles Ararat put before you and triumph. I am confident you will not only survive. You will thrive. Remember always your roots and the planet that sent you forth. Future generations will venture back to the stars, and our two civilizations will once again be joined. In the meantime, send us updates that will allow future explorers from Earth to better prepare for life on other planets. We will keep you in our prayers and send monthly updates as we head back to Earth. Anyone who wants to say goodbye and Godspeed should come to the shuttle boarding air lock within the next half hour."

Morgan and Sarah joined most of the *Mayflower*'s management team and many others in the companionway to the air lock to wish the colony members well. As Graysun and Kayane drifted through the crowd, Kayane called to Sarah, "Pray for me." A few feet farther on, Kayane saw Carter and Ethel

Leindecker, the couple that had adopted Kayane's three children. Morgan thought Kayane was going to cry as she drifted past them, but all she said was, "I know my children are in good hands. Thank you."

As Luis Sanchez passed by his parents, Sandra was crying. She still had not gotten over Luis's decision. "I'll be fine, Mom," Luis said. "Don't worry."

Captain Larson and his wife, Deanna, were near Morgan in the companionway. As Vickie Larson floated past them, the captain smiled and said, "I am proud of you, Vickie. I only wish I could stay here with you."

Deanna, on the other hand, was crying. Vickie paused and gave her mother a brief hug before continuing on to pass through the air lock. Deanna turned and pushed her way through the crowd, not waiting for the rest of the volunteers to board.

John Malcolm was also nearby, and he waved to his wife, Rebecca, and blew her a kiss. John had accepted their separation ever since Rebecca had volunteered and handled his last opportunity to see her gracefully.

Judy and Mark Polachek had asked the captain to grant them a divorce after Mark had been chosen for the colony. Judy said she wanted the freedom to remarry if she found someone in the future, and Mark agreed that she should be free to do as she wished. The captain granted their divorce, noting it was the first one he had been asked to grant since the *Mayflower* left Earth. Judy was not there as Mark entered the air lock.

Ida Brunken looked very sad as her son, Henry, worked his way past her to the *Orion*. Henry was her only child, and she was getting past the age where she could have another. He nodded to his mother but said nothing. Morgan was surprised that he didn't see Nels there. "Sarah, do you see Nels anywhere?"

She looked around but couldn't find Nels either. Morgan asked the captain if he knew where Nels was.

"No, and I'm surprised. I, for sure, thought Nels would be here to encourage his son to carry on his legacy. It's hard to understand what Nels is thinking sometimes. Perhaps seeing the colony depart without him was more than he wanted to endure. He's probably brooding somewhere by himself."

Two hours later, the *Mayflower* was in the right orbital position for the *Orion* to depart. It fired its deceleration rockets and began its descent toward Ararat. The *Orion* used a glider-type landing procedure, much like the NASA shuttles of the late twentieth century. The shuttles in that program were designed to glide down from space and land on concrete runways or dry lake beds. These runways were very long, 15,000 feet for the concrete runways at the Kennedy Space Center and Edwards Air Force Base and up to about 35,000 feet of dry lake bed runway at the White Sands Missile Range in New Mexico. The shuttles landed at higher speed than commercial aircraft of the time, about 215 miles per hour. Once on the ground, the shuttles would deploy air brakes and a parachute to bring them to a stop.

The shuttles on the *Mayflower* were modified considerably from the design used on Earth. Since there would be no prepared runways and it was unknown if suitable flat areas of sufficient length would be available, they were modified for either water landings or short runway sites. In the case of Ararat, a dry salt lake bed about three miles from the colony site was found that had about 5,000 feet of available area. The *Mayflower* had dropped surface transportation equipment at this location when the base camp was established after arrival in orbit around Ararat. This equipment was being used to travel to and from the colony to haul personnel and materials scavenged from earlier one-way flights.

About one hour after the *Orion* departed, it landed safely on Ararat. Day one of the history of the colonization of Ararat had begun.

CHAPTER 7

Soon after the *Orion* landed, Captain Larson received a surprising call from Graysun Williams. "Nels Brunken stowed away on the *Orion*," Graysun said. "We found him in a small storage locker in the back of the shuttle as we were disembarking. He was a little bruised because he didn't have a proper deceleration chair but had surrounded himself with personal belongings. They provided enough padding that he avoided serious injury."

Graysun also told the captain that before the colony members had an opportunity to decide what they should do with Nels, he informed them he had no intentions of living with the colony. Beyond that, Graysun suggested that Captain Larson talk directly with Nels and broke the connection.

The captain called Morgan and Dr. Sanchez to his quarters. When they arrived, he briefly filled them in on what he knew and said he wanted them to be present when he talked to Nels. Morgan noticed that Sandra's eyes were reddened. She and her husband had pleaded with their son Luis to change his mind and stay on the *Mayflower*, but Luis was determined be a part of the colony. Morgan tried to understand Sandra's anguish over Luis's decision. How would he and Sarah react if one of their children was for all practical purposes gone forever?

"Captain," Nels said when a communications channel was opened, "I want to apologize for not telling you what I planned to do, but I knew you would try to stop me, and I couldn't let that happen. I decided to do this a few days after I learned I was not included on the colony crew list."

"What are you planning to do?" the captain asked.

"I am going to show the colony that humans can survive on the surface of Ararat without artificial breathing equipment or pressurized living spaces. I am going to give them hope for the future."

"Why? They already have hope and a great deal of determination."

"To a certain extent, yes, but they are relying on their technology to survive. They are planning to live in a ground-based version of the *Mayflower* habitat. What if there is a breakdown in their oxygen system? What if their hydroponic systems fail? They don't have the luxury of the backup systems available on the *Mayflower*. I want to show them that they don't need to be dependent on all that technology."

"How do you plan to do that?" Morgan asked.

"By going native. I studied the surface of Ararat carefully and found a natural stream of fresh water a little north of the base camp. The Ararat ecosystem in that area is fairly well developed. I brought a minimum supply of personal belongings with me to set up a camp. I have already hiked to the site and am setting up shop."

"Are you having any difficulty with the atmosphere?" Sandra asked.

"Not so far," he replied. "When I decided to do this, I didn't know how I was going to get to the surface, but I knew I had to be in the best possible shape. I began an extensive physical fitness program similar to what I did before I embarked on a mountain climbing expedition back on Earth. By being prepared then, I was able to climb to Mount Aconcagua's 22,800-foot summit in Argentina without supplemental breathing equipment and was over 24,000 feet on Mount Everest before I put on a mask. And remember, the exertion factor of mountain climbing is much higher that what I am facing here."

"What about food?" Captain Larson asked.

"That's another area where I owe you an apology," he said. "I brought a small supply of emergency rations with me, enough for about a month. I did not take any of the seed stock of Earth plants that were destined for the colony. I intend to find native plants and perhaps some animals that are edible. I do not believe we should introduce any Earth organisms on Ararat if at all possible. I want to show the colony that it is not necessary to do so. If I can survive, they will know that they can adapt to Ararat's environment. If people are going to live in the stars, they need to find how to do it consistent with what the stars have to offer."

"A month's supply doesn't give you much time," Morgan said. "We had just begun our studies on Ararat's plants and animals. We did find a few native plants that appear to have nutrients of value to the human digestive system, but nobody tried to live on them, and no detailed chemical analysis of them was done. The ocean may provide a better place to start. I found some aquatic plants that looked like they could provide sustenance. Marlene Deveroe, who is part of the colony, did extensive bio-chemical research on two species of seaweed similar to Earth's kelp. She found that both plants would be comparable to quinoa in meeting a human's dietary needs. Nobody, however, consumed any of it, so we do not know if our systems can effectively process them."

"I reviewed all of the data she developed with Purple," Nels responded. "The one thing I have asked of the colony is that they make a boat available to me. Graysun said he was not prepared to make that decision, and I would have to wait to hear back from him. I want to harvest some of the kelp-like plants and see what my stomach does with it. In the meantime,

I found some small tuber-like growths on a leafy plant near my camp site. I ate one a few minutes ago. It hasn't killed me so far."

"Well," Captain Larson said, "you have always done things your way. All I know for certain is that we are not coming to the surface to retrieve you. You have made your choice, and you will have to live or die with whatever outcome results."

"We all die sometime. At least I will die doing what I always wanted to do, exploring the unknown."

"Please keep us apprised of any discoveries you make," Morgan said. "Purple will store that information for future generations. By the way, did you tell Ida what you were doing?"

"I left a message with Purple to be delivered as soon as the *Orion* departed. She suspected something like this. She will understand." With that, Nels terminated his communications link.

As Morgan and Dr. Sanchez moved to leave the captain's quarters, they heard him mutter, "I wish I had had the courage to do what Nels has done."

A few hours later, the colony informed the *Mayflower* and Nels that he would have a boat to use in exchange for information on the ocean's aquatic resources, but he would receive nothing else from the colony and would not be permitted to enter the colony's habitat under any circumstances.

With the colonists gone and all the supplies intended for them dropped to the surface, the *Mayflower* crew began the preparations for departure for Earth. However, enthusiasm for getting under way was lacking. It was one thing to ready the *Mayflower* structurally for acceleration and the accompanying structural stresses. It was quite another to convince the passengers they needed to be physically prepared. The older crew members in particular were lackluster in preparing their bodies for the stresses of one gravity. Dr. Sanchez and Melissa Grant were doing what they could to motivate those who were risking injury when the Perry-Warner drive was activated, but the process was slow. Two weeks after the *Orion* left, they both told the captain the *Mayflower* should not depart anytime soon. Captain Larson, who had become withdrawn and insipid since his conversation with Nels, said it didn't really matter to him. Just let him know when they wanted to leave.

Communications with the colonists were almost nonexistent. As soon as they had landed, they stopped using their personal communicators to establish links with the *Mayflower*. Instead, they established a single open link through the shuttle *Explorer*'s computer for *official* communications. In the first thirty days since the message about Nels, only two messages from the colony had been received, both short updates regarding the expansion of the colony's living space. The *Mayflower* continued to send daily status reports to the colony, but there was no acknowledgment that those reports were received.

About five weeks after the *Orion* departed, Morgan was reviewing some studies on Earth's ocean pollution problems when Laura scrambled into the ecology center. Ever since she had gotten over her initial anger regarding Henry's lackadaisical attitude regarding their relationship, she had been very upbeat about getting under way. Her physical conditioning, always good, was superb. There was no doubt in Morgan's mind that she was looking forward to the challenges she would face upon arriving back in the solar system.

"You look like you have lots of news," Morgan observed. "What's up?"

"Two things," she replied. "First, I just had lunch with Erica Norquist. You remember her? She is the girl that backed out of the colony at the last minute. She told me what her reason was, and now I understand why we are not hearing from the colony."

"I'm all ears," Morgan said.

"Well, you remember right after the colonists first met as a group, they said they were working on an organizational structure but would not say anything until they were established on the surface? Erica told me it was much more than any of us could have imagined. They decided to completely abandon the *Mayflower* charter and prepare a new one. It took them most of the two months they were preparing for departure to agree on everything, and when they did, it had to be accepted by all. Erica was the only one who could not agree with what they had decided."

"What are some of the details that bothered her?" Morgan asked.

"A whole host of things. Actually, I can't believe she was the only one that objected. It's not surprising that they set a prime objective on survival. But the rules and regulations they established in an effort to guarantee that prime objective are draconian. For example, they agreed to abandon the bond of marriage. They decided the need to maximize variability in reproduction was in conflict with the bond of marriage, and the only way to avoid disputes was to eliminate the concept of a family unit."

"There were three married couples as part of the crew. Did they agree to that?"

"According to Erica, yes," Laura said. "But those couples agreed not to let on what they were doing while they were still on the *Mayflower*. Basically, everything they said before departing about family and children was designed to deceive us."

"Graysun and Kayane Williams certainly fooled Sarah and me," Morgan said. "When we had supper with them a few days before they left, they talked like they were ready to embark on a new adventure. But I do remember that Kayane seemed guarded during the conversation. I recall that when Kayane started to talk about children, Graysun cut her off."

"There's much more," Laura continued. "Erica says they agreed to give up all liberty and freedom of choice in favor of the needs of the group. She could understand the need for some guidance because of the small population, but she said they went way too far. Get this. They decided the primary role of women was reproduction. While they recognized that some of the original women had vital skills, those skills would be turned over to males as the population grows. Female children would be raised to bear children. The males would be raised to manage the colony."

"The women agreed to that?"

"And much more," Laura said. "Erica said the women agreed to give up all rights to equality. The men would be the only ones who have a say in the decision-making process. Basically, the women agreed to become subservient to the men. That was more than Erica could agree to and why she was eliminated from the colony population."

"Amazing. Did she know how the men were going to run things?"

"She was not sure. The men had a separate caucus once these principles were decided upon, and the only thing Erica heard was that there would be no leader appointed. Decisions would be made by the majority of all the men over eighteen in the colony."

"Well, I guess it is their decision to try and do what is best for their situation," Morgan said. "But if they are successful, I wonder what their civilization will look like in a few hundred years. By giving up all our standards of cultural and moral norms, I can't imagine it will be anything like what we set out to do when we left Earth.

"By the way, you said you had two pieces of news. What is the second one? Could it possibly top what you just told me?"

"On a personal note, it's bigger," Laura said smiling. "I am engaged. I plan on getting married soon after we get under way."

"Wow! That is a surprise. I knew you were able to get over Henry quickly, but I didn't realize you had already found someone else. Who is the lucky guy?"

"Bradley McMullen. I've been friends with him for a long time. When Henry dumped me without a thought, I talked with Brad about returning to Earth. He has the same positive outlook I do about going back. It didn't take long for us to fall in love. We decided, 'Why wait? Let's get our family started now.' That way, we will be able to enjoy our grandchildren on Earth before we are too old."

Morgan knew that Bradley was a good choice for Laura. He was the same age, twenty-five, and was trained as a hydrogeologist. He had told Morgan in the workout room a few weeks before that he was looking forward to getting back on Earth. He wanted to work toward improving supplies of quality water to the many places that had let their treatment systems fall into disrepair.

"Not that you need it from me, but you certainly have my blessing. Bradley is a neat guy."

"My parents think so too. Don't be surprised if Bradley asks you to be his best man. You may remember that his father died soon after we left Alpha Centauri."

"I would be honored," said Morgan as he unstrapped from his workstation. "I'll see you later. I want to fill Sarah in on what Erica told you." Morgan called Sarah and found out she was in the hydroponic garden. He left the ecology center and worked his way through the corridors to the lower level where the *Mayflower* food was grown.

Morgan found Sarah in her office outside the gardens. She looked up from her workstation as Morgan entered the space and pulled himself into the other chair. "Hey, sweetie, I wasn't expecting you down here today. What's up?"

"Laura just told me she is getting married to Brad McMullen as soon as we get under way."

"Wow, that's good news," Said Sarah. "It sure didn't take her long to get over Henry Brunken. He was kind of a creep the way he immediately abandoned her in favor of joining the colony. I'm impressed by Laura's maturity. She has adjusted to the idea of returning to Earth as well as anyone I know. I've talked with Brad several times, and he seems to be a very levelheaded guy."

"I agree. She said she wants to get her family started now so that they can enjoy their grandchildren on Earth while they are still young. I wish more of the young adults on the *Mayflower* were making similar plans. Many of them were postponing committed relationships while waiting to find a new permanent home. Now it appears they want to wait until they get back to Earth. That's another eight years."

"Remember when Melissa Grant described this group when we were discussing our options? She said they wanted the journey to be over regardless of where they wound up. I suppose many of them are simply putting their lives on hold waiting for that end. I'm not sure that's a good idea. The shock they will get when they try and assimilate into Earth's population will be enough to deal with without trying to cement a permanent relationship at the same time."

"It will be tough for them," Morgan agreed. "But time and hormones will likely result in more bonds being formed as we head back. On another subject, have you had a chance to talk to Erica Norquist since she changed her mind? I know she works in the galley area under your management."

"She mentioned to me that the colony was headed in a direction she could not go. But she didn't give me any specifics.

I tried to call Kayane to find out what was going on, but her communications link did not open. Neither would Graysun's. I don't know why they are not using them."

"Erica confided in Laura at lunch today," Morgan said. "The colonists have changed a lot, including apparently turning off their communicators. It's no wonder they do not want to talk to us. They may be afraid we will try and influence their decisions. What I have is third hand, but it's worth repeating as best as I can." Morgan went on to relate everything Laura had told him. Sarah listened with an increased amount of incredulity as the story unfolded. By the time he finished, she was shaking her head in disbelief.

"What in the world happened to them," she said as Morgan finished. "They have sold their souls in an effort to enhance their chances for survival. What is the purpose of surviving if in the process you give up the very essence of your character? I cannot believe Kayane would have agreed to that."

"Me neither, but apparently, she did. Are you ready for departure?" he asked, referring to the hydroponic gardens.

"Yes, all the gardens have been positioned to assume normal gravity once we get under way. I wish I could say the same about the people that work here."

"It's like that throughout the ship, particularly among those over thirty-five," Morgan said. "The captain had better do something, or we will have a number of injuries when we get under way. I'm going to head up to his office now to talk to him about trying to motivate everyone to get physically ready for acceleration. I'll also fill him in on what we have heard about the colony."

"See you later for dinner," Sarah said as Morgan moved out of her office toward the upper decks.

Morgan pondered how to approach Captain Larson as he headed toward his office. It was difficult to see how the captain could motivate the crew when he showed no enthusiasm himself for returning to Earth. But Morgan knew they could not stay here in orbit around Ararat forever. The younger members of the crew, like Laura, were ready and willing to return to Earth. Melissa had told him a few days earlier that they were becoming frustrated because the captain continued to delay the departure. Morgan had to convince him to set a definite date for getting under way. Those crew members that refused to prepare adequately for the gravitational effects of acceleration would simply have to face the consequences.

Morgan called the captain and told him he was on the way to talk to him about a couple of issues. The captain said he was in his cabin and would meet him in his office in fifteen minutes. So Morgan diverted briefly to the ecology center. Laura was still there, reviewing the environmental status of Earth's oceans and atmosphere with Purple.

Laura looked up as Morgan drifted in. "I sure wish we were getting reports from home. All the data in our computer will be over thirty years old by the time we get back. It looks like unless we receive some new information from Earth, I will be thirty years out of date too."

Morgan looked at Laura with a new sense of understanding as to what it meant to start the return journey as soon as possible. "You called earth *home*, Laura. I don't remember you saying that before. Sarah said the same thing when we found out we were going back. I'm glad you are looking at the return that way. As to being thirty years out of date, that might be an advantage. You will be able to clearly see how the environment has changed since we left. Purple's data will not be distorted by the passage of time."

"I hadn't thought of it that way. Thanks."

"Sarah is excited for you and Brad. We hope your plans will encourage others to do the same. I'm on my way up to the captain's office to talk to him about setting a firm date for getting under way. We need to do something, or the crew will never get ready for departure. Why don't you come along and tell him what you heard from Erica Norquist? I don't think he is aware of what is happening with the colony."

Laura looked a little apprehensive. "Are you sure, Morgan? I'm not one of his division chiefs."

"Nonsense," said Morgan. "We are not that formal on this ship. You've already demonstrated you are part of the team with your work on the colony review process."

Laura smiled at the compliment as she unstrapped and followed Morgan to the captain's office.

Captain Larson was already seated at his workstation when they arrived. His clothes were disheveled and his hair unruly. He said, "Sorry, I look a mess. I was lying in my bunk when you called. I haven't been feeling very well lately."

Morgan decided to ignore the remark. There was no point in trying to encourage the captain. Until he no longer viewed the mission and therefore himself as a failure, he was likely going to stay his current state of the blues. "Captain," Morgan said, "have you talked to Erica Norquist since she left the colony group?"

"I asked her that day why she had changed her mind, and she said only that the colony was not a good fit for her. I haven't talked to her since then."

"She opened up to Laura today. Some of the things she said were really weird. Laura is here with me to relate what she heard." Laura then proceeded to tell the captain everything she had learned from Erica. As she spoke, Captain Larson became more and more interested in what he was hearing.

When she finished, he said, "Ever since the decision was made to establish the colony, I have been moping around because I wanted to be a part of the group that stayed but knew

I could not abandon the *Mayflower*. From what Erica has told you, I can see that my frustration was misguided. I accepted the assignment as leader of this mission because I believed mankind had lost its way. I saw this as an opportunity to try once again to establish a nation where liberty, freedom, and equality were the cornerstones. I believed that the moral code we all adopted was the cement that would bind those cornerstones together to become the foundation of a nation devoid of the corruption and misery of every nation on Earth. These ideas are nothing new. Leading up to the revolution in America in the 1700s, the founders knew liberty and equality of the common man could not be achieved without a strong moral foundation. I remember reading about Samuel Adams in school. He stated, 'Neither the wisest constitution nor the wisest laws will secure the liberty and happiness of a people whose manners are universally corrupt.' Religion and biblical principles were fundamental in early America. George Washington said in his farewell address in 1796, 'Of all the dispositions and habits which lead to political prosperity, religion and morality are indispensable supports. And let us with caution indulge the supposition that morality can be maintained without religion. Reason and experience both forbid us to expect that national morality can prevail in exclusion of religious principle. It is substantially true that virtue or morality is a necessary spring of popular government.' These men knew that liberty and freedom would not survive without a strong moral base. As morality eroded away in America, so did its greatness. I wanted to rekindle the vision of the eighteenth-century colonies."

Morgan was impressed by the captain's remarks. He knew the captain was a history buff but was not aware of the depth of his knowledge concerning the founding of the United States.

"I knew that the colony would have to make some adjustments," Captain Larson continued, "to compensate for its small initial population, but I never thought it would come to this. This is not what I wanted. From what Erica Norquist has said, the colony is adopting a system of rule completely foreign to our mission objective. What good is the colony if it repeats the mistakes of history? If I could get them back, I would. But that will not happen. I am glad that Erica at least did not agree to sell herself out, but I am amazed she was the only one. I am dumbfounded that Graysun and Kayane Williams agreed to draconian measures like these."

"Apparently they did," said Morgan. "Sarah has tried to talk to Kayane, but they must have their communicators turned off."

"I haven't been able to talk to my daughter, Vickie, either," said Captain Larson. "I thought they had shut down the communicators because they were too busy. Now it appears they want to make sure nobody in the colony discusses what they are doing with us on the *Mayflower*. Purple, can you activate Vickie's communicator?"

"I could if it was just turned off," the computer responded. "But my information is that it has been destroyed."

"What about the others?"

"All of the communicators assigned to the colony personnel have been destroyed. The only link I have is with the computer they took out of the *Explorer*. It is still receiving information. Per your request, I asked the colony to establish a link with Vickie. I just received a message that no link between individuals is permitted."

"What about Nels? Is his communicator operating?"

"Yes," Purple responded. "He has been sending information to my files every day. He is in his shelter right now if you want to speak to him."

"Nels," Captain Larson said, opening a channel to him, "have you talked to the colony people lately?"

"Not since the day I got the boat," Nels responded. "I tried to contact Marlene Deveroe to discuss what I have learned about the kelp-like seaweed, but she hasn't responded."

"I'm asking Laura Simmons to fill you in on what she knows," Captain Larson said. He nodded to Laura to proceed. Laura opened a channel to Nels and briefed him on Erica's revelations.

After she finished, Nels said, "Interesting. I have been wondering who is really running the show in there. I find it hard to believe they all willingly agreed to such a complete change of lifestyle. I think my son would go along with it, but all the women? I hope it will work out for them."

"What about you?" the captain asked. "How are you adapting to the surface."

"Quite well. I have found several plants that are nutritious and one edible small mammal-like creature that I have trapped. The seaweed didn't turn out to be palatable. That's why I was trying to contact Marlene. She may know of a way to extract something useful from the seaweed."

"Let us know if there is anything we can do for you. We will be here for a while yet."

"Will do," Nels said, signing off.

"Captain," Morgan said, "the other subject I want to discuss with you is our departure for Earth. The ship is ready to go, but the crew isn't. We need to prepare them for acceleration. A few weeks ago, you said that it didn't matter when we left orbit, just let you know when the crew was ready. That is not working. Many of the older crew are putting off conditioning workouts while the younger ones are getting antsy that we are not already on our way."

"Melissa told me the same thing yesterday. Do you have any suggestions?"

"Yes. First, set a definite date. Second, set an example for all the crew. Get yourself ready."

"You are right, Morgan. I will talk to Melissa and Dr. Sanchez and announce a departure date tomorrow after I have their input. As to your second point, I will start setting an example today by going to the workout room for a couple hours. Actually, after hearing what the colony is doing, returning to Earth doesn't seem as bad as I thought."

The next morning, Captain Larson announced that the *Mayflower* would get under way for Earth on August 20, 2085, ten weeks in the future. He said that should give everyone enough time to prepare physically. But he reminded all crew members that they were free and could choose not to get in shape. If that was what they chose, they were likely to be very uncomfortable and possibly injured when the Perry-Warner engines were started. It was up to them.

Captain Larson worked hard to set an example over the next few weeks. He appeared in the workout room every day and worked hard to build up his muscles. Many of the older crew members responded positively to his initiative. By the middle of July, Dr. Sanchez announced that ninety percent of the crew was physically ready to depart Ararat's orbit. She said most of those lagging behind were working on their fitness and felt they would be ready by the scheduled departure date.

In late July, Nels called the captain and said he had some disturbing news. He reported that there had apparently been a revolt of some sorts in the colony, and he was going over there to investigate. The captain summoned all of the division chiefs to the conference room. As soon as everyone was present, including Samuel Workman who had replaced Graysun Williams as systems officer, Captain Larson opened a general channel with Nels's communicator.

"Nels, I have all the division chiefs here with me. You told me a little while ago that something was happening at the colony. Can you bring us up to date? What is going on?"

"About an hour ago, Marcus Clauson arrived at my camp. As you know, he is a fitness expert and in great shape. Even so, he was having difficulty breathing. After he had rested and could talk, he told me two other colony members were outside their enclosure and needed help. I went out and found them. I just got back to my camp. They were unable to walk here on their own as they were unprepared for exposure to Ararat's atmosphere."

"Who are they?" Dr. Sanchez asked.

"Two women. One is Kayane Williams, and the other is Susan Petersen." Morgan knew Susan as a young lady who had become proficient as a plant ecologist. She had told Morgan that she wanted to be part of the colony so she could begin a systematic classification of Ararat's plant life. She said somewhat humorously that she wanted to go down in history as the Carl Linnaeus of Ararat.

"What happened?" Captain Larson asked.

"From what they have said, conditions in the colony were becoming very contentious. All of the colony members had gone along with the strict rules they developed before they left the *Mayflower*, but some of them, including the three here with me, were not committed to those rules. They simply did not want to risk being rejected as Erica eventually was. They thought they could soften the harsh organizational system once they were on the surface. Apparently, when some of the women raised the issue, the response was extreme. They were told there would be no changes in their status, and if they continued to question the colony's charter, they would be shunned. Kayane knew that it would be certain death if she were expelled from the colony's habitat. No one had a personal communicator to call the *Mayflower* or me for help. But Marcus Clauson thought he could make it to my camp on his own. So the three of them agreed to escape. All they took with them were a few personal belongings. I found the two women a few hundred yards outside the colony. They were in pretty bad shape and wouldn't have lasted much longer. I was able to get them back here on a sled I had built."

"Have they said what they want to do now that they are out of the colony?"

"I asked them," Nels said, "including whether they wanted to go back to the *Mayflower*. They all said no. They are all committed to Ararat. They just aren't willing to give up their souls as part of that commitment. They want to live here in my camp."

"Is that agreeable to you?"

"It certainly isn't something I was planning. I need help, but I can make it work."

"What do you need?" Captain Larson asked.

"Breathers, for starters," Nels responded. "The two women are not doing very well, particularly Kayane. The colony is apparently doing nothing to begin adaptation to the Ararat environment. They even abandoned the initial atmospheric conditions the advance ground crew had established, including mixing in the natural air on Ararat. Marcus said they were maintaining the colony's environment just like that on the *Mayflower*. Also we will need food. None of them will be in shape to help me gather food for some time. I have found enough for me but not enough for three more mouths yet. Also I will need some construction tools so I can expand my camp. The colony used almost everything from the *Explorer*, but the *Orion* is sitting abandoned on the salt flat. Some of the other construction materials you downloaded also appear to have been abandoned by them. I can easily get enough to create enough additional space. My guests could also use some additional clothing and personal effects. Beyond that, I am not sure. We haven't talked about long-range plans yet."

Captain Larson looked around the table to see if anyone had any objections to Nels's requests. Seeing none, he told Nels they would arrange a drop immediately. John Malcolm said he would include communicators to replace those destroyed by the colony. Randy Edwards suggested they also include a solar-powered rover, and the captain agreed. There were still six of these small two-seat rovers on board the *Mayflower*, and Randy could see no reason all of them would be needed on the return trip. Samuel Workman said he would include an oxygen recharge system with the four breathers he was including in the drop. Most of the construction tools had already been given to the colony, but Samuel was sure he could scrounge up enough for Nels to expand his camp for its new residents.

Two days later, Kayane Williams called Sarah while Morgan and Sarah were relaxing in their quarters. Sarah asked how she and the others were doing.

"Mentally, much better," she said, "but physically I'm having trouble. I can't walk more than a few steps at a time. I'm also having terrible headaches and can't keep much food down. Thanks for sending supplemental breathing masks. I don't think I could have made it without the help. I need to use mine constantly right now. Susan is like me, flat on her back most of the time sucking oxygen. Marcus is doing better. He has been able to do some simple things to help Nels. He has even been outside in the area near Nels's camp gathering a little food. Marcus needs to rest a lot but is trying hard to adapt without using supplemental oxygen.

"Nels is amazing. He is so fit. It looks like he was born in this environment. He has set up a schedule to wean us off the breathers over a period of about a month or two. In the meantime, he has us on a conditioning program to prepare our bodies for physical activity. I can't believe how he has taken us under his wing like a mother duck. Nels is really in his element here on the surface. But I think he was lonely before we arrived. He didn't think the colony would shut him out completely. He is happy to have our company and says he has a new purpose in life. According to him, his original plan was to simply demonstrate to the colony that humans could adapt to the environmental conditions on Ararat. Now he sees his mission is much bigger. He is talking about our little group as an alternative colony that will not abandon the principles of our charter, including our moral code. We are all determined to do what Nels says and become active according to the timetable he set for us. We want to be full partners in the success of our little group."

"Do you think that is possible with just the four of you as a founding population?" asked Sarah.

"If I put on my hat as a geneticist, I doubt it. But Nels's optimism is overwhelming and rubbing off on all of us. He says that all that statistical projection stuff is worthless in the face of the human spirit to survive. I never knew Nels to be a religious person, but he believes God put him here to show the colony how wrong they were.

"The reason I called is to tell you what happened from my perspective. I think we owe it to all those on the *Mayflower* to know how superficial man's stated standards of behavior can be. When we began discussing our need to sacrifice in order to protect our survival, I went along. But it soon became apparent we were allowing our moral fiber to deteriorate in the name of survival. Most of the men began to say that we women had to focus on reproduction. The concepts of family, love, and physical relationships were counter to the goals of the colony. Graysun was the leader of this way of thinking. He said our marriage could not interfere with our *prime purpose* of bearing children. I could not believe how quickly he changed. He told me that past relationships were trivial in relation to the greater good of the colony. All of the men except Marcus Clauson and several of the women voiced the same opinion. But Graysun and I kept up the charade of a couple while we were on the *Mayflower*. I really wanted to be a part of the colony and hoped I could convince Graysun to respect our relationship once we were on Ararat. But as soon as we landed, all pretense of our marriage ended. I and the other women became the chattel of the colony. Initially, I tried to reason with the Graysun and the other men, but they became increasingly hostile to me. So I talked quietly to the women. Several were upset at their diminished role, but they didn't see any other choice. Then Susan Petersen told me she was going to leave. She said she would rather die than become for all intents and purposes the property of the colony. She gave me the idea of joining Nels Brunken. I confided in Marcus, and he agreed to go with us. We didn't tell anyone else. I'm not sure whether they would have tried to stop us or simply pushed us out the door. So here I am. I've lost my children. I've lost my husband, but at least I kept my moral compass, and I have my dignity."

"Did you have any sense Graysun would turn on you like that?" Sarah asked.

"No, not at all. I knew that he had had a rough childhood. He was always a driven person. That is why he was able to overcome his poor start in life and become a successful systems engineer. He never displayed any behavior inconsistent with the mission of the *Mayflower* to me. But somewhere buried deep in his DNA was this domineering trait that came to the surface when the colony option appeared. It was deep enough in his subconscious that neither I nor the selection committee for the *Mayflower* mission had any inkling it was there. I'm just glad I was able to get away from him."

"I would have thought your skills as a geneticist were crucial to the colony," Morgan said.

"Apparently not. I had set in place some preliminary plans which will work for a while if they want to use them. But from the way they were talking, they will probably go to a totally random system. Besides, they have a pretty good library in the computer they got from the *Explorer*. If they need some help, they will find a way to get it."

"With two women leaving, doesn't that hurt the colony's chances of survival?" Sarah asked.

"Not as much as one would think," Morgan said. "When Purple ran those calculations, it was still considering aspects of the moral code in its calculations. I checked with Purple today, and it said that after it included the conversations with Nels, the genetic material the colony had would largely offset the loss of the two women from a genetic viability standpoint. Also just because the women left the colony, it doesn't follow that they left the Ararat-colony gene pool. They still have Kayane's frozen eggs. And they are still on Ararat, so they still are part of the planet's gene pool. Also, survival chances had included some risk of early mortality. If no one dies before contributing to the genetic variability of Ararat, the three that left are still accounted for. As it stands right now, the overall chances are essentially the same as what Purple calculated before."

"Marcus said the men had anticipated the possibility some may decide not to accept their course of action. All the younger members that were not included in the genetic material stored on the *Mayflower* were required to provide samples before we disembarked including Erica Norquist. Besides, the colony doesn't care about the statistics," Kayane said. "They say they will grow and flourish, period. You know, I think they might. I just can't be a part of it."

"It's good to hear from you, Kayane," Sarah said. "We hope you will feel better soon. And tell Nels we are so thankful he was there for you. Morgan and I are praying you will be able to live a long life on Ararat."

"Thanks for your support and prayers. I will tell Nels just that. He is so different than he was on the *Mayflower*. He used to complain all the time, particularly after the captain decided we would return to Earth. Now he is happy and content. I think we will get along just fine."

"I'm glad for him and for you, Kayane. Take care of yourself. Call us again soon and keep us advised as to your adaptation to Ararat."

"I will. Give my kids a hug for me," Kayane signed off wistfully.

CHAPTER 8

On August 20, 2085, at 8:00 a.m. ship's time as scheduled, the *Mayflower*'s Perry-Warner engines were activated, and the ship began to move out of orbit around Ararat. Like almost all of the crew members, Morgan, Sarah, and their children were in their quarters lying down as the effects of gravity were begun to be felt.

"How long do we have to stay here?" Emily asked.

"Dr. Sanchez says we should wait at least an hour after acceleration begins," Sarah responded. "Even though you, children, have all worked hard to build your muscles up, it has been over two years since you have experienced the effects of weight. If you get up too fast, you could become dizzy and fall. When you do start to move around, remember to take it slowly. You have to retrain your muscles and your vestibular system, or you could lose your balance."

"What's the vestibular system?"

"It's in your inner ears, Emily. It senses movements and then sends signals to your muscles to help you stay upright under gravity. While we've been weightless in orbit around Ararat, our bodies have had no sense of up or down. It will take them a little while to adjust so that you don't fall down."

Seeming satisfied, Emily was willing to lie quietly, listening to some music on her communicator. Then Jessica asked, "How fast are we going now?"

"That's an interesting question, Jessica," Morgan responded. "Ben, you have been studying physics this year. Do you want to try out your knowledge?"

Ben beamed at being given the chance to show off a little bit. "Sure, Dad. Let's see. We have been under power for about thirty minutes now. We are accelerating at 980 cm/sec^2 or about 32.2 ft/sec^2. That means right now we are going about 17,666 m/sec or about 39,518 miles per hour. That assumes that we were standing still when we started. I know that is not true, but the math is too difficult for me to do in my head."

Morgan smiled. "Speed and velocity are measured against something. Your answer actually gives the speed in relation to the place in space where we went under power. But that place is also in motion. We were in a low altitude orbit around Ararat. Our orbital speed was about 13,000 mph. Then, of course, Ararat was orbiting Epsilon Eridani at about 80,000 mph. If that's not enough, the stars in this section of the galaxy are orbiting the center of the galaxy at about 495,000 mph, not to mention that the Milky Way galaxy is part of the local group of galaxies that is also moving. Since all of these orbits are roughly circular, the motions are constantly changing in relation to each other. By the time the *Mayflower* reaches its drifting speed of 0.8473 the speed of light in three hundred days or about 568 million miles per hour, these other velocities that existed when we started will have very little influence on our actual speed over the ground, so to speak. Purple includes them in its calculations for our precise direction of travel and the precise time to begin deceleration. I think your answer to Jessica was very good as it calculates how much our speed has changed since we started accelerating."

"I don't really know what speed is," Emily interjected. "I mean, I understand it's how fast we are going, but it doesn't mean anything to me. I feel the pull on my body when the Perry-Warner engines are running, but I don't feel speed."

"That's because speed is always in relation to something else. You were born on the *Mayflower*, and you are accelerating just like the ship. If you look out one of the portholes, the stars are so far away that you can't see how you are moving in relation to them. Think about it this way. When you get up and get your legs under you, you will be able to walk through the corridors of the *Mayflower*. If you look at the corridor walls, you will see you are moving in relation to them. What you are seeing is your speed in relation to the corridor walls. Walking is at about three or four miles per hour. You can see that speed by looking at a particular place on the wall as you pass."

"I get it now, Dad," Emily said. "When I was using the treadmill as we decelerated coming to Epsilon Eridani, it said I was running about nine miles per hour. I wasn't moving in relation to the fitness room, but I was in relation to the treadmill track."

"That's a good observation, Emily," Sarah said. "We've been lying here long enough. Anybody ready to get up?"

Without taking time to answer, Jessica popped up from her bed and immediately fell back down. "Wow, my head was spinning. That was neat."

Ben and Emily were more deliberate, rising slowly and gaining their balance before they tried to walk. Jessica stood up slower than her first try, and soon the three children were walking slowly around their quarters. "Come on," said Ben. "Let's see who else is moving around." Without further delay, they walked through the cabin's hatch and disappeared down the companionway.

"Be careful, particularly around the ladders between decks," said Sarah.

"How are you feeling?" Morgan asked her.

"Not as young as I used to," laughed Sarah as she sat up. "I think I'll sit here a few minutes before I try and stand."

"I hear you," he replied. "I'm not looking forward to doing this again after over six years weightless during the coasting period of our return flight. Speaking of which, any new thoughts about returning to Earth?"

"Just that I'm nervous about how different the children will find living on Earth will be compared to the life we have on the *Mayflower*. Emily's question about speed demonstrates that they know nothing about life on a planet's surface. Our educational program on the *Mayflower* has focused on science and math, and all the children are well trained in those areas. But they haven't learned much about everyday life. They have never dealt with money. They have never shopped. They have never crossed a street. They have never encountered a stranger. We had always thought they would easily adapt to colony life as all the residents would be having the same experiences. Now we have to educate them on how to live among billions of other people. Many of those people have very different standards than we do. It's not just learning to cope with things like crowds. It's also how to identify potential harm, whether it's from natural disasters, traffic, or people."

"Education is going to have to be our major emphasis on this return flight," Morgan said as he dropped his legs over the edge of their sleeping platform. "Even you and I need to retrain ourselves in the daily living skills we will need when we get back."

Morgan thought about the weeks leading up to the departure while he sat still adjusting to the ship's acceleration. Once the captain set the firm departure date, preparations began in earnest. Nels and Kayane called frequently with progress reports. His conditioning program was working well. By the time the *Mayflower* was ready to begin its homeward flight, Kayane said

Susan was able to spend up to two hours at a time out and about without extra oxygen. Susan had started on classification of Ararat's organisms. She reported excitedly that Ararat's plants had reproductive systems remarkably like taxonomically similar plant species on Earth. She had already identified several types of simple fungi-like plants involved in the decomposition of dead plant-like material on the ground. The ones she had examined appeared to reproduce with spores somewhat like Earth's mushrooms. The larger plants she had looked at so far all seemed to be like Earth's grasses and palm trees. On Earth, these plants are classified as monocotyledons, members of the class angiosperms. These are flowering plants with a single seed leaf upon germination. Many on Earth are valuable sources of food such as corn, wheat, and onions. She was working to find similar edible types on Ararat.

Nels indicated a week before the departure that he wanted to move his base camp farther up the coast as soon as the women were able to make the journey. Using the rover the *Mayflower* had dropped to him, he had explored the area for three days and found the environment toward the north more profuse and diversified, including signs of larger animals that had not been detected during the evaluation of Ararat by the *Mayflower*'s crew. He also planned on building a more extensive camp using equipment from the abandoned shuttle *Orion* and some of the construction materials the colony had not used. "I had originally planned on a simple nomadic lifestyle," he said. "But now we need a permanent camp to work from."

The colony had still not opened a communications channel with the *Mayflower*. Purple continued to send daily updates to the colony computer, but there was no way to determine whether they were being reviewed by any members of the colony. John Malcolm had said the *Mayflower* would lose the ability to talk to Nels and his band about five days after the Perry-Warner engines were started. The personal communicators did not have the power to maintain signal strength over vast distances. Once that happened, the only way to communicate with Nels and his group would be through the long-range equipment the colony or Nels had scavenged from the shuttles.

As Morgan was about to stand up for the first time, Purple announced on a crew-wide channel that a message had been received from the colony. The computer had checked with the captain and received permission to let the entire population of the *Mayflower* hear it.

"Captain and crew of the *Mayflower*," the message began, "we know you have begun your journey back to Earth. We wish your flight to be successful and that you all find conditions on Earth acceptable when you arrive. As for us, we are moving forward according to our plan. We decided to cease all personal communications with you as it would serve no purpose. You undoubtedly disagree with the way of life we have chosen. We do not seek your opinion regarding the choice we have made. It is our belief it was a necessary step to secure our long-term survival. Our survival is our only goal, and we will do anything necessary to achieve that goal. Unfortunately, three of our former residents broke their covenant with us and chose to leave. We understand that they are still alive with Nels and have told you what they found unacceptable in our colony. They made the mistake of not being honest before we left the *Mayflower*. They thought they could change the covenant we all agreed to. They were mistaken. We doubt they will last long on their own, but that was their choice. They will not be allowed back into our colony under any circumstances. We do not want anyone not fully committed to our mission. As for us, we will survive, but you will not hear from us again. When you get back to Earth, tell them that we did colonize the stars. When you are able, send another ship to see what we have created. Until then, please refrain from sending us meaningless messages. If you do, we will be forced to break this one remaining channel of communications. That is all."

Morgan looked at Sarah who was now standing and exercising her legs. She shook her head in disbelief. "I don't think I would want to be on a mission that came back here in a generation or two," she said. "It's unbelievable to me what they are doing."

"Me neither," said Morgan as he slowly rose to his feet. "I wonder—" he continued when he was interrupted by a call from Nels. Sarah indicated she was also on the channel with Nels.

"Purple included our communicators in hearing the colony's message. Kayane is so sad over what the colony has become. She said Graysun was one of the promoters of the colony's covenant. I can say I would not have accepted their approach, and if I had dropped out, I wouldn't have been able to stow away. Then I would have been my old grumpy self on the *Mayflower*. I am happy where I am and that I now have others to share life with on Ararat. Kayane has something she wants to say to you."

"Surprises never cease," she began. "And I've got a doozy for you. I'm five months pregnant."

"Holy cow!" exclaimed Sarah. "That is a surprise. How are you feeling?"

"Better now. That was part of the reason I was not feeling well when I left the colony. It was also one of the reasons I did leave. I knew I was pregnant when we came down on the *Orion* and that Grayson was the father. I could not bear the thought of raising *our child* in an environment where its father had become foreign to me. I didn't tell anyone at the colony because I was afraid they would prevent me from leaving. I doubt Grayson has any idea I am pregnant."

"What does Nels think?"

"He's actually glad. He says there are now two colonies on Ararat—the Nels colony and the weird colony. He says we are out to outdo the whooping cranes. We are starting from a population of four and one half. At first, I wasn't sure what Ararat had in store for us, but now I am optimistic there is a future for us on this planet. Marcus and Susan are compatible and have decided to eventually have a child of their own. We are also preparing a code of conduct similar to the *Mayflower*'s. We are determined to keep our core beliefs intact. Who knows, if Earth does send another expedition to Ararat, they may find two populations living polar-opposite lifestyles."

"Give our love to your little band," Sarah said. "And keep in touch as long as we can talk to each other. John Malcolm says we will be out of communicator range in about five days."

"Will do. Give my kids a kiss and tell them I love them," Kayane responded, signing off.

"What were you saying when Nels called?" Sarah asked Morgan.

"I don't remember. I guess it wasn't that important." Morgan did a few knee bends to let his leg muscles know they were going to be working for a while.

"What do you think? Do you think Nels and his little band have a chance?" asked Sarah.

"Actually, I do. Remember, the probabilities of survival we discussed were statistical probabilities. They were computed by Purple. Purple is a very intelligent computer, but that intelligence is artificial intelligence. Purple is capable of analyzing data, computing statistical probabilities, making assumptions, logic-based decision-making, and reasoning with the information available to it. But the computer does not have all the capabilities of the human mind. It doesn't have emotions. It doesn't have instinct. It doesn't have wisdom. It doesn't have sagacity. The human mind can use these characteristics and other capabilities we don't even understand to make decisions and take courses of action that seem illogical or counterintuitive but proved to be correct. If they use these human skills to their advantage, they can overcome what Purple saw as insurmountable odds."

"But if that is the case, why didn't we all stay?"

"Because when it comes to survival, those that volunteered undoubtedly have a better set of those known and unknown capabilities than the general population of the *Mayflower*. Luis Sanchez is the youngest member of the colony at nineteen. All of the volunteers passed the extensive screening for the selection of the *Mayflower* crew, even Luis who was seven when we left. Now look at how quickly they abandoned every aspect of our moral code when faced with the challenge of living on Ararat. I don't think many of us could have accepted that. Purple's calculations are more accurate the larger the sample size it is considering. We would have tried to do things consistent with our standards, and that would have worked against our chances of survival."

"Okay," Sarah said. "I can understand that. But what about Kayane and the others that left the colony?"

"They demonstrated another trait of man that would be impossible to predict statistically. They were willing to give up the security of the colony to protect their beliefs. They had already shown a unique capability to face the uncertain future on Ararat in preference to returning to Earth. Now they have chosen a risky future again in preference to submitting to the will of the colony. To me, that shows a tremendous amount of individuality and determination. I think the biggest challenge they face is a premature death, either from an accident or from some factor in the Ararat environment that kills them."

"And then there's Nels," she said. "He has built his whole life around conquering difficult challenges. He will be a great teacher for the rest of his group."

CONRAD A. FJETLAND

"I agree. I don't doubt that if anyone could survive on Ararat, Nels could. Now that he has taken the others under his wing, he has an even greater purpose for the future. Remember how I described how man had found different ways to adapt physically to high altitudes on Earth? We now have two different approaches to life on Ararat. I think they both have a chance of success. Unfortunately, unless the colony reverses its position on communications, we will probably never know. Earth could have valuable information for future expeditions if the colony were to send information regarding how they are doing. Hopefully, they will eventually change their minds."

"I know there is nothing we can do to help them now," Sarah said. "But I hate the thought of never knowing their fate.

"My legs feel ready to go now. Thank goodness, we worked hard to stay in shape during the last weightless period. What about you? Are you ready to go for a walk and test your sea legs?"

Morgan looked admiringly at his wife. She had indeed stayed in shape. She had weighed about 125 pounds and was five feet seven inches tall when they left Earth thirteen years before. The several extended weightless periods had done nothing to alter her appearance. She showed no signs of the puffy-face and bird-leg syndromes that are common under extended periods of weightlessness. These are the result of changes in the distribution of blood and other body fluids in the absence of gravity. Morgan at 185 pounds when the *Mayflower* left Earth had also avoided these problems by sticking to an aggressive exercise program. They were both about two inches taller because of the relaxation of the compression of the spine, but Morgan knew that would change in a few days now that they were again subject to the effects of gravity.

"Yes, let's go," he said. "I will keep one hand close to the bulkheads for a while in case I get dizzy, but right now, I feel fine."

As they stepped into the corridor, two young boys ran by, narrowly missing them. Morgan recognized one of the boys as the younger son of John Malcolm. "I'm not ready for that." Morgan laughed.

"Nor am I," Sarah said. "Children that age have known nothing other than life on the *Mayflower*. Adapting to gravity after weightlessness is just part of their normal experiences. They also have the advantage of being young at heart."

As they walked slowly down the passageway toward the central companionway to the galley area, Sarah called Mario Hernandez, who was on duty in the hydroponic gardens, to make sure everything had gone smoothly during the transition to gravity. He informed her that one of the quinoa trays had tipped over, but nothing was lost, and it had been easily righted.

They encountered several children walking and sometimes running up and down the corridors, but only a few adults were out so far. As they reached the ladder down to the galley, Sarah asked, "Are you up to some stairs yet?"

"Sure," Morgan replied. "Let's get a cup of coffee."

They worked their way down through the three decks of living quarters to the galley level. They found about twenty others were already in the galley as they entered. Morgan went to get two cups of quinoa coffee while Sarah joined a group of five at a nearby table. "Anybody heard about any problems with acceleration?" Sarah asked as she sat down.

Monica Everly, a twenty-year-old assistant of Sarah in food production, said that her father had injured his shoulder by falling. "He stood up too quickly," she said, "and fell right over. He's sore, but I don't think it's serious." Two others at the table related similar stories, but none of the injuries seemed serious so far.

Morgan arrived at the table with two steaming mugs of coffee. He sat down next to Sarah and handed her one of the mugs. After taking a long sip, he said, "Ah, there's nothing like a drink of hot coffee from a mug where you don't have to suck it out of a weightless bottle."

"You do realize that that's not real coffee, don't you?" Monica quipped. "It's just another version of quinoa with a little chemical flavoring to make it taste like coffee."

"I know," he replied. "But I can dream. Just think in nine or ten more years, I can have the genuine article. That's at least one thing to look forward to."

"I'm looking forward to seeing the real mountains," said Bob Workman, a nineteen-year-old fitness trainer. He was the oldest son of Samuel Workman, the new systems officer. "I was only seven when we left Earth, and I don't really remember much about it. Some of the videos are really beautiful, but they are just images. I want to see what mountains actually look like and walk on their surfaces."

"That's a good point, Bob," said Sarah. "We always talk about all the bad things on Earth, but there is beauty there. There are many places where man has not destroyed that natural beauty. I hope you do get to experience some of nature's bounty."

"At least it wasn't all destroyed when we left," Monica somberly remarked. "Who knows what they will have managed to do by the time we get back."

"Morgan, what did you think about the statement from the colony we all heard a few minutes ago?" Bob asked, changing the subject.

"I guess if I had to sum it up, never underestimate the ability of man to do the unexpected," he answered thoughtfully. "One of the things we all cherish on the *Mayflower* is our freedom of choice, liberty, and our moral code. But the colony has demonstrated that these can be fragile concepts. I am sure you have all heard what Erica Norquist and Kayane Williams have said about the colony's choices. I suppose one could argue that the colony members exercised freedom of choice by agreeing to give up all they did to arrive at a collective arrangement. In the long run, it may be what they had to do to secure to their continued existence."

"All I know is that it is not consistent with our mission. I thought we were sent out here by the consortium to establish a population of man that would not repeat the mistakes made by every civilization on Earth. It sounds to me like they have already started making those same mistakes."

"You are right, Bob," Morgan said. "They may have improved their survival chances, but at what cost? What will they be like in a few generations? Unfortunately, unless they decide to reopen communications, we may never know."

As they finished their coffee, Morgan and Sarah received a call from the captain. He wanted all the division chiefs to assemble in the conference room at 1:00 p.m. He said he wanted to receive verbal reports from each division regarding any problems that might have occurred as a result of acceleration.

"That's a little strange," said Sarah. "He could get all that information from the computer. I need to go down to the hydroponics deck to make sure nothing else has happened."

"I guess he wants our personal touch. There's really nothing to report from my division. I'll check with Laura before heading back to our quarters. Shall we meet there at noon for lunch?"

"Rather than me climbing up to our quarters just to turn around and come back down, why don't you meet me here?" said Sarah as she walked out of the galley area.

"Good point. Will do," replied Morgan.

It was four decks up to the office deck above the living area. The *Mayflower* had an elevator, but everyone was encouraged to use the companionway ladders anytime less than five decks were being climbed. It was all part of the effort to help maintain healthy fitness levels. Even though Morgan was in good shape, by the time he reached the ecology center he was struggling to catch his breath. He leaned against the bulkhead outside the lab for a couple seconds before entering.

Laura was there, studying reports contained in Purple's data files. She looked up as Morgan walked through the opening into the lab. "Take it easy, Morgan. We've only been under gravity for a couple hours. You look like you just climbed a mountain."

"Just four decks," he responded. "You are right. I've got to go a little slower until I have my leg strength and lungs back in shape. I guess I'm not as young as I used to be. What are you looking at now?"

"Air-quality issues when we left. The United States and some of the European countries had reduced emissions from fossil fuels by the mid-twenty-first century, but their efforts were more than offset by increased emissions by Asian and South American countries. I was only thirteen when we left Earth and don't remember much about it. How bad were the conditions?"

"Pretty bad," Morgan said. "In the twentieth century, dirty air was considered a local issue. Smog, as it was called, was first considered a problem in cities like London. There, it was caused by burning of large quantities of coal for heat, emitting soot and sulfur dioxide into the atmosphere. Then cities like Los Angeles, Mexico City, and Hong Kong had air-quality issues resulting from fossil fuel consumption in internal combustion engines and factories. These pollutants become concentrated under certain conditions, like temperature inversions in the atmosphere that did not allow the pollutants to disperse. But on a global scale, concerns about dirty air were more of an academic exercise than a real problem. It began to change in the first quarter of the twenty-first century. Increasing levels of these pollutants were being detected far from industrial cities. But governments could not agree on what to do about it. Everyone wanted someone else to do something. Those that did soon found they were put at an economic disadvantage when they forced reductions on their people. The problem was still getting worse when we left in 2072. It's hard to say what we will find when we get back."

"I hope they have found a solution, but if not, it's another area I would be interested in. I found a scientific paper in Purple's files that indicated a new anaerobic bacterium discovered in a hot sulfur springs has potential for reducing sulfur-dioxide pollutants. What about you? What do you want to do when we get back?"

"Ecosystem dynamics has always been my main scientific area of interest. Sarah and I will be nearly fifty when we arrive. That's a little old to begin thrashing around in the bush, especially since we will have been living a largely sedentary life here on the *Mayflower* for over twenty years by the time we are back. I think we will look for a teaching position somewhere. I may even look into some sort of a management position. Being part of the *Mayflower*'s management team has opened my eyes to new areas of interest.

"The captain has called all the division chiefs to gather at one this afternoon to give him a status report. There's not much going on in our department, but I will talk to him about preparing for our arrival." Morgan turned to leave and head back to meet Sarah.

"Stop by after the meeting and give me the hot scoop," Laura called to him as he disappeared down the corridor.

Morgan decided to stop by his quarters to rest a bit before returning to the galley. He was still a little wobbly on his feet, so he wanted to get off them for a few minutes. Just as he sat down, Sarah surprised him by walking into their cabin. She was not breathing hard like Morgan had been when he climbed to the upper decks of the *Mayflower*. "I thought you were going to wait for me in the galley. I assume you decided to use the elevator since you're not out of breath," he said as she walked in. "I climbed the four decks to my laboratory, and I was beat when I got there."

"I had a little extra time, so I changed my mind," she responded. "You are right about the elevator. It's the equivalent of seven decks up from the hydroponic gardens to our space." She smiled. "I knew better than to try that for a day or two. Let me know when you are ready to get some lunch."

Thirty minutes later, Morgan and Sarah returned to the galley and enjoyed a relaxing meal, their first under gravity conditions in over two years, before reporting to the conference room. When all were assembled, Captain Larson walked in and took his position at the end of the table. The captain looked rather chipper compared to his demeanor since the decision to return to Earth had been made. Morgan noted that the captain had not replaced Nels's position. He assumed the captain had decided there was no immediate need for a planetologist now that they were committed to returning to Earth. Nels's duties, however, had also included interstellar navigation including making sure the flight path did not enter any areas where the *Mayflower* could intersect higher than base levels of space junk like rocks or ice.

"I have three subjects I want to discuss with you," he began. "First, I have received reports from Purple regarding our initiation of acceleration, and I know you are all aware of your areas of responsibility, but I want each of you to have a complete picture. Randy, will you go first?"

"Sure, Captain. The six Perry-Warner engines all started exactly on time as expected. However, there was a minor power anomaly in one of them. This anomaly was apparently the result of a minute calculation error of some of the mass we downloaded to Ararat. Purple indicated that the shuttle *Orion* apparently loaded more fuel than was reported. Purple corrected this anomaly within a few nanoseconds, but it did result in some damage. I will defer to Samuel Workman to describe that damage."

"The anomaly was corrected so fast by Purple that there was no visible damage," Samuel began. "But Purple said there was some structural shifting on the hydroponics deck. The external skin of the *Mayflower* flexed on the port side about a tenth of an inch before it returned to its normal shape. I had my technicians inspect the affected area. It was about three square feet. The X-rays they took of the skin where it flexed showed some microcracks, so we have welded a plate over the spot. Subsequent analysis by the computer shows the strength of the patched area equal to the rest of the *Mayflower*."

"Thanks, Sam," Randy said. "As for the rest of the engineering systems, everything is in order. We are accelerating at exactly one standard earth gravity. Power output is normal, and fuel is adequate for the return flight."

"Sam, do you have anything else to report?" the captain asked.

"Our life-support systems are all operating normally. The consumption of oxygen has risen about five percent under acceleration, which is expected. All of the recycling systems are functioning properly."

"Okay. Sarah, how are things in the hydroponics?"

"We had one quinoa production tray tip over near the area where the technicians were fixing the ship's skin, but I don't believe the two events are related. The load on the tray was not properly distributed. It has been righted, and no production was lost. We have started increasing production to compensate for the crew's increased oxygen use. I also checked on the shrimp. As before, I don't think they even notice when we go to gravity conditions."

"Sandra, any serious medical issues?"

"Yes," Sandra Sanchez replied. "So far, my staff has treated two broken legs and three hip injuries. All of them involved crew members over thirty-five years old. One five-year-old boy fell down a companionway, but it appears only his ego was bruised. He had forgotten how to walk down the ladders. I know of several other bumps and bruises, but no other serious injuries. I am urging everyone to take it easy for a few days while our bodies adjust. I don't want to see any heart problems or strokes from overexertion. The enhanced conditioning program the last couple of months really helped us avoid more serious health-related issues."

"John, do we still have contact with Nels's group?" the captain asked.

"Yes, we can talk with them for four more days. After that, we will be too far away for the signal strength from their communicators to reach us. However, we can broadcast from our ship's radios to them. The communicator reception capabilities should be good enough to receive our signals from as far as a light-year away. Nels told me a couple days ago that he had removed the long-range equipment from the *Orion*. None of his group is trained in the use of this equipment, so I asked Purple to send him detailed information on the requirements and operation of the system. Once out of communicator range, our only way to reach each other will be through the interstellar radios."

"What about the colony? Have we heard anything further?" Judy Polachek asked.

"That was their last message," John answered. "After that, the captain instructed me to discontinue sending daily updates.

Hopefully they will keep listening. When we have something important to communicate, we will send it."

"Thanks, John. Melissa, what about your areas of responsibility?"

"Morale is pretty good right now. I was in the galley for about an hour before lunch, and most of those I talked to were glad we were finally under way. Quite frankly, Captain, when the crew saw that you had shed your dour attitude and publicly set an example of preparedness for acceleration, it rubbed off on many others who were feeling the same way. The trick will be to maintain this newfound energy as time goes by. It will be critical during the over six years of weightlessness."

"I agree," the captain said. "And we will discuss that further in a few moments. Judy or Morgan, do you have anything you need to report from your divisions? I know not much goes on in the environmental or farming areas during flight."

Both Morgan and Judy said nothing of note was going on in their areas and probably would not be for years to come.

"All right. The second matter I want to bring up is preparation of the crew for arrival at Earth. I know we have talked about this somewhat before, but we need to give it a lot more attention, or our people will be psychologically unprepared for life on Earth. Most of those under eighteen have no idea about such simple things as how to cross a street or how to get a job. We have all been preparing for life in a small colony. Now we have to think about assimilating into a population that will probably be over sixteen billion by the time we get back. Management of the education program necessary to properly prepare everyone for our return will be a full-time job. I talked to Melissa about this before we left Ararat's orbit. She has agreed that her former duties will be split, and she will begin to work full time on education. She has recommended that her assistant, Christopher

Vollbrecht, take over the duties as morale officer, and I concur with her recommendation."

"Thank you, Captain," Melissa said. "I will do my best to prepare everyone for our arrival back home."

"I know you will, Melissa. Now for my third subject, I appreciate that many of you observed a more positive attitude in me. I worked hard to improve my public persona. After what happened with the colony, I have accepted that returning to Earth is not only best for this crew, but it is also the best alternative for me. But I have also learned that my focus has changed. I no longer believe I am the best person to carry out the functions of captain of this ship. However, I have always had a great deal of interest in human history. I had always thought it was primarily an academic subject for the *Mayflower*, but once the decision was made to return to Earth, I realized that all the younger people on this ship needed to have a thorough understanding of history as part of their preparation for life on Earth. So I have decided to retire as captain and spend the next few years as a teacher. I have reviewed the charter, and it provides a procedure for replacement of the captain. As you know, for almost all decisions on the *Mayflower*, the captain has the ultimate authority. The one exception is for the captain's replacement. I do not have the authority to name my replacement, nor do I want that authority. That responsibility rests with all adults over the age of eighteen. Once I notified Purple that I intended to retire, the computer opened a place for nominations to replace me. At the conclusion of this meeting, Purple will deliver an announcement I have prepared to the crew. Each crew member will be invited to nominate a possible successor. The nomination process will stay open for five days. It will then be followed by an election. The charter provides that to be selected as the new captain, a nominee must receive more than 50 percent of the votes of those eligible to vote, not of those who actually voted. This provision was designed to guarantee a high level of participation in this very important decision-making process. If no nominee obtains 50 percent support, then a runoff election will be held as often as necessary among the top three vote getters. Purple will announce when a new captain has been elected. Until that happens, I will remain in the post. That is all for now. The meeting is adjourned. Purple, please deliver my announcement to all aboard the *Mayflower*. Thank you all for your support and leadership for the years since we left Earth."

CHAPTER 9

Morgan awoke to an alarm call from Purple. "Captain Parker, there has been a decompression event beginning in compartment 4-65. I have initiated standard lockdown procedures of all internal air locks."

Morgan rubbed his eyes and unstrapped from his bed. He looked at the wall calendar and saw it was 3:15 a.m., August 10, 2087. As he drifted over to his clothing from the previous evening, Sarah awoke. She looked alarmingly at Morgan and asked, "Why did Purple awaken you?"

"The computer detected an air pressure anomaly in one of the crew quarters on deck four. We are under lockdown. I am getting dressed, but I will have to wait here until Purple analyzes the extent of the problem and takes appropriate action." He grabbed his magnetic boots and day wear and began dressing. He didn't always wear the boots but knew he would want to be able to attach to the ship's floor panels when he left the compartment to check the extent of whatever had happened. The boots had been designed for use under weightless conditions when one wanted to anchor in one place. The magnetic field could be turned off as needed so that one could drift through a passageway without being drawn to the bulkheads and then activated when one wanted to be anchored in a specific place.

Morgan pushed himself out of the sleeping part of their quarters and strapped into the double lounger to wait for an update from the computer. Sarah came out of the sleeping room a few minutes later and joined Morgan in the lounger. As they sat quietly waiting for Purple's report, Morgan reflected back on the two years since they had left orbit around Ararat.

Captain Larson's announcement that he was resigning as captain had come as a shock to Morgan and just about everyone else on the *Mayflower*. Three crew members were nominated to replace him including Morgan. The other two clearly expressed that they did not want the responsibility and asked crew members to not vote for them. Morgan was not anxious to have the job either but realized he would have little to do during the flight back to Earth. Laura was more than qualified to teach the environmental subjects that were being offered on the return flight. As a result, Morgan was almost unanimously elected as captain on the first ballot. Laura Simmons replaced Morgan as chief ecologist. Howard Larson eagerly gave up his access by verbal command to the computer, although he couldn't shake the title as captain. After some discussion with Laura, they agreed that she would not need to have that authority over the computer on the return flight, so only Morgan, Randy Edwards, and John Malcolm retained the verbal command authority. Howard quickly transformed into a history instructor. He seemed much more relaxed in his new role. The only disappointment he occasionally expressed was that he missed his daughter, Vickie.

Morgan and Sarah heard from Kayane several more times before the *Mayflower* was too far from Ararat for her communicator to reach them. She said all was well in their small camp. She was slowly adjusting to the oxygen levels and felt she could wean herself from supplemental equipment within another month or so. She said Susan and Henry were doing much better. Susan had found a grain-like plant that she was focusing on to see if it would provide a reliable source of food. Nels communicated daily with Captain Larson until the *Mayflower* was out of range. Nels told Captain Larson that he had been working with John Malcolm to get the long-range receiver he had removed from the *Orion* working but that the transmitter side was a problem. The power requirements of the transmitter were beyond what he was able to remove from the abandoned shuttle. After the election was settled, John sent them a message that Morgan had replaced Howard as captain, but by then, the *Mayflower* was beyond Nels's communicator capability to respond.

The flight under acceleration had gone smoothly. No further serious injuries occurred after the ones that had happened the first few hours. One male, age fifty, died unexpectedly 112 days into the flight, but Dr. Sanchez's autopsy showed it was a defective heart valve and not related to gravitational stress. With the loss of the thirty-eight colony members and Nels, there were 613 people on board when the Perry-Warner engines were started. Sixteen babies were born over the next three hundred days, so along with the one death, the population was 628 when the *Mayflower* reached its maximum speed and began coasting. Another twenty were born in the year since they had resumed weightless flight.

One of those born was a daughter for Laura and her husband, Bradley McMullen. They were married just two weeks after leaving Ararat's orbit. Morgan was asked and gladly served as Bradley's best man. The service was performed by Miguel Sanchez. The wedding helped break Miguel out of the depression he had been in since learning that his oldest son, Luis, had volunteered to stay on Ararat. Since the wedding, Miguel had spent most of his spare time studying the Bible and documents of other Earth religions. He had started teaching a program on the relation between religion and society on Earth.

Morgan's thoughts were interrupted by Purple's status report. The loss of pressure was caused by a small piece of space debris. It impacted the *Mayflower* near the upper left corner of the ship. It passed cleanly through the outer skin and nonpressurized storage compartments on the first three decks. The small stone, about the size of a millet seed, then went cleanly through cabin 4-65, the first pressurized space it encountered. The cabin's automatic seals were immediately released and sealed the hole in the ceiling before the loss of air became significant to the three occupants who were sleeping at the time. The stone then passed through crew compartments on decks five and six. The cabin on deck five was not occupied at the time, and since the hole in the ceiling in cabin 4-65 was patched, no air was lost. Unfortunately on deck six, the stone intercepted one of the occupants, a seventeen-year-old boy named Larry Spencer, and he was killed while he was sleeping. After leaving the three crew decks, the stone continued through a corner of a storage locker adjacent to the galley. It then went cleanly through all three double decks of the hydroponic gardens and deck fourteen, devoted to shrimp production. Damage to the hydroponic equipment was limited to small holes in production trays on each deck. On the shrimp deck, it penetrated the floor between two tanks. Finally, the stone went through deck fifteen, the equipment deck, and engineering spaces for the Perry-Warner drives on deck sixteen. The engines were not damaged, but one of the oxygen-regeneration pumps was punctured on the equipment deck. Another automatic seal was dispatched to the exit hole at the base of deck sixteen, resulting in only a minor loss of air. Purple concluded by reporting that the situation was now under control and all emergency hatches had been reopened.

Morgan thought about the comments Randy Edwards had made over two years before concerning the integrity of the *Mayflower*'s hull. Randy had expressed concern that the outer skin of the ship was being eroded by cosmic dust, and the possibility of a hull failure was increasing as they continued to travel at high speeds through space. It was one of the reasons they had decided not to travel to Tau Ceti as originally planned. Morgan called Randy and asked him where he was.

"I'm on my way to the equipment deck to look at the oxygen pump that was damaged," he said.

"I need to first stop by the Spencer's cabin on deck six. Dr. Sanchez is there with the Spencers, and I want to see if there's anything I can do for them. I will meet you in a few minutes on deck fifteen." Morgan told Sarah that everything was under control and she should go back to bed. The food production night shift had already addressed the minor damage on the hydroponics decks. He said he would join her for breakfast later that morning.

As Morgan floated into the Spencers' quarters, he found Avery and Tammy Spencer strapped into their lounger and Dr. Sanchez booted to the floor in front of them. Morgan turned on his boots and joined Dr. Sanchez. "Purple filled me in on what occurred here," he began as sympathetically as he could. "I am so sorry that this happened. Please tell us if there is anything we can do to help you in this difficult time."

"It's unbelievable," Tammy sobbed. "Larry was just two when we left Earth. He had no memories of it and was so much looking forward to returning. Now he's gone. When I think of all the things that could happen to one of my children, being killed by a meteor was the farthest from my mind."

"Doctor, make sure everything is taken care of. I need to get down to the equipment deck where Randy Edwards is assessing the damage to some equipment. Avery, Tammy, please do not hesitate to call me or any member of this crew if you need anything."

"Thank you, Captain," said Avery somberly. Morgan preferred to be called Morgan rather than captain, but he didn't say anything. Usually, only Purple addressed him as captain.

Morgan worked his way down to deck fifteen, the equipment deck, and found Randy by the damaged oxygen pump. "Hey, Randy," he began, "Purple gave me a general update. What is the situation with the oxygen pump?"

"It sure could be worse. We have two additional pumps on line, and this one can be repaired. The stone passed through the pressure chamber. I will have one of the techs weld it later this morning. How are the Spencers?"

"About what one would expect," replied Morgan. "The loss of a child is always hard, and an accident like this is so unforeseen. It makes it that much more difficult."

"We probably have been luckier than we deserve. This is the first breach of the hull since we left Earth. Space is not a pure vacuum as much as we would like it to be. That is why the exposed surfaces of our hull are thinning due to erosion. Even out here far from any star, there are one or two hydrogen atoms in every cubic meter of space. At the speed we are traveling, they cause erosion when they impact the hull. Fortunately, larger particles are rare this far out in space. But comets do spin off debris, and we apparently impacted a small piece. It passed through the ship so fast that it didn't even have time to heat up.

"That was the first deployment of the automatic pressure patches," Randy continued. "They worked as designed. Purple estimates we lost less than a cubic foot of our air. It's interesting that the first pressurized cabin the stone penetrated was on deck four. Remember the discussion we had about placing the patches in every compartment? Some thought they only needed to be in spaces adjoining the outer skin, but I argued for them in every compartment. The three spaces above quarters 4-65 were originally pressurized, but after the equipment stored there was off-loaded to the Ararat colony, there was no need to keep air in them. So the patches there did not sense any drop in pressure."

"Have you looked at the patches yet?" Morgan asked.

"Not the one in 4-65. But I did go down to the engineering space, and I doubt I could have found it without Purple's help. It was a very small hole, and the patch seemed to fill it completely. Just to be safe, I will have plates welded over the entrance and exit holes as well as the hole in the top of 4-65. I will also fix the holes in the storage compartments in case we decide to pressurize them."

"Let me know if you encounter any problems," Morgan said. "I'm heading up to the operations center to talk to the computer and Phil Cavuto to see if there is more space debris along our path. If there is, we may have to alter our course. We cannot afford to take a hit through the heart of the *Mayflower*."

Morgan turned off his boots and pushed toward the companionway to the top of the *Mayflower*. Soon after he had taken over as captain, Morgan had appointed Phil Cavuto to replace Nels Brunken as the chief planetologist. The chief planetologist's job included navigation through interstellar space. The protocol for a decompression event would have required Purple to awaken Phil as well as Morgan and Randy. Morgan called Phil and asked him to come to the operations center where he would join him in a few minutes.

As he entered the central companionway that allowed him to move directly from deck fifteen to the operations center on deck one, he considered the design of the *Mayflower* in relation to the risks of interstellar travel. There was, of course, no need to build a streamlined ship for travel in space. The virtual vacuum eliminated any need to consider aerodynamic factors. The design became a compromise among efficiency of construction, use of the ship's components upon arrival at its destination, the erosion factor, and stress considerations when under power with the Perry-Warner engines. Further, the designers knew that it would be home to over five hundred people for many years, so it had to be livable.

The designers decided on a configuration using right angles where surfaces joined. This allowed for economy of space and ease of dismantling when the ship arrived at its destination. Stress factors dictated it be longer than wide. The surfaces primarily exposed to erosion at what would be the top under acceleration and drifting and the base under deceleration would be armored, and the rest would not. When construction was completed, the *Mayflower* was about 192 feet long with each deck measuring 136 feet by 168 feet. It could be best described as a cuboid or rectangular prism.

The top deck contained the operations center and extensive storage space. Decks two and three were devoted to offices and laboratory space. Purple's core was located in the operations center. The *Mayflower's* classrooms were on deck two, and the hospital was on deck three. Also within decks two and three was the ship's gymnasium. It consisted of a small exercise room containing equipment designed for workouts under weightless conditions as well as under acceleration. Adjacent to the workout space was a double-deck play area. This area was padded on all surfaces and provided a place for competitive three-dimensional games. Both the children and the adults enjoyed vigorous contests of weightless dodgeball or lacrosse. Leagues that had been formed on the flight from Alpha Centauri to Epsilon Eridani provided an excellent way for crew members to work off excess energy.

Extensive storage compartments were around the perimeter of decks two and three. These storage compartments could be opened to the outside to allow drops to a planet's surface. That was the case of the three storage areas first punctured by the space stone.

Decks four through six were divided up into living quarters. Each deck had sixty-eight units. Each unit was ten by seventeen feet. Interior units like Morgan's had a living space in front and two small sleeping areas behind. Some of the units located along the outside hull were configured differently depending on who was occupying them. The units were in groups of four with a men's and women's bathroom for each group. The designers had built a total of 204 living quarters into the *Mayflower*, allowing for some population growth as the journey progressed. At the time the stone intercepted the *Mayflower*, 187 units were being used.

The galley, food-storage and food-preparation spaces, were on the deck below the living area. Below the galley deck were three double decks devoted to quinoa production. These decks were designed so that they could be reconfigured as necessary to raise quinoa under either gravity or weightless conditions. Shrimp production was on deck fourteen below the quinoa decks. Deck fifteen contained equipment that maintained air and water quality and recycled nutrients in the ship's closed system. Finally, deck sixteen was devoted to the *Mayflower*'s Perry-Warner engines. Also on this bottom deck was fuel storage for the drive and the ship's shuttles.

Two large companionways and four elevators passed through the center of the *Mayflower* from top to bottom. The elevators were only used to move bulky objects during weightless conditions but were essential for crew members when under acceleration or deceleration. Passageways and corridors were eight feet wide throughout the ship. The central companionways were fourteen feet wide. This width gave enough room to allow crew members to navigate past each other under weightless conditions. There were also smaller companionways between specific decks where frequent direct access was needed. All of the companionways were equipped with ladders that were stowed when the *Mayflower* was not under power and deployed when gravity conditions existed. There were numerous handgrips in the companionways and all corridors for propelling oneself through them under weightless conditions. It was also possible to walk in the corridors by using magnetic boots, but few crew members did that.

Phil was already there when Morgan drifted into the operations center. Phil was a young astrophysicist when the *Mayflower* departed from Earth. He had worked closely with Nels during the flights to Alpha Centauri and Epsilon Eridani and was a natural to take over the interstellar flight duties after the loss of Nels.

The only other person in the center was the duty watchman. When the Perry-Warner engines were not running, only one person was on duty at time in the operations center. The only function that was conducted there was a routine monitoring of *Mayflower*'s flight path. All other activities on the *Mayflower* were carried out elsewhere on the ship. Morgan acknowledged the watchman and strapped in to his seat in front of a large display screen.

"Was this piece of space debris a random event, or are we looking at a heightened possibility of more encounters?" he asked Phil.

"I have looked at all of the information we have for the course we are on. There is nothing on our charts or detected on our sensors that indicates any increase above the base level of particles larger than a molecule. Purple's monitoring of hull erosion from hydrogen and occasionally helium atoms does not show any change in the frequency of contacts resulting from the deep space norm of less than two atoms per cubic meter of space. Also there is no change in background radiation or magnetic fields. The temperature of space in this area is 2.7 kelvin which is normal for deep space. All things considered, this appears to have been a chance event. I see no advantage to changing our course or speed. We are just as likely to encounter another object big enough to penetrate the hull on a new course as we would be if we stay on our current flight plan."

"Purple, what is your analysis of the situation?"

"Phil Cavuto has stated the facts very well," the computer responded. "My monitoring of the hull erosion actually shows a slight decrease from that observed between Alpha Centauri and Epsilon Eridani. Any change in course or speed would be more likely to increase the risk rather than decrease it."

"Okay, we will stay the course. But I want to expand our monitoring. I would like to know of any objects bigger than an atom that pass within one mile of our hull."

"We can do that, Morgan," said Phil.

Morgan left the command center and worked his way back toward his cabin. It was 7:25 a.m. when he pulled his way through his quarter's hatch. Sarah was strapped into the lounger waiting for him when he arrived. "Are the girls going to the morning meal with us?" Morgan asked.

"They are in the women's room getting ready. Emily has been taking a lot longer lately. I think she may be trying to impress one of the boys near her age."

Emily had turned fourteen a couple months before. Morgan had also noticed how she was paying a lot more attention to her appearance. Hair was not an issue when under weightless conditions; everyone wore their hair closely cropped. But she had been spending a great deal of time on her skin condition since her birthday and was using some modest makeup. The *Mayflower* had eliminated a lot of health diseases for its crew, but adolescent acne was not one of them. Acne is caused by increased levels of testosterone or other androgens during puberty and the resulting interaction with naturally occurring bacteria on the skin. Dr. Sanchez had determined that its occurrence on the *Mayflower* was statistically no different than that found in the general population on Earth before the *Mayflower* left.

Just then, Jessica entered the living space and said, "Emily's still fussing around in front of the mirror. She said she will be here in a minute." Sarah heard her mutter under her breath. "Whatever that means."

"Be nice," Sarah said.

"I try, but she pays more attention to boys now than she does to me. It's not fair."

Morgan smiled. "I know it doesn't seem fair right now, Jessica. But in a few years, you, too, will be a teenager, then you will understand how important it is to look your best."

"Tommy Malcolm says I'm cute right now," Jessica bragged. Tommy was the younger son of John Malcolm and one year older than Jessica. "I think his brother Walter likes Emily." Walter was three months older than Emily.

"I'm ready," said Emily as she pulled into the cabin. "Is Ben going to join us?"

"I don't think so today," Sarah said. "He will probably eat with his friends after his morning workout." Ben, now eighteen years old, had moved out of his parent's quarters and was living with three other single men on deck five.

As they all headed down the companionway on the way to the galley, Morgan looked at Sarah and remarked, "We are getting older, aren't we? We have two teenagers now and a third one not far behind. I'm beginning to understand why my mother said, 'Just remember, what goes around comes around,' when I was being a stupid teenager."

"You, a stupid teenager." Sarah laughed. "I don't believe it. You have always told me you were an angel."

"That was just the good face I put on to win you over. I had my moments when I was a kid. But let's forget that for now. We don't want to give the girls any bad ideas."

They obtained their food dispensers and strapped down to one of the galley tables. "Walter told me about Larry Spencer," Emily lamented. "Could that happen to us, Dad? Would it hurt?"

Morgan thought about how he should answer. How does one explain totally random events that seem to have no rhyme or reason? How does one answer that ageless question, "Why do bad things happen to good people?"

"I talked with Purple and Phil Cavuto," Morgan decided to begin slowly. "They both agree that it is extremely unlikely we will encounter another piece of space debris large enough to puncture the hull. I don't think you or anyone else has to worry about being hit by a space rock. But that doesn't mean accidents don't happen. Life is full of risks. Overall, we are just as safe here as we would be on Earth. But remember, several crew members have died since we left Earth. These things happen. That is why we should always have our hearts ready for the future. Remember when you were studying Ecclesiastes in your Sunday school? In chapter 9 verse 12, King Solomon wrote, 'No man knows when his hour will come.' What King Solomon was saying is that men are not in control of their destiny. God is. We are not wise enough to know the future. God controls the future. But our faith tells us that ultimately justice will be done. I guess the best answer is that you will not likely be hit by a space rock, but we don't have any way to know what will happen in the future. But as long as you do your best to live according to God's word, you don't have anything to fear about living in his kingdom."

"Okay, I guess," she answered thoughtfully. "Mr. Sanchez said something like that a few weeks ago." Typical of a young teenager, she quickly broke out of her somber mood. Finishing her breakfast of quinoa pancakes, she left the table and headed to the companionway with Jessica right behind her. "I have an anatomy test in twenty minutes. See you later."

"You did a good job with that," Sarah said. "I never knew anybody my age that died when I was a child. I can see how Emily was worried."

"I didn't either. Truthfully, I didn't know how to respond. The words just seemed to flow out." Morgan pushed away from the table and took his food dispenser to the recycle chamber. "We have our weekly staff meeting at nine. The space rock should make it a lot less boring than the last few have been. See you there in an hour," he said as he pulled toward the companionway.

Morgan returned to deck six and the Spencer's cabin. The Spencers were not there, and Dr. Sanchez had already had the body removed. Morgan assumed she would want to do an autopsy before the body was released to the chapel for a memorial ceremony. The impact on Larry Spencer made such a small hole in his head that almost no bleeding had occurred. Morgan called Avery Spencer and asked where he was. All communicators had the ability to tell exactly where its owner was, but for privacy reasons Morgan, and Captain Larson before him, had that feature turned off. Purple, of course, knew where each communicator was at any time but, in accordance with the captain's command, did not disclose that information. Avery responded that he and his wife were on their way from the hospital to the chapel with Larry's body. Morgan again expressed his sympathy and left their cabin for his office on the second deck. At 9:00 a.m., he arrived at the conference room. As usual, according to the ship's custom, all of his senior officers were already present and strapped in.

"Good morning, everyone," Morgan began as he fastened himself into his seat. "I know you have all been informed about the impact the *Mayflower* had with a small piece of space debris, but I want to go over the details here to make sure we all have the same information. Unfortunately, the impact included a fatal injury to Larry Spencer as he slept, so I will start with Dr. Sanchez."

"Larry was apparently on his side in relation to his quarter's floor when he was hit. The stone was about one millimeter in diameter. It struck Larry on the left temple and exited the right temple. The hole was so small that only one or two drops of blood leaked out of the exit wound. Quite frankly, this is about the only place on the human body that an impact like that would likely be fatal. Even if it had passed through Larry's heart, I think his body could have kept him alive until repairs were made. I performed a quick autopsy to determine what happened. Unfortunately, as it passed through the posterior portion of his brain's frontal lobe, it completely disrupted the ability of his brain to function. It was like the stone short-circuited all the brain's functions. If I had to describe what the result was, Larry didn't die. He stopped living."

"Have any plans been made yet?" Sarah asked.

"I released Larry's body to his parents just before I came here," Sandra said. "They were taking it to the chapel and would have a memorial service this afternoon. After that it will be sent to recycling. I don't know who they are asking to speak at the memorial."

"I just heard from your husband, Dr. Sanchez," Christopher Vollbrecht said. "He is going to say a few words at three this afternoon. They only want a few of Larry's friends to come to the ceremony. It shouldn't last more than fifteen minutes."

"Thanks, Christopher," Morgan said. "I am sure many of the young people on board are shocked by what happened. My son, Ben, is just a little older than Larry. Ben and Larry played on the same lacrosse team. I haven't seen Ben yet this morning, but I am sure he is very upset by Larry's passing. We have had a few deaths since we left Earth, but this is the first teenager to be lost. You may have to provide some counseling for his friends."

"I agree, and I've already set up some time to do just that. Purple will send private notices to all of the crew members inviting them to come and talk if they want to."

"Doctor, is there anything else we need to talk about?"

"Yes. We have been weightless for about fourteen months since shutting down the Perry-Warner engines. Once again, we are seeing crew members reducing and in some cases even quitting their physical fitness programs. We have more than five years of weightless conditions left before we near the solar system and begin deceleration. That is more than a year longer than our weightless period between Alpha Centauri and Epsilon Eridani. Anyone who is not in shape when we decelerate will likely be seriously injured and could even possibly die. We need to place more emphasis on fitness. If someone allows themselves to get completely out of shape for years, they will not be able to recover. They need to stay fit and not believe they can put it off until later."

"I'm not sure what more we can do," said Melissa Grant. "Everybody knows how important continued fitness is. Some just don't care enough to put forth the effort."

"Our charter gets in the way sometimes, doesn't it?" Morgan offered. "We have a strong commitment to personal choice. Mandatory rules would fly in the face of that. But we need to do something. Purple, do you have statistics on everyone's use of the fitness center and how efficient they are with their time there? If so, how are we doing as a crew?"

"Of the 647 humans currently aboard the *Mayflower*," the computer began, "forty-eight are too young to have an established fitness program. The remaining 599 are composed of 442 aged eighteen and over and 157 between three and seventeen years old. At the present time, 378 of the adults and 152 of the adolescents are meeting their fitness standards. Thirty-five of the remaining adults are within 10 percent of their standards and twenty-nine are significantly below standard. Of the adolescents, the five that are below their requirements are all within 10 percent of their goals. As a crew overall, the number of individuals below their personal standards is slowly increasing. If the current trend continues, almost half the crew will not be in sufficient shape to avoid injury when gravity conditions resume. These are statistical projections based on the data I am receiving. Only 412 of the 599 crew members with scheduled fitness programs have the data function of their communicators activated."

"Well, we certainly can't use that information to approach those that Purple knows are slacking off," said Melissa. "That would be a major violation of their privacy, not to mention our charter. Purple will never release an individual's health records unless that person authorizes it for Dr. Sanchez."

Privacy concerns had become a major issue early in the twenty-first century. As the digital age bloomed, more and more information was available about every aspect of one's life. Further, as computers became more advanced, the ability to analyze that information became easier. By the middle of the twenty-first century, almost everyone carried some type of communicator. These devices allowed their owners to have constant access to all sorts of information, but they also provided everything from the owner's location to his current state of health to master data storage systems. The intent of gathering this information was to use it for the health and welfare of the people. Governments, however, quickly found that it also provided increasing ways to exercise control over the people. Attempts to rein in the unauthorized use of personal information were usually overridden by arguments that it helped provide for the common good. Unfortunately, when the government is in charge of deciding what is best for the common good, the individual frequently winds up with the short end of the stick. For the vast majority of the population, the complete lack of privacy had become a way of life. Little did they know how they were being increasingly controlled and guided by the information in the hands of those who they thought were there to protect and serve them.

John Chu, the first of the five founders of the Space Colonization Consortium, was at the time the head of Earth's largest telecommunications company. John had seen over the years how governments used their power to expropriate private information from his customers. First, they gathered data under the guise that it was needed for security purposes. Then through regulations, they required that all personal communicators provide a minimum level of information on its user. By the time the Perry-Warner drive system was developed, all communicators reported the user's physical location, vital signs, level of activity, and conversations that were not even taking place through the communicator. Most people were unaware that they were being constantly monitored, and those that did seemed to accept it like lemmings charging toward a cliff.

Part of John Chu's mission in establishing the consortium was to restore the right of an individual to his privacy. The *Mayflower*'s charter included strict guidelines regarding the use of personal information. All communicators on the *Mayflower* had the capability to provide vital information to Purple, but Purple could not release it unless it received specific authorization from the individual and then only to Dr. Sanchez. Further, only the captain had the authority to request general trend data, like that just provided regarding fitness. Finally, every crew member had the ability to not only turn off the data aspect of their communicator but also to turn it off completely. While

Purple could activate a communicator in an emergency, that ability was limited to voice communications only.

Another modification Chu made to the communicators on the *Mayflower* was the ease with which one person could communicate with another. Since the population size was small, any person could call another by simply saying their first name, and a direct channel would be opened between the two parties. To make this system work, forty-two people had to change their first name when the *Mayflower* departed Earth to avoid duplication. As a result, first names were commonly used throughout the ship. A name registry was kept on the ship so when there was a birth, the parents could select a new name that was not in use. By saying *family*, a channel could be opened among all family members. There were also group designations for those in similar work areas, for instance *hydroponics* or *engineering*. The captain had a special command, *crew*, that would open a channel to every member of the *Mayflower* crew. The communicators also had a feature that prevented a channel being opened when a party being spoken to was within twenty feet, allowing personal conversations to take place without a channel being opened.

"I have no intention of personal intervention in any individual's fitness regimen or lack thereof," Morgan responded to Melissa. "Freedom of choice and privacy are basic tenets of this mission, and it is my duty to protect those principles. But I can set a better example, and I want all of you to do as best as you can to do the same. Our job is to lead, not push. If a crew member doesn't want to be ready for deceleration, he will know the consequences. That is their choice, not ours. Sandra, do your best to tell them of the dangers of loss of muscle tone when they come in to you and your staff for treatment. I think that your advice as medical officer is consistent with our charter.

Does anyone have any suggestions that could encourage more participation in exercise activities?"

"I have one," Christopher said. "I have been thinking of establishing some sort of rewards for the games being played in the gymnasium. Perhaps we can schedule a weightless Olympics games. We can also set up different flights based on age or skill levels to encourage everyone to participate."

"Great idea, Christopher. I will volunteer for an over forty team. Now let's move on. Randy, please fill everyone in on the damage to the *Mayflower* as a result of the impact."

Randy proceeded to recount deck by deck in detail what happened as the small stone passed through the ship. He also described what repairs had already been completed and what remained to be done. He finished up by saying, "All in all, we were very fortunate. There easily could have been damage to more critical components of this ship. I am also very pleased with how well the automatic seals worked. They had never been tested under operational conditions. They worked very fast and kept air loss to a minimum."

"What about the compartments on the first three decks?" asked Sarah. "They are depressurized now, but I may need them for storage later. This event has shown how vulnerable our food supply is. I want to increase production and build up a surplus beyond that available from our emergency rations."

"Already scheduled for later today," said Randy.

"Let me know when you want to start," Sam Workman said to Sarah. "If we are going to significantly increase quinoa production, I will need to make some adjustments in our carbon dioxide, oxygen, and water-vapor levels in our air system. When we store quinoa, we remove hydrogen, carbon, and oxygen from our short-term biochemical cycle."

"Melissa, anything to report regarding our educational program?" Morgan asked.

"Training the younger crew members for life on Earth is proving to be difficult," she began. "I'm sure glad that the founders decided to store hundreds of videos in Purple's data banks. They are better at showing them what daily activities on Earth will be like than anything we could say in a classroom setting. We are starting classes in basic economics and the use of credit chips. I'm holding off on social-skills training for a couple more years. I know I will have a lot of difficulty blending back into society. It will be even harder for those that have no background memories of what to do or say when confronting social interactions with strangers.

"Many of the younger crew members are very concerned about career training," Melissa continued. "Before we left Epsilon Eridani, everyone was gearing toward a profession related to building and growing a colony. Take my son as an example. Carlos was ready to assume a terraforming career for our colony. How does he use that education on Earth? He's not sure what he should prepare for, something in agricultural science or perhaps a career in heavy construction."

"Erica Norquist was talking to me along the same lines," Sarah said. "She is one of my assistants in galley operations. She doesn't see much of a future in knowing how to serve quinoa fifty different ways. I jokingly told her she should consider opening a quinoa restaurant on Earth. I don't think there will be a lot of competition."

"That actually might be a good idea," Melissa replied. "Captain Larson is planning to present a series of talks on using the experiences of life on the *Mayflower* to become speakers on a college lecture circuit. We don't usually think of ourselves this way, but we are a significant long-term experiment in human behavior under controlled conditions, not to mention having the only personal experience in interstellar space travel. I am sure we will all be celebrities when we get back."

"John, anything new to add on the communications front?" Morgan asked.

"Not really," John Malcolm answered. "It is unlikely we will hear anything from Earth for some time. We are still way too far from the solar system to pick up any general broadcasts. I did send a message that we were returning, but in view of the lack of any contact since very early in our flight to Alpha Centauri, I doubt that anyone even knows where we are right now. They would need to know our exact trajectory to send us a beamed message, and we haven't received one. As for Ararat, Nels and his group may still be able to receive our messages. I sent him one a few days ago. I haven't felt anything warranted a message to the colony in view of their admonishment about communications."

"Anything further that needs to be brought up?" Morgan looked around the room to give everyone an opportunity to speak. Not surprisingly, neither Judy Polachek nor Laura Simmons had said anything. Their areas of responsibility did not normally come into play when travelling between the stars. When no one offered any further comments, Morgan adjourned the meeting.

Sarah pushed alongside Morgan as they left the conference room and worked their way to the central companionway. "We've got six more years before we enter the solar system," Sarah said. "Do you think we can keep the spirits of the crew up for that long? Purple's projection of the health of the crew concerns me. I don't see how we can start slowing down if it's going to harm half of our people."

Morgan was not sure how to respond to Sarah's comments, so he said nothing for a moment as he contemplated what would have to be done. "We really have no choice, Sarah. The engines have to be turned on in just over five years. To do anything else would be fatal for all of us."

As he turned toward the companionway that would take him to his office, he wondered if morale would go up or down in response to some of the ideas they had just discussed. How individuals took care of themselves as they neared the termination of their long journey would have a major impact on their well-being once they reached Earth's surface. Only time would tell.

CHAPTER 10

Morgan and Sarah looked up from lunch as Ben excitedly pulled into the galley. "Mom, Dad, it's a girl! You are grandparents." He shouted as he flew passed, too fast to catch a handhold to stop at their table.

"Whoa, slow down," Sarah said. "You don't want to break your head on your first day as a parent."

Ben finally seized a table well past Morgan and Sarah and was able to scrub off his inertia. Gathering his composure, he worked his way back to his parents. As he grabbed onto a handhold next to his mother, he was still out of breath from his high-speed flight from the ship's hospital to the galley.

"I wanted to tell you in person," he panted. "I didn't think a communicator was an appropriate method for delivering this news."

Morgan looked proudly at Ben as he caught his breath. Ben, now twenty-three years old, had grown into a fine young man. He was extremely fit, typical of the crew members near his age. He had been married nineteen months before, March 30, 2091, ship's time, to Anne Montgomery. As Ben's breathing finally began to slow, Morgan said, "Okay, now tell us all the details."

"Her name is Brittany Sarah Parker," Ben beamed. "Everything went perfectly. Dr. Sanchez says she would weigh seven pounds three ounces if we were under deceleration. Anne is doing fine. All the hard work she did preparing for a weightless birth really paid off. Brittany was born about an hour ago. October 7, 2092, what a glorious day! I'm so excited! I need to go and find Anne's parents. They should be waiting in their quarters for news."

Ben released his grip and pushed toward the companionway. "Tell the Montgomerys we are excited for them," Sarah called after Ben as he drifted away. "We will be up to see our granddaughter as soon as Samantha lets us know it's all right." She turned her head toward Morgan. "Well, Grandpa, how do you feel?"

"Older," he said, "and proud. Ben has really transitioned well into adulthood. He and Anne will be fine parents."

Morgan relaxed at the table and thought about the last five years. Nobody could explain exactly why, but something happened to the morale of the crew after the *Mayflower* was struck by the space rock in 2087. Morgan remembered how concerned he and the rest of the management team were at the time. Fitness was declining, and morale was low. But the impact turned out to be the event that reversed the trend. Morgan had thought that he and his principal assistants needed to step up and set an example for all to follow. But it was the young adults like Ben that showed the way. Whether or not it was the death of Larry Spencer, no one was sure, but something had triggered a new commitment to returning to Earth in the younger generation on the *Mayflower*. It started with just a handful working out every day. Within a few months, their enthusiasm had rubbed off on most of the crew. About a year after the impact, Dr. Sanchez reported that she was no longer concerned about fitness for most of the crew.

It wasn't just fitness either. Attitudes about putting life on hold until they were back on Earth began to change. Ben had said one day that his friends no longer wanted to wait until they were on Earth to start families. While no one said so, it was apparent they were concerned they would not relate well to anyone not a part of the *Mayflower*'s journey. They thought the best way to assume life outside the *Mayflower* was in a committed relationship with responsibilities for children of their own. So many crew members in their twenties formed relationships and began to get married. Ben and Anne actually waited longer than many of their friends. Even Emily, now nineteen, had recently announced she would be getting married to Walter Malcolm soon after they began deceleration.

Career decisions had also changed soon after the death of Larry Spencer. The realization that they were not going to be colonizing a barren wilderness led many to abandon previous disciplines in favor of those they would find useful on Earth. Food and shelter would not be fundamental needs. There would be no need for finding mineral resources and developing raw materials into essential supplies. Figuring out how to blend into Earth's society became a new focus. Several crew members decided to abandon physical-science careers for more socially oriented disciplines. Many were planning careers in education based on their experiences in space. Others had a strong interest in making sure a space program continued. The *Mayflower* was nearing the end of its life expectancy, but there was a belief a return should be made to Epsilon Eridani when possible. John Malcolm had formed a group, including Ben, which was developing a new method of long-range communications in the hopes they could contact Nels's group or the colony. Financial disciplines, something not needed on the *Mayflower*, became a focus for several crew members.

There hadn't been any further emergencies since the encounter with the space rock. Now they were just seven days away from the beginning of deceleration. It was amazing that they would be in Earth's orbit in just 307 days. There were currently 739 souls on board the *Mayflower*. Another ninety-eight had been born since the impact, and six had died. Dr. Sanchez had determined that three of the deaths were due to untreatable cancers. One had choked to death, and two were from heart problems. *At least the Mayflower's journey could be considered a success from two perspectives,* Morgan thought. They were returning to Earth with more people than had departed, and there had not been a single incident of acrimony resulting in serious injury or death. The skeptics on Earth who predicted that hundreds of people could not exist in such a confined space for many years without resorting to violence were certainly proved wrong. Morgan mused that those skeptics had mistakenly based their assumptions on the general nature of society at the time, a world seriously lacking high standards of decency and morality.

What those skeptics failed to understand was the nature of those selected for the *Mayflower's* epic journey. Societies for ages had tried to instill moral values through legislation, but it never worked. Whether it was laws against alcohol, prostitution, drugs, pornography, or any other *social* shortcoming, laws and regulations didn't work. They only led to increased crime and *back-alley* sources of what much of humanity craved.

Those who planned the *Mayflower* expedition knew that morality came from faith and a pure heart, not through government laws and regulations. The moral code was not law; it was simply an outward expression of what all crew members accepted as the way to life in God's universe. Honesty, propriety, and respect were fundamental tenants of the *Mayflower*, and each member of the crew had vigorously worked to ensure they were maintained. Discourse was resolved through civil processes considering the opinions of all, not through intimidation or violence. Even so, the experience of the colony's formation showed how fragile moral standards could be when faced with adversity.

204

As if she was reading his thoughts, Sarah said, "I am very pleased how well our children and actually all the children on the *Mayflower* have turned out. But it will be much more difficult to raise a child among Earth's masses. I know that Ben and Anne will raise Brittany properly. It won't be easy for them, but they have the right core beliefs and foundation."

"Once we are done with this mission and back home, we will have lots of time to be doting grandparents," offered Morgan. "I suspect you will be hovering over all your grandchildren like a mother hen."

"I'll be hovering over you too. Don't you forget it." She laughed.

"You have raised an issue we need to consider however. We have been preparing to blend back into Earth's society. The more I think about it, the more I realize how difficult that will be. And I'm not just talking about those who have grown up on the *Mayflower*. It's going to be a challenge for all of us. Remember, we will have aged twenty-one years since we left, but Earth's population has grown thirty-three years older. Add to that the four years we were isolated from the general population after we were selected for this journey, and we have missed a whole generation. As I think about how much the world changed from when we were born to the time we left, I wonder if we will even recognize the world we find when we arrive."

"What alternative do we have?" Sarah asked seriously.

"I'm not sure, but we may want to consider staying together instead of dispersing. It's an option I have been kicking around for a few months. If we could find a suitable place where we could set up our own community, perhaps we should think about doing it. No one would be required to stay in the community, of course, but I suspect many would want to."

"I think that would be a good option," Sarah said. "We could start out being our own community and slowly blend in with society. But we don't want to put any limitations on our people."

"Well, we still have almost a year to decide what to do," said Morgan. "And a lot will depend on the reception we get when we establish communications with Earth. Hopefully we will find the consortium is still active, and they will be able to help us with the transition. In the meantime, I will let the crew know it is time to start thinking about options. Right now, I need to go up to the command deck. Randy Edwards and Sam Workman are supposed to meet me there to begin the rotation of the *Mayflower*. I'll see you for dinner. I want to try out Erica's latest creation—quinoa Swedish meatballs."

"She said they are pretty good. But then we haven't had real meatballs in over twenty years. My idea of what really tastes good was lost years ago," quipped Sarah as Morgan headed toward the central companionway.

Sam was already there when Morgan arrived, and Randy drifted in a few minutes later. "Purple has checked all its systems sensors and indicates the ship is ready for rotation. I did a visual inspection myself and did not find anything out of order," said Sam as Randy arrived at the command center.

"I tested all of the rotational thruster jets over the last two days and confirmed Purple's report that they will function normally," said Randy. "We are ready to rotate at your command, Morgan." Morgan appreciated Randy's thoroughness. In some respects, he was an old-school engineering officer. He used all of the ship's computer and electronic monitoring capabilities but still wanted to independently confirm that what those monitors were reporting was accurate, reliable, and trustworthy. His favorite saying was "trust but verify" which he had learned in school came from an old Russian proverb. The proverb became famous when United States President Ronald Reagan frequently used it in the 1980s during diplomatic discussions with the leader of the Soviet Union, Mikhail Gorbachev. Randy believed that anything built by man was subject to breakdowns and malfunctions. The best way to make sure things were working as designed was to apply liberal doses of ears, eyeballs, and human ingenuity.

"It looks like we are at the beginning of the end of our odyssey," said Morgan to Randy and Sam. "Only seven more days until we begin decelerating into the solar system.

"Purple, begin rotation of the *Mayflower* into position for the initiation of deceleration using the Perry-Warner engines."

"Thrusters have been fired to rotate the ship counterclockwise," said the computer. "In twenty-five hours, six minutes, and thirteen seconds, I will fire the opposite thrusters to stop rotation in the correct position for deceleration."

Randy looked up from the data screen he was holding. "All the fired thrusters shut down as designed. We are now rotating into position for initiation of deceleration. I will be here tomorrow to monitor the completion of the rotation of the *Mayflower*."

The *Mayflower* was already prepared for the gravitational effects of deceleration. That process had begun over a month ago and had gone smoothly as most of the crew was motivated by the belief that in less than a year they would be able to disembark. In reality, the rotational process provided almost no effects that could be detected by human senses. The thrusters only fired for a few seconds, and the amount of thrust was so small that it was only noticeable to one who was floating unattached to any surface of the ship. In those cases, they noticed a slight drift toward one side of the ship. As soon as the thrusters shut off, conditions were the same as before in drifting mode.

It was still about an hour before he was to meet Sarah for dinner, so Morgan decided to stop by his old ecology lab. Laura was there as he had expected, using the whiteboard to teach her daughter Cindy how to write. "Morgan," she said, looking around from the whiteboard, "did we start rotation yet?"

"We did about twenty minutes ago. How are the kids doing?"

"Super," she said, smiling. "Can you believe it? Cindy will be six in a few days, and Erin is now four. But that's not the biggest news. Brad and I have another one on the way."

"Wow," Morgan said. "When did you find that out?"

"Yesterday. I asked Dr. Sanchez to do a test-strip swab. She said I was two weeks along. It's going to be another boy. I think Brad is more excited than I am. We are glad he will be born before we enter orbit around Earth."

"Congratulations one more time. You and Bradley make a fine team. I know you will be able to find good careers back on Earth." Morgan knew that Laura wanted to work in a university and had been honing her skills as an ecologist for years. She had studied virtually everything in Purple's storage banks and had been picking Morgan's brain ever since they had left Earth. Her primary concern, he thought, was that she didn't have a formal degree, and many universities were more interested in a person's curriculum vitae than what they actually knew. In addition, she did not know what scientific developments might have taken place since the *Mayflower*'s departure in 2072. She was concerned that she would be woefully out of date, a concern that Morgan did not share. He knew her knowledge of the Ararat ecosystems was far more valuable, if any university could cast aside its stodgy rules in favor of obtaining a uniquely qualified talent.

"Uncle Morgan," said Cindy, "when will we be in the solar system? My mother told me we were going to start slowing down in a few days to begin our approach to Earth. I looked up the solar system and learned a bunch about Earth and the other planets, so I began wondering when we would be there, and I could see them."

Morgan was not surprised by Cindy's question. Like most children on the *Mayflower*, she could already read. Her formal education had started when she was four, but Laura had been reading to her from digital books stored in Purple's files since she was a baby. Cindy began reading on her own before she turned five and was now proficient in using her data screen to access the computer's files.

"That's a very interesting question, Cindy, and not easy to answer. Let's start with a question. Do you know what an astronomical unit is?"

"Yes, I read that it is the average distance from the Earth to the Sun."

"Very good. Do you also know what a light-year is?"

"Yes, it's the distance light travels in one year. I also learned," she offered enthusiastically, "that we are going really fast, over four fifths the speed of light, and that's why we need to start slowing down now. Mom says it will take us almost ten months to slow down enough to enter orbit around Earth. She told me an orbit is like going in a big circle around something."

Laura looked at Cindy and smiled while Morgan did a few preliminary calculations in his head. "You've been doing a lot of reading, haven't you?"

"I like to read," Cindy responded, "like you do."

"Okay," Morgan said. "Let's see how well I can answer your questions. First, when we begin to slow down, we will be about a third of a light-year from the Sun. That's about 22,250 astronomical units. So we are still a long way away. You mentioned you knew about the eight planets around the Sun. The farthest from the Sun is Neptune. Neptune is a little over thirty astronomical units from the Sun. But there is much more to the solar system than the planets. For example, there are what are called minor planets in orbit around the Sun. One, called Pluto, used to be counted as one of the regular planets when it was discovered in the 1930s, but later, scientists decided that it really should be called a minor planet, although they still debate it at times. There are lots of these minor planets, and many of them are much farther from the Sun than Neptune. As an example, one called Eris is in a lopsided orbit that carries it beyond one hundred astronomical units from the Sun. Eris was discovered early in the twenty-first century when it was about ninety-six astronomical units from the Sun. Eris is bigger than Pluto but still a lot smaller than the Earth. Eris even has a moon of its own called Dysnomia."

"Wow, I want to read about that," said Cindy.

"There are comets in orbit around the Sun that go even farther into space before returning to the Sun thousands of years later. So it is difficult to say exactly where the solar system ends and outer space begins. Some people like to call the edge of the heliosphere as the outer boundary of the solar system. That is the place in space where the Sun's solar wind pressure is no longer greater than the general intergalactic pressure of the galaxy. That occurs about 120 astronomical units from the Sun. Whatever we call the edge of the solar system, it is still a long way from where we are. The calculations are beyond what I can do in my head, so why don't I ask our computer to calculate when we will cross the heliosphere boundary called the heliopause and when we will cross the orbit of Neptune? Purple, how many days before Earth's orbit will we cross the solar system's heliopause and Neptune's orbit? Calculate to two decimals, please."

"Captain Morgan, we will cross what is commonly called the heliopause, the outer boundary of the heliosphere 22.15 days before entering Earth's orbit. We will not actually cross Neptune's orbit but will arrive at a distance from the Sun equal to Neptune's average orbital radius 11.07 days before entering Earth's orbit."

Morgan smiled at Purple's usual precise answer regarding Neptune. The angle of approach meant that they would be thirty degrees off from Neptune's orbit and would not actually cross the orbit. "So you see, Cindy," Morgan said, "we have a lot of time before we enter the solar system. Do you have any other questions?"

"Not right now. I'm going to do a lot of reading so I know everything about the solar system before we get there," she said enthusiastically. "I'll bet I will have more questions tomorrow."

"She never ceases to amaze me," Morgan said to Laura.

"Me either. I also talked to Dr. Sanchez about the children when the engines are fired. There are one hundred and eighteen that have never experienced the effects of gravity. Some are over six years old. She said the fitness staff has been working very hard to prepare them, but it's hard to teach something they have never experienced. I remember several were injured when we approached Epsilon Eridani, and that time, weightlessness was under five years. We are going to have a lot of kids who want to run around who have never walked. As you can imagine, Cindy and Erin are two of them. I am worried about how well they will adapt."

"You are not the only one worried," Morgan said. "Make sure you use the elevators to take them to the training site the fitness people have prepared once we fire the engines. They are ready to teach all children under ten how to walk. The reports I have received show that the exercise programs have adequately prepared their muscles. Learning to balance will be the primary problem most of them face. Everyone, including adults, will need to take it slowly at first. I remember how I overdid it when we left Epsilon Eridani, and that time, it was less than two years weightless."

"I think Brad and I are ready," Laura said. "I know one thing for sure—we are ready to get off this ship. Deceleration is a milestone we have been waiting for a long time."

"See you later. I need to get to the galley to join Sarah for Swedish meatballs."

"Good luck with that," Laura joked as Morgan grabbed a handhold and pulled himself out of the ecology lab.

The next day, Morgan returned to the command center for the firing of the thrusters to stop rotation. Purple was programmed to fire them automatically when the *Mayflower* was in the proper position. Sam Workman and Randy Edwards were also present.

About thirty seconds before the thrusters were supposed to fire, Purple said, "Captain Parker, I have aborted the procedure to stop the rotational process. My sensors indicate two of the clockwise thrusters will not shut off properly when fired. That would result in an increased spin in the other direction."

"Is it something you can fix?" asked Morgan.

"No," responded the computer. "My sensors indicate the valves are clogged. It is not something I can correct. It will require human repairs."

"That means we will have to do a space walk," said Randy nervously. "And we will continue to rotate until it's fixed."

Morgan, Randy, and Sam discussed for a few minutes whether there were any other alternatives, but they couldn't come up with one. Space walks were always a dangerous activity. Since they had left Earth, the only space walk conducted was by Randy and an assistant when they measured hull erosion while in orbit around Epsilon Eridani. That assistant, Richard Rundquist, was now at the colony on Ararat.

Morgan asked Purple how much time they had to fix the thrusters and stabilize the *Mayflower* for ignition of the Perry-Warner engines. The computer said that ideally the ship needed to be in proper orientation forty-eight hours before ignition to allow time to correct for any anomalies, but if necessary, the time could be reduced to twenty-four hours. Thus, the repairs should be completed within four days or at least no longer than five days.

The two faulty thrusters were on the forward part of the ship, one outside deck two on the port side and the other outside of deck three on the starboard side. Thus, two separate space walks would be required. After studying the thruster plans on his data plate, Randy decided the best course of action was to replace the control valves. The thrusters were too large to be easily disconnected from the hull. Sam volunteered to assist Randy on the space walks.

The next two days, Randy and Sam rehearsed the procedures for the space walk and for replacing the control valves using a spare thruster stored on the equipment deck. The control valve was mounted on the outside of the thruster and connected the supply line of liquid nitrogen to a heater that vaporized the nitrogen, providing the thrust through a nozzle. Randy did not know why Purple determined they would stick when opened, but he speculated that somehow a tiny amount of nitrogen had remained in the valve when they last used the thrusters departing from Epsilon Eridani's system. Once the valve was opened, the nitrogen crystals would block the valve from returning to its closed position. Replacing the valve required disconnecting the supply line coupling, another coupling to the heater, and removing four mounting bolts. Connections to the computer and electrical supply were through contact points on the valve and thruster housing. If everything went smoothly, the rehearsals indicated it would take about three hours from the time they exited the ship to completion of the replacement. Randy decided that they would try and replace both valves on the third day with two space walks, saving the fourth day for any contingency.

The morning of the third day, Randy and Sam suited up and were ready to go at 8:30 a.m. They carried a full eight-hour supply of oxygen along with a safety tether and a 100-foot emergency safety line. The tethers and the safety line had locking carabiners on each end for attachment to their space suits and handholds on the ship's hull. Randy carried the valve, about the size of a shoebox, while Sam had a set of power wrenches and some spare bolts. Morgan asked if they wanted to take additional oxygen bottles, but Randy said they already had enough stuff to keep track of. Morgan stood by near the hatch, monitoring the communications between Randy and Sam.

The first thruster was about fifty feet from the deck two hatch on the port side. Spaced every three feet around the hull were the handholds and brackets where safety lines could be attached. The outer hull was made from a titanium alloy for its strength-to-weight characteristics. The alloy is nonmagnetic; thus the handholds and brackets were the only way to remain fastened to the *Mayflower*.

The procedure for moving on the outside of the hull that Randy and Sam had rehearsed was to always be attached by at least one of the safety lines. When they exited the hatch, they attached a tether to the bracket by the hatch and then reached to the next handhold three feet away. When they pulled themselves to that handhold, they would attach the emergency safety line to the bracket by that handhold and then reach back and disconnect the tether. Then they would reach to the next handhold and repeat the process. Randy went first, followed by Sam.

Even though they had rehearsed in their space suits, they found moving across the hull difficult and slow. Every movement they made resulted in a countermovement of their bodies. To remain steady, they had to use one hand to hold on to the ship at all times. The carabiners were difficult to close properly with one hand. It turned out that it took over an hour for Randy and Sam to reach the thruster and get properly attached to brackets on each side.

Removing the valve also proved difficult. Ironically, the designers of the *Mayflower* had chosen to use thrusters instead of zero-propellant maneuvering technology because they thought the older thruster system was more reliable. They knew that once the *Mayflower* left Earth, no outside help would be available, so they wanted to keep as many operational components as possible simple and trustworthy. They did not anticipate repairs to the thrusters or their valves would ever be necessary. Morgan was surprised to learn that the designers had not incorporated any way to shut off the nitrogen supply if the control valve failed to close. The designers rejected zero-propellant technology because they were concerned that some situations around unknown planets might exceed the capability of that system. In addition, they did not consider thruster fuel a serious problem as the amount required to rotate the *Mayflower* in space was insignificant to the overall mass of the ship, and it could be replenished when orbiting another planet. So the thruster system was adopted. Unfortunately, it was designed too simply. The twenty thrusters for counterclockwise and twenty thrusters for clockwise rotation all had to fire together. There was no way to isolate one malfunctioning thruster from the rest of the system. So repairs were necessary.

Randy and Sam had to hold on tightly with one hand while gripping one of the handles on the power wrench with the other to keep the wrench from twisting and flying off when it was activated. Several times one of them lost his grip on the wrench resulting in the wrench slipping from its position on the bolt. Repositioning the wrench took additional time. Another two hours had passed by the time the four bolts were out and the supply line was disconnected. Once the old valve was free, Randy hooked it to his emergency safety line while the new valve was installed. Morgan objected to this breach of protocol, but Randy said he wanted to examine it when he got back on board. He explained to Morgan that he was still secured by his tether and would reattach the safety line as soon as the new valve was installed. He would then carry it back the same way he brought out the old one.

Mounting the new valve was clumsy, but it went a little quicker. Randy and Sam found it easier to tighten the bolts most of the way with a hand wrench. They only used the power wrench for the final effort to secure the bolts. Once they were done, Randy asked Purple to run a diagnostic test on the new valve. Purple responded immediately that the thruster should now function properly.

Randy let Morgan know they were starting the return journey to the air lock. It was two fifteen in the afternoon by the time they arrived back and were safely inside the ship. The installation process took almost six hours. Both of them were exhausted by the time they got their suits off. Morgan decided that it would be too risky to try and install the other valve that afternoon. He said that Randy and Sam needed to be rested, and they still had tomorrow to install the other valve. They agreed and said they would be ready to go at eight the next morning.

When Randy and Sam arrived at the deck-three air lock the next morning, Morgan was already there. "Your suits have a full load of oxygen again. That should give you plenty of time even if you run into more trouble than you did yesterday."

"Thanks," said Randy. "We should be able to do this one quicker than yesterday. I took the valve we removed down to the equipment deck and checked it out. I couldn't find anything wrong with it. It tested out fine. There are only two possibilities I can think of. First, as soon as it was brought into the ship, whatever was clogging the valve thawed out. That seems to me to be the most likely scenario. The second possibility is that the computer's diagnostic test of the thrusters was faulty. If that were true, it would be worrisome. We rely on Purple for almost every aspect of our daily lives, and its capabilities are essential if we are going to properly return to orbit around Earth. I want to bring the other valve back and see if it performs the same way."

"Purple," said Morgan, "please run a self-diagnostic test and identify any issues you find."

"The test is under way," said Purple. Morgan and Randy waited a few moments while the computer analyzed its internal systems. "I find a few small irregularities, but I do not find they are related to the thruster test. These irregularities are associated with my storage files. I find several files have corrupted data as a result of minor programming error. I corrected that error when I first found it three years ago. I do not find that those problems will have any impact on my ability to control the essential functions of this ship."

"Purple, continue to monitor all functions and notify me of any changes to your normal operational protocols."

"Randy," Morgan continued, "as much as I don't like the additional risk associated with it, I would like you to bring the other old valve back and examine it. Sometimes we forget that Purple is just a machine. We need to know if any problems are developing."

"I was planning on doing just that," said Randy. "Let's go, Sam, and get this job done."

They exited the air lock a few minutes before eight. The faulty thruster was closer to the starboard air lock on deck three than the deck two thruster by about ten feet. That, in combination with what they learned the day before, allowed the replacement to move along somewhat faster. Randy informed Morgan that he had the old valve off and were starting to install the new one about two hours after they exited the ship. An hour later, Randy notified Morgan that the new valve was installed. Purple tested it and reported that the valve functioned normally."

"Looks like we are done," Randy said to Sam. "I think we will be back on board in time for lunch."

Sam was on the side closer to the hatch. He reached over to the first handhold and attached his safety line to the adjoining bracket then unhooked his tether and pulled over to the handhold. Randy reached around to the handhold on the other side of the valve and when he had hold of it, disconnected his tether. As he prepared to reattach it to the adjacent bracket, the old valve slipped from his grasp. Without thinking, he reached for it, causing him to push away from the ship's hull.

"Sam," he said, "I'm off the ship, and my safety line is still hooked to the valve. My trajectory is taking me away from the valve's path. I can't catch it to get hold of the safety line. Sam, do not try and come to me. I will be beyond the length of your safety line before you could get here. I'm going to try my suit thrusters to fly back."

"Eng. Edwards," Purple said, "your suit sensors tell me you are moving away faster that your suit can propel you back. Do not try to fly back to the thruster valve. Take an angle course back to the aft portion of the ship near deck fifteen. It is your best chance of regaining contact with the *Mayflower*. But you must act immediately. You are approaching a critical angle of no return."

"I am turning my suit now. Here goes." Randy fired his suit pack and started heading back on a trajectory that he thought would bring him into contact with the aft portion of the ship. "It looks like I will hit the ship between decks fifteen and sixteen."

"You will be going relatively fast when you get there," Purple said. "Do not try to slow down. If you do, you will miss the ship. Be prepared to grab any handhold you can when you hit the hull."

Morgan and Sam stayed quiet while Randy tried to maneuver into position and Purple guided him. They knew there was nothing constructive they could add, and Randy needed his full attention on getting back to the *Mayflower*. Instead, Morgan called his chief shuttle pilot, Antonio Grant.

"Antonio," Morgan said, "we have a man, Randy Edwards, outside the ship and adrift in space. How long will it take you to prepare and launch a shuttle?"

"About three hours," Antonio replied. "The shuttles are currently set up for the ignition of the Perry-Warner engines in a couple days. Everything is currently locked down. I will start getting the *Gemini* ready immediately. How much time do we have?"

"Edwards has about four hours of oxygen left. We hope to catch him on the aft portion of the ship, but if we miss, you will be his last chance."

"I've called all the shuttle personnel to help me. I'll let you know when we are ready," Antonio panted as he rushed to the shuttle *Gemini* attachment site.

"Purple, how long before Edwards reaches the hull?"

"Twelve minutes and sixteen seconds, Captain Parker," responded the computer. "He will be closest to hatch 16-3."

Morgan quickly dispatched his two safety men to the air lock adjoining hatch 16-3. They were already suited up. "Open the hatch and be ready to grab Edwards or throw him a lifeline. But under no circumstances are you to unclip your safety tethers or go outside the hatch. We don't want to further complicate this mess. Keep me informed." Morgan then headed to the operations center to monitor the situation. He asked Sarah to join him there.

"Randy, how are you doing?" Morgan asked lamely.

"Right now, it looks like I will hit the ship. I just hope I can grab a handhold when I do. As for how I'm doing, I'm scared. I know if I miss, it will be a long time before I find anything else to grab onto. Did Sam get back on board all right?"

"He did. Antonio Grant is preparing a shuttle just in case you can't grab on. Also the safety crew will be there to help you."

A few minutes later, one of the safety crew said, "We're in position. I can see him approaching. He is moving pretty fast. He is going to hit about sixty feet aft of the hatch. We are streaming out safety lines. Hopefully he will be able to catch one."

"Here it comes," grunted Randy. "I'm coming in pretty hot…three, two…damn, I missed the handhold and bounced off the hull pretty hard. There's one of the safety lines. I can't reach it. I missed everything, Morgan. I'm sorry."

"Don't give up yet, Randy. The shuttle is on its way. Purple is tracking you and feeding your coordinates into the *Gemini*'s navigation system."

"Thanks, Morgan. Right now, I need to open a private channel to Samantha. Let me know when the shuttle launches."

Morgan knew that Antonio Grant was doing everything he could to launch the *Gemini*; it wouldn't do any good to bother him with questions. Instead, he asked the computer how much breathing time was left in Randy's suit.

"Captain Parker," the computer responded, "he has been consuming more oxygen than normal the last hour. His breathing has slowed down now. At the present rate of consumption, he will run out of oxygen in three hours and ten minutes."

There was nothing that Morgan could do to speed up the rescue mission. He talked quietly with Sarah as the time passed. They reminisced about their friends Randy and Samantha. Finally, Antonio Grant called. "We are ready to go, Captain. Once we leave the *Mayflower*, it will take a few minutes to stabilize the *Gemini* from the rotational forces we are currently experiencing. How much time does Randy have?"

Morgan looked at his data tablet where he was monitoring the operation. "Only twelve minutes," he said.

"I'll do my best to get there in time," Antonio said.

"Randy, the shuttle is launched. It should be there in a few minutes."

"I don't think I'm going to make it," gasped Randy. "Air is gone. Please watch over Samantha and my family for me. Godspeed for the rest of your journey."

"Go as fast as you can, Antonio. Randy is running out of air," pleaded Morgan.

Thirty minutes later, Antonio Grant said, "We have Mr. Edwards on board. We were not in time. Dr. Sanchez is with me and tried to revive him, but we were too late. Randy is dead."

CHAPTER 11

Morgan contemplated their imminent arrival at Earth as he walked toward the communications center. The *Mayflower* was only ten days from orbit around Earth. He had just left a meeting on the bridge with Tyler Haroldson who had replaced Randy Edwards as chief engineer. His discussion with Tyler reminded him how much the management group had changed since they left Earth. He, of course, had replaced Howard Larson as captain of the *Mayflower*. Larson was still on board but was now focused on preparing for an anticipated lecture tour on Earth. Laura Simmons McMullen was now part of the leadership group, having replaced Morgan as chief ecologist. Samuel Workman had replaced Graysun Williams, who had stayed on Ararat. Nels Brunken was also left behind on Ararat; he had been replaced as planetologist by Phil Cavuto.

Sadly, Randy Edwards was also no longer part of the *Mayflower* crew. After his death, Morgan asked one of Randy's assistants, Tyler Haroldson, to assume the duties as chief engineer. Tyler had joined the *Mayflower* crew as the ship's Perry-Warner drive engineer. Morgan originally considered asking Miguel Sanchez to be the chief engineer, but Miguel was increasingly focusing his attention on religious studies and told Morgan he did not want the additional responsibilities as chief engineer.

Another new member of the group was Christopher Vollbrecht. He had taken over duties as morale officer when

Melissa Grant gave up those duties to focus on education in preparation for the return to Earth. So only four of the original team remained in the same positions that they had when they left Earth—Sarah Parker as nutrition officer, John Malcolm in communications, Sandra Sanchez as chief medical officer, and Judy Polachek as chief agronomist.

Morgan was surprised that he was not more excited about the imminent conclusion of their long odyssey. He and Sarah had talked many times about returning to a simple academic life on Earth, and he knew she was looking forward to it. Morgan, however, was not sure anymore that academia was a goal of his. Over the years, he had grown comfortable with his responsibilities as captain. He liked the challenges it presented. He had never considered himself a leader prior to Captain Larson's resignation but found those skills had indeed been buried deep in his DNA. His handling of both the mundane daily duties of command of the *Mayflower* as well as the several crises that had occurred during the return flight had kept him energized. Perhaps if most of the crew decided to stay together on Earth, he would still play some sort of leadership role.

He really began to understand his aptitude for leadership and management after the death of Randy Edwards. The shock of the loss of Randy hit everyone hard, but there was no time to grieve. The old valve that Randy and Sam Workman had removed was still attached to Randy's safety line, drifting near the hull. If the thrusters were fired, it would become a dangerous object banging on the side of the ship, and the thrusters had to be fired the next day. After a brief discussion with Sam, Morgan decided he would accompany Sam outside to remove the floating valve. Morgan had never done a space walk before, but he did not want to ask any other crew member to risk his life when he was the one who asked Randy to bring the old valve back aboard. He and Sam suited up that afternoon and went outside. When they reached the safety line, they pulled the valve back to the hull, detached the line, and gave the old valve a big shove to get it clear of the ship. Morgan no longer desired to bring it aboard. Morgan and Sam were back inside in less than an hour. The thrusters fired properly the next morning, and the *Mayflower* was in position when deceleration commenced. All of the Perry-Warner engines operated normally without any indication of the anomaly experienced when they left Ararat's orbit.

Randy had been a popular member of the crew, and his sudden death, so close to the completion of their return to Earth, had a great impact on the crew. Miguel Sanchez delayed a memorial service until the *Mayflower* was under deceleration for a day to give those wanting to attend time to adjust to gravity conditions. The service was held in the galley, and over one hundred crew members crowded into the space to offer their respects and condolences. Samantha and her three children, all in their twenties, each related their favorite stories about their husband and father. Samantha was gracious, not blaming anyone for his loss. "He talked to me continuously while he was waiting for the *Gemini* to come for him. Near the end, he knew the *Gemini* would not get there in time. He said he was doing his job, and no one was at fault for the accident. He didn't even blame himself. 'Sometimes bad things happen. It's just part of life,' he said. Just before he died, he urged me to celebrate our life together and not grieve his death. And that is what I am going to do. We had thirty-one wonderful years together. That is what I am going to focus on, not his loss." Samantha closed her comments by asking everyone to join her in singing "Amazing Grace." Samantha was smiling gracefully as the service ended, and Randy's remains were sent to the recycling system.

His discussion with Tyler and Purple had gone well. Tyler had assumed the verbal command authority with Purple when he took over the duties of chief engineer. Tyler confirmed the computer's report that the Perry-Warner drive system was in perfect order and ready to shut down ten days later. Tyler had completed an extensive analysis of the system and found no indication that the anomaly experienced in one of the engines when they left Ararat would manifest itself again. Tyler also reported that Purple had been able to program an approach to a geosynchronous orbit over the central North American continent that would not need to use the thrusters. That way, they wouldn't have to worry about another thruster problem like that experienced when they rotated the ship. "The flight plan is designed so that we will not need to use the thrusters," he said. "The engines will shut off at 9:52 a.m., August 10, 2093, ship's date, as we glide into a circular orbit 26,199 miles above the state of Kansas. In that position, we will be able to off-load anywhere in the United States."

Morgan was relieved that the thrusters were not needed. Lately more and more systems on the *Mayflower* were showing their age. At least he would not have to worry about problems entering orbit around Earth. He was, however, beginning to worry about what reception they would receive when they arrived in that orbit. As he entered the communications center, he asked, "John, have you made contact yet?"

"No, and I am very concerned," John Malcolm replied. "It does not surprise me that there has been no response from Brad Johnson at our base. It has been thirty-three years Earth time since we left. But we crossed inside the sphere of Neptune's orbit yesterday, and we are well within range of picking up nondirectional high-powered transmissions. I know it's not our ship because I have received some data transfers from weather satellites in Earth's orbit. I also received a brief data transmission from a weather station in Alberta, Canada. But I have been unable to detect any broadcasts from any communications media. I have no explanation for the lack of these detectable signals. We will be close enough to pick up personal communicators in five more days. Perhaps then, we will know what is going on."

"Is it possible that new technology has been developed in the last thirty years that could not be received by our ship's systems?" Morgan asked.

"I suppose new methods could have been developed," John replied. "But I can't imagine any new stuff could have completely replaced all of the existing communications networks on Earth in thirty years. Also that doesn't explain the satellites and weather stations that are still transmitting."

"What about an electromagnetic bomb or some other type of weapon?"

"I seriously doubt it could be the reason. Electromagnetic weapons have been available for a long time, and one was used by terrorists about twenty years before we left Earth. I believe it was in Southeast Asia somewhere, and it wasn't nearly as effective as many believed it would be. In my opinion, to cause a complete worldwide failure of all electronic communications through some sort of weapon is beyond the means of even the evilest members of mankind. War in general is a possibility perhaps. But it would have to been far beyond anything we could imagine to knock out communications worldwide."

"Is a solar event a possible explanation?"

"Again that doesn't explain the operating satellites and weather station," John said. "The bottom line is I don't know why I am not hearing anything. I will keep listening, but I fear something serious is wrong. In any event, we will know more when we enter orbit in ten days."

"Thanks for the update. I don't understand it and am also worried," Morgan said. "Let me know as soon as you hear something. If we don't have communications established by the time we are within personal communicator range, people are going to get very nervous. Also go back and review all of Brad Johnson's transmissions and see if you can find any clues."

John nodded his agreement as Morgan walked out of the communications center. He decided to stop by Christopher Vollbrecht's office to talk about the communications issue. Vollbrecht was not there when Morgan arrived, so Morgan called him on his communicator and found out he was in the galley having a cup of coffee.

"Stay there, Christopher, I will join you in a couple of minutes," Morgan said as he headed to the central companionway. He hustled down the ladders from deck two to the galley on deck seven. He liked the exercise he got climbing up and down the central companionway instead of using the elevators. Morgan wished all of the crew members would use opportunities like this to keep fit. Unfortunately, not everyone realized the importance of fitness, and several were putting it off again. The price for ignoring fitness was high when the *Mayflower* initiated deceleration for the approach to Earth after more than six years of weightless flight. Twelve crew members died of heart failure and other complications soon after the engines were started, and another twenty received serious injuries. He was reminded of the old twelfth-century English saying, "You can lead a horse to water, but you can't make it drink it." In other words, people will only do what they want to do no matter how important the alternative is.

Morgan wondered if his children would appreciate an old saying like that. They, of course, knew what horses were from their studies, but they had never seen a real horse other than in videos or any other animal other than a shrimp for that matter. Would they even understand the concept of leading a horse to water and why the horse might not drink? It was sobering to think about how much there would be to learn about life outside the confines of the *Mayflower*.

As Morgan entered the galley, he saw Christopher Vollbrecht at a table drinking quinoa coffee along with his wife, Erica Norquist. Christopher and Erica were married on Valentine's Day of 2088, ship's time. They now had a three-year-old daughter named Wendori. Morgan understood she was pregnant with her second child due in four more months.

Morgan walked over to the coffee dispenser and drew a steaming cup of quinoa coffee. Then he pulled up a chair and joined Christopher and Erica. "Only a few more days, Erica," Morgan began. "Are you excited about returning to Earth?"

"More than you can imagine," she responded. "I was just seven when we left Earth, and I don't remember very much about it. But part of my excitement comes from knowing how close I came to not even being here. When I told the colony volunteers I was concerned about some of the policies they were discussing, I was merely expressing my opinion. I still wanted to stay on Ararat and was shocked when they told me I was no longer part of the colony. At first, I was really disappointed. Now I realize how lucky I was. I am looking forward to a simple family life on Earth, something I could never have had in the colony."

"Are you still planning on opening a quinoa-based gourmet restaurant on Earth?"

"Actually, I am. That is why I have been experimenting with different recipes. Some of them have turned out to be pretty good."

"I remember your Swedish meatballs a few months ago," said Morgan. "They were really tasty. I don't know how you did it."

"I'll never tell," laughed Erica.

"She is not the only one that was lucky the colony rejected her," Christopher said. "She didn't know it at the time, Morgan, but I was already in love with her when she volunteered. I was devastated when she said she was staying on Ararat. When I found out she wasn't going to be leaving the *Mayflower*, I was determined to try and win her over to me. Now here we are, happily married and expecting a little boy to be added to our family."

Morgan smiled. "I'm truly glad that things worked out so well for you two and that you are excited about your new life on Earth. That's in a way the reason I wanted to talk to you, Christopher. You have the best sense of the mood of our crew. I wanted your assessment of the crew's feelings about the lack of communications from Earth."

"Sounds like you are going to be talking shop, and I have to get back to work anyway. People have to eat wherever they are," Erica said as she excused herself.

"Right now, I'm seeing some concern about our failure to make contact with Earth," said Christopher. "For most, it's not a major issue yet, but it's building. I spend a lot of time wandering the ship and keeping my ears to the deck, so to speak. The crew members have come up with a hundred and one possible explanations for the matter. They will need answers soon." Christopher paused before continuing. "There is one issue, however, that has many of the crew members near my age on edge, including me. How will we fit in to Earth's society when they get back on the surface? For a long time, we weren't worried about life on Earth. We just wanted to get there. We were busy with our life here on the *Mayflower*. But now the reality of a new life is upon us. I was born on Earth on March 3, 2062, but I have no recollection of social protocols and standards. Also although I am thirty-one years old now, someone on Earth born the same day I was will be forty-four. That's going to be hard to adjust to. I think there is a growing consensus that we will have to stay together. There are too many things we won't know to be turned loose in society. We feel we will be social misfits."

"I think you are right, Christopher. Once we leave the *Mayflower*, I will also be just another confused Earthling trying to adjust to a world I probably won't recognize. We will know in a few days exactly what kind of a world awaits us. In the meantime, why don't you do a formal survey to see whether there is a predominate opinion for our future, and if so, what is it? Our charter did not anticipate a return to Earth. Any decision will have to be made by the crew and the consortium, if it still exists."

"I've already started doing that. I will have some answers and recommendations for you by the time we are in orbit."

Morgan excused himself and returned to the central companionway. He climbed down to deck eight where Sarah's office was. Sarah had recently said she was a little concerned about quinoa production. Sarah was at her workstation when Morgan entered the office.

"Any word from Earth yet?" she asked.

"No. John Malcolm is getting quite concerned, and I must admit, so am I. We discussed a few possible reasons, but none of them seemed likely. At any rate, you mentioned a problem with the quinoa production last evening. Is it anything serious?"

"I don't think so. I noticed that our yields started to decrease a few weeks ago. It wasn't much at first, but it seems to be getting worse. Yesterday's harvest was almost three percent below production levels required to maintain the food requirements of our current population. That's not enough to cause any shortages for the amount of time we have left on the *Mayflower*, but it does make me curious. I asked Judy Polachek to take a look at the matter a few days ago. She knows more about agricultural and soil sciences than anyone else on this ship and was excited to have a research project to focus on. She hasn't had much to do since we abandoned our mission to colonize a new planet."

"I agree it's nothing to worry about right now. We still have that extra six months supply in reserve that you produced shortly after the meteor hit our ship. But I'm glad production didn't start to decline before we left Epsilon Eridani. It would have had a significant impact on our decision process."

"You've got that right, Morgan. I wonder if the colony is having similar problems. In fact, I wonder if they are even still alive."

"We will send them a message as soon as the first crew members off-load to Earth. It will be the first message to the colony since we let them know about the decompression event. We didn't even notify the colony about Randy's death, and I don't know if Nels is receiving our messages or if he is able to talk to the colony members. Hopefully, they are still there and will receive our transmissions. Who knows, perhaps they will even respond some day and let us know their status."

Sarah and Morgan looked up as their daughter, Emily, poked her head into the office. "Hi, sweetie," said Sarah. "How's married life? Am I going to be a grandmother again?" Emily had married Walter Malcolm last April first on Walter's twentieth birthday; Emily was still nineteen at the time. Originally, they had planned to tie the knot the previous November, but the death of Randy Edwards had resulted in a delay in their plans.

Marriage at a young age had become increasingly common as the *Mayflower* approached Earth. Christopher Vollbrecht said it was a subconscious response to the unknown they would face when assimilating back into Earth's society. The young adults felt they would be better prepared if they were already in a permanent relationship. Sarah and Morgan talked with Emily and Walter to make sure they were ready for a lifetime commitment, and Emily and Walter convinced them they were right for each other.

"Mother!" Emily blushed. "We've only been married four months. I'll let you know when I know."

"I'm just teasing," Sarah laughed. "On a more serious note, have you seen Dr. Sanchez yet for your vaccine? We are heading that way in a few minutes."

"Yes, Walter and I had our shots yesterday. It wasn't a big deal."

A great deal of effort went into eliminating human diseases from the crew of the *Mayflower* before it left Earth. A combination of vigorous inoculations and screening of all of the original crew members had been largely successful. Only the common cold was successful in evading the screening process. Caused by numerous different strains of the rhinovirus, no cure had ever been found. Colds were experienced by most of the crew members at one time or another, but the controlled environment on the *Mayflower* had reduced the frequency of colds to about one third found on Earth. Colds under weightless conditions were more of a problem because a sneeze or cough would spread the virus much farther. No other infectious disease had been detected on the *Mayflower* since leaving Earth, but a supply of all known antibiotic and antiviral vaccines had been brought on the mission and stored in the event a disease outbreak occurred.

When the decision to abandon the mission and return to Earth was made, Dr. Sanchez and her staff developed a plan to prepare all crew members for the eventual exposure to Earth's infectious diseases. These diseases fall into three categories: those caused by bacteria, those caused by viruses, and those caused by protozoans. Several of the most dangerous diseases had been eradicated from the human population prior to the departure of the *Mayflower*. Small pox, caused by a virus, was declared eradicated in 1980, although some samples were kept into the twenty-first century under the guise of research. Another viral disease, polio, was last detected in 2021 and was declared eradicated in 2025. Two bacterial diseases diphtheria and whooping cough had been eliminated from all developed nations by the mid-twenty-first century but were still occasionally reported in remote portions of the globe when the *Mayflower* left in 2072.

Several other diseases such as malaria (a protozoan disease), typhoid fever, and tuberculosis (bacterial diseases) were still prevalent in many parts of the world but were no longer found in North America where the *Mayflower* was expected to return. Dr. Sanchez decided that it would be unnecessary to protect the crew from these diseases. She determined that the main disease threat to the *Mayflower* crew would come from two known sources—influenza and tetanus. In addition, there was always the possibility that some new disease had developed, but there was nothing she could do about such an occurrence.

Influenza is caused by a variety of viruses found in humans, birds, and mammals. Influenza spreads through the air from coughing and sneezing and direct contact with animal droppings. Seasonal epidemics and occasional pandemic outbreaks continued in the twenty-first century in spite of aggressive vaccination programs. Part of the problem in controlling influenza is the frequent evolvement of new strains of the virus, sometimes directly from humans and sometimes from animals that then spreads to humans. Thus, new vaccines have to be continuously developed to keep up with the mutation rate of the virus. As a result, Dr. Sanchez concluded that using the influenza vaccines on the *Mayflower* would likely provide little benefit and could cause some harmful side effects. She informed Morgan before deceleration to Earth began that it would be best to wait until they arrived on Earth and then treat everyone with the latest vaccine available.

Tetanus, however, is different. It is caused by a species of bacteria *Clostridium tetani* found throughout the Earth. *C. tetani* endospores are common in the intestines of cattle, sheep, dogs, and many other animals. It is found in fecal droppings and manure-treated soils. The endospores metabolize when they find a suitable anaerobic environment. Prime habitat for the spores is found in objects such as barbed wire fences and nails, particularly when rusting of the metal begins. Then when a human is scratched or punctured by such an object, the spores are introduced into the body, and the tetanus infection begins to attack the body's muscle systems. The mortality rate approaches 50 percent in unvaccinated people. Because the *C. tetani* bacterium is so common and widespread, eradication is not feasible. Vaccination is the solution to prevention of the disease. Unlike many diseases, vaccination does not provide permanent immunity from tetanus. Booster shots are required every ten years to ensure continued protection. Thus, everyone on the *Mayflower* needed either an original vaccination or a booster shot.

While some development of an oral vaccine had occurred on Earth before the *Mayflower* left, Dr. Sanchez chose the proven method of direct injection into the thigh muscle. Everyone on the *Mayflower* was encouraged to receive an immunization shot at least two weeks before they returned to the surface of the Earth. She had started the program a month before the *Mayflower* was scheduled to enter Earth's orbit.

"I've got to run," Emily said. "Walter and I are helping Samantha Edwards in the nursery. Walter really likes working with the babies. He says he wants to go to medical school when we get to Earth. I think he will make a great doctor."

"I agree. Walter has a wonderful bedside manner and has learned a great deal about medicine already," Morgan said. "What about you? Are you still going to pursue a teaching career?" Morgan asked.

"I think so. From what I have learned from the computer's files, the public education system was not very good when the *Mayflower* left. I don't think I could put up with the education standards that were in place for the general population. I liked my school years here on the *Mayflower*, so maybe I will find a similar environment in a private school somewhere. Hopefully, they will accept my *Mayflower* credentials as equivalent to a college degree on Earth." Emily, like most children on the *Mayflower* her age, had completed her primary and secondary education in her early teens and had finished all the required courses for a college degree by the time she was nineteen. She had focused on primary education and had received her *Mayflower* certification from Melissa Grant just before her marriage to Walter.

"As soon as we land, I intend to convince the powers that be on Earth that an education on the *Mayflower* is equal to or better than anything any college on Earth can provide," said Morgan. "I think you and all those educated here will find you are more than qualified for your field."

"Thanks, Dad. I'll see you later," she said as she darted out of Sarah's office toward the central companionway.

As Sarah watched Emily disappear around the corner of her office hatch, she asked, "Are you confident, Morgan, that the governments and universities on Earth will accept Melissa's diplomas? There will probably be a lot of institutional resistance."

"I think most governments will come around once they see how well educated our people are. It may be necessary to take a course or two in current affairs to catch up with new and emerging issues, but other than that, our children have an excellent education. The universities are another matter. Many of them will get hung up on pedigrees. Walter, for example, may find it difficult to find a medical school that will let him in right away. They will be concerned about the lack of a piece of paper from a recognized premedical school. Hopefully they still offer some sort of an admission exam for advanced degrees. I am confident that people like Walter will excel on such exams, and they can find enlightened schools that will overlook normal entrance requirements. Laura McMullen, for example, already knows more than most PhDs with ecology degrees did when we left, including me. All she will need is a short review of recent developments, and she could teach at any university in the land."

"At least you and I know the system," Sarah said. "For our children and all the others who grew up on this ship, the *Mayflower* way of doing things is the only one they know. I hope they will be able to adjust."

"Me too. Come on, we've put off our visit to the clinic long enough. Let's get it over with."

Morgan and Sarah walked to the central companionway and climbed to deck three where the hospital and clinic were located. As they entered the corridor on deck three, Sarah said, breathing easily, "I sure couldn't have done that a few months ago. Avoiding the elevators has really helped me get my legs back."

"I agree. I'm looking forward to taking up a little jogging when we are back on the ground. Hopefully we won't be weightless for more than a few days."

Dr. Sanchez looked up from her workstation as Morgan and Sarah entered the clinic. "Are you finally here for your tetanus shot?" she said jokingly. "My daughter Julia is doing the honors. She is in the first room to your right. Please stop back when you are done. I want to chat for a few minutes."

"Ubetcha," said Morgan. Like her husband, Miguel, it had taken Sandra a long time to get over the loss of her son Luis to the colony. It wasn't until they were halfway through the coasting phase of the return trip that she seemed to get back to normal. Undoubtedly, Julia's decision to follow in her mother's footsteps had played a major role in her rejuvenated outlook on life. Now twenty-six, Julia had taken up the study of medicine and had all the knowledge and experience to be a doctor.

Morgan and Sarah walked into the first patient room off the central clinic office. Julia had heard them talking to her mother and was standing near the door waiting for them.

"Hi, Captain and Mrs. Parker," she said as they entered.

"Please," Morgan said, "it's Morgan and Sarah."

"I understand you are engaged to David Cornwell," Sarah said. "Have you set a date yet?"

David Cornwell was three years older than Julia. David had grown up on the Cornwell family farm in Illinois before his parents volunteered for the *Mayflower* crew as agricultural specialists. They both worked in the hydroponic gardens. David was twenty years old when the decision to return to Earth was made and had seriously considered volunteering for the Ararat colony, but he didn't think his desire to follow in the family footsteps as a farmer was possible on Ararat. But he had not been happy about returning to Earth either and kept mostly to himself for several years on the return flight. He gradually came out of his shell when he and Julia became friends a couple of years ago. Now twenty-nine, he was one of the oldest crew members that had not yet married.

"No, but we will pretty soon," Julia sighed. "David says he wants to see how we will fit in on Earth before we get married. He wants to farm but doesn't know whether he will be able to do that. His family farm was sold when we left Earth, and he doesn't think he will be able to afford to buy enough land to support a family. He says he needs to know what his future is going to be before we start a family. I keep telling him it doesn't make any difference, but he's pretty stubborn. I expect we will know in a few days. Have we established communications with our Earth base yet?"

"No response to our calls so far," said Morgan. "I know everyone is getting antsy about that, so I will make a general announcement as soon as I have something to report."

"Thanks, any news will be good news. Okay, who is going to be first?" she said, holding a sterilized swab.

A few minutes later, Morgan and Sarah were vaccinated and returned to the central medical office. Sandra had pulled up a couple chairs and indicated they should join her. "A lot of people are asking questions, Morgan," she began. "They want to know what conditions are like on Earth. Do you have any idea why we haven't been able to open a line of communications yet?"

"No. I just talked with John Malcolm, and the only thing he's been able to detect from Earth's surface is an automatic weather station in Canada. He said we should be within range of personal communicators in five more days. Hopefully someone will be talking to us by then."

"You need to do something soon, Morgan," Sandra said. "The rumors are flying, and some of them are not good for the crew's morale. Miguel mentioned to me last evening that one of the men in his Bible class was talking about Bible prophecy in Revelations coming true. Talk like that could cause unrest if it becomes widespread."

"I had planned to wait until we were within personal communicator range before I said anything, but you are right. I will make a general announcement as soon as I get back to my office. Do either of you have any words of wisdom for that announcement?" he asked, looking at Sarah and Sandra.

"The truth is the best approach," said Sandra, and Sarah nodded her agreement. "Tell us what you know as well as what you don't know."

"Thanks, ladies. Are you coming with me, Sarah?"

"No, I'm going back to my office. I'll see you in our quarters before dinner time."

As Morgan left the medical clinic and climbed to his office in the command center, he composed in his mind what he was going to say. After talking with John Malcolm, Christopher Vollbrecht, Dr. Sanchez, and his wife Sarah, he knew that he had to say something. The trick was going to be to give as much information as possible without creating any undo panic. It was still possible that everything would be cleared up in a few days as they drew closer to Earth. He was going to have to choose his words carefully.

"Crew of the *Mayflower*," he began, "this is Captain Parker. We are now just ten days away from Earth's orbit. I know that you are excited about our long journey nearing its end. At the same time, many of you are aware that we have not yet been able to establish a communications link with anyone on Earth. This is a concern of mine as it is for many of you. I do not know why we haven't received any responses to our hails so far. Further, the only electronic signals we have received to date are from weather satellites in orbit around Earth and from an automatic weather station in Canada. I cannot explain why we are not getting more. We are well within range to pick up transmissions from radio, television, and other high-power electronic media. We are not, however, within personal communicator range. That will come in about five days.

"Here is what I do know. The fact that the Canadian weather station is broadcasting means there has not been a global catastrophic event. There are at least some signs of normal functions taking place. We have also received some pictures through our high-powered optics that show weather patterns that appear normal. Our sensors do not indicate any elevated radiation levels. The Earth is still there, and as we draw closer, we will know more. Until then, I urge you not to jump to any conclusions. We have been gone for thirty-four Earth years now, and there are many possibilities that could explain our communication difficulties. As soon as I know more, I will tell you. Thank you for patience as we complete our long journey."

Morgan sat back in his chair as he finished and wondered if he had done more harm than good. The bottom line was that there was a lot more that he didn't know than what he did know. He hoped the crew would be patient as he and his staff found answers to all those unknowns. As he left the command center, he decided to stop by his old ecology center and see if Laura had any thoughts about the issue. He hadn't talked to her for several days.

Laura was there along with her son Erin. "Hey, Laura," said Morgan as he entered the small office, "I'm glad you are here. Hi, Erin, where are your sister and brother?"

"Daddy and Cindy went to pick up Jaxon from the nursery. I'm old enough to come here from school on my own," Erin proudly said.

"That you are. You're almost five now, aren't you? I keep forgetting when your birthday is. Can you remind me?"

"September 15, silly. You didn't really forget, did you?"

"No, not really. I'm sure your Aunt Sarah and I will have something special for you," said Morgan.

"Uncle Morgan, I have a question. When will my birthday be on Earth, and how old will I be?"

Morgan paused, trying to figure out how to answer those questions. "Those are great questions, Erin. Let's see. You will still be five years old, and your birthday will still be September 15. But it's August in the year 2093 here on the *Mayflower*, and on Earth, it's March 2106. Maybe your parents will decide to have another birthday party for you in six months. Won't that be special?"

"That sounds great. Maybe by then they will have something other than quinoa to make me a birthday cake."

"I sure hope so," said Laura. "I remember what good old-fashioned chocolate cake tasted like. You will love it. Who knows? I have been taking some cooking classes. I may even be able to make it for you myself."

"Wow, that would be special," Erin said as he turned back to the story he was reading.

Laura turned to Morgan, suddenly looking very serious. "That's just one small example of the problems we will face once we get off the *Mayflower*. Do we automatically become twelve and a half years older? Have you thought of how to address that little problem? Unless we have been working in the galley, none of us under thirty-five have ever cooked a meal. There are so many issues that we will have to face—money for example. We don't use money here, and those who grew up on this ship have never had to purchase anything. I know we have spent a lot of time on teaching social skills, but there is nothing like experience. I was just thirteen when we left Earth and don't have enough experience myself to teach my kids. I guess what I am saying is I'm a little scared about how we are going to reenter Earth society."

Morgan was a little surprised at Laura's comments. Normally, she was very calm, cool, and collected. He was glad that Christopher Vollbrecht was already working on recommendations for reentry into society. "I think everyone is on edge right now, and the lack of any response from Earth isn't helping any. That is why I made the announcement. The crew needs to know what is going on. I just wish I had something more to tell them."

"You did say something positive, Morgan. You said that the Earth is still there and has not undergone a catastrophic event. Some people were beginning to doubt that. I'm sorry I unloaded on you. I guess it's my motherly instincts coming into play. I am sure all these things we are worrying about will turn out to be no big deal."

"No problem," said Morgan. "I need input like that. What you said has been on my mind also. I think we all were expecting to make a grand entrance with flags waving, like a winning sports team returning to their hometown. It's hard to accept that perhaps nobody has even noticed our return. At any rate, we are learning more each day."

Morgan glanced at the screen above his old workstation and saw it was approaching the dinner hour. "I need to get going, Laura. I told Sarah I would join her for dinner. Say hi to Cindy for me. I'm sorry I missed her and Jaxon. Cindy always has interesting questions for me."

"I will," Laura said, looking cheery once again as Morgan walked out of the ecology center toward his quarters where Sarah said she would meet him.

CHAPTER 12

Nothing was heard from Earth as the *Mayflower* drew within five days of Earth. Nothing was heard when four days out or three days out. By two days out, neither Morgan nor John Malcolm expected to hear anything, and they were right. Their expectations were based not only on the lack of electronic transmissions. The *Mayflower* was within range of its optics to begin to see detail when they were five days out from orbit. It was what they didn't see that was disturbing. There were no lights in the nighttime sky. None. Anywhere. The Earth was dark. Morgan did as promised and announced to the crew that it appeared the power grid was out, not only in North America but throughout the world. Concern began to change to fear and worry. By the time the ship was two days away from its scheduled orbit around Earth, they could see enough detail that it was apparent there had been no global environmental disaster. Sea levels appeared normal; forests and lakes were still where they were supposed to be. Greenland was still covered by glaciers. There was snow cover over the northern plains and Great Lakes, as expected that time of year on Earth. While this news was somewhat encouraging, it did little to alleviate the crew's anxiety.

Finally on August 10, 2093, ship's calendar and March 22, 2106, according to the Earth calendar, the *Mayflower* arrived in a geosynchronous orbit high above the state of Kansas. It was twenty-one years and ten days by the ship's calendar since the

Mayflower departed. In the meantime, the Earth had aged thirty-three years. The Earth appeared normal from over 26,000 miles up with one exception; there was no sign of human activity.

As soon as the *Mayflower* was stabilized in orbit and the ship's routine had completed its transformation to weightless conditions, Morgan asked the division chiefs to assemble in the command-deck conference room. He told them he wanted to discuss how to investigate the conditions they were finding on Earth, the status of the ship's systems, and what, if any, options they had.

Morgan noticed the troubled look on everyone's face as they strapped into their seats. He said, "Well, this certainly isn't the welcome we were expecting, is it? I have to be honest and tell you the future of us all appears to be in jeopardy unless we can figure out what we are going to do. Do any of you have any idea what is going on? I am open to any possibilities."

Samuel Workman spoke up first. He and two of his staff had been monitoring the optics continuously since the *Mayflower* had crossed into the inner solar system. "I have not seen any sign of people. Certainly, the lack of lights and apparently the lack of any electrical grid is significant. Further, we looked at major manufacturing sites in China, Europe, and South America and could not see any activity such as smokestack emissions. Large agricultural areas in the Midwestern United States, Europe, and South America show no signs of recent activity. The patterns that would be visible at this altitude from organized farming are not there. However, that does not mean there aren't any people alive on Earth. There could well be small bands living a relatively primitive existence that we are unable to detect from this altitude. But from our observations, it appears that human civilization as it exited when we left is no longer present."

"Have you seen any signs of life other than humans?" asked Morgan.

"It does appear that plant life is still present. Forest areas are green, and some of those agricultural areas I just mentioned do appear to have some plant life, particularly in the Southern Hemisphere and southern parts of North America. The upper Midwest is still emerging from winter conditions. As for animal life, we haven't seen any signs yet."

"Is it possible," began Melissa Grant carefully, "that it is us and not Earth that has undergone some strange transformation? For example, do we really know it's the year 2106 on Earth? What if our understanding of the physics of interstellar travel is all wrong? Maybe it's a thousand years in the future, or maybe it's a thousand years before we left?"

"That's good, Melissa," Morgan said. "As I said, we need to consider every idea no matter how strange it sounds. Phil, as our resident physicist what do you think?"

"Anything is possible," Phil replied. "I had been thinking about possibilities like that myself. I also thought about an alternate universe possibility like we had passed through some sort of a portal and are looking at a different Earth than the one we left. The more we learn about how our universe functions, the more we find that we don't understand it completely. But to me, those theories are still in the realm of science fiction without any hard science to support them. The science as we know it does not support a time shift or alternate universe possibility. Also the basic infrastructure is still in place even if it's not operating. We can see the cities. We can see artificial reservoirs. We even have a couple satellites functioning and a weather station or two operating on Earth. So I must conclude we are back at the same Earth at the relatively correct time as the Earth we left. If Samuel's observations about the winter conditions are correct, Purple's calendar calculations are on the money."

"Okay," Melissa said. "Since Morgan is encouraging us to put everything on the table, what about a war?"

"Let me try that one," said Morgan. "I have thought about it for several days. When our main concern was the lack of communications, I discussed the possibility of some sort of electromagnetic bomb with John. It didn't seem likely that such a weapon could have worldwide impact, but it is possible. But that would not explain all the visual evidence we have gathered since then. The weather stations are another stumbling block to that theory. A nuclear war resulting in mutual worldwide destruction would have left visible signs. A more conventional war would likely also have left a lot of damage that we could see. If there was a war, where are the winners? Would a war really come down to the last two humans killing each other? Of course, there may still be a remnant population, but we haven't detected one from this altitude. We won't know that until we get a closer look."

"How about a biological or other kind of weapon?" asked Sarah.

"That is possible, but I find it hard to believe," answered Sandra Sanchez. "First of all, even the evilest people usually develop an antidote or some sort of a survival plan to go along with their weapon. It makes little sense, at least to our western civilization way of thinking, to kill yourself along with your enemy. Second, could a weapon be so effective as to have worldwide implications? How would it be delivered to all corners of the world in such a way that no reaction to its coming was made. If I were in New Zealand, for example, and learned that a biological weapon was being used in Europe or Asia, I would take immediate action to protect myself. I did a search in Purple's memory banks to see if there was any documentation of something that had that capability. If it was a weapon, it was unknown when we left Earth. But we can't rule out man's ability to create the ultimate weapon. Purple's data banks include some research going on regarding electrical interference with brain activity, but it was focused on paralysis, not harmful uses."

"What about a natural disease?" asked Judy Polachek.

"A pandemic disease outbreak is a possibility. But a disease that kills everyone or virtually everyone in a short period of time? It's very hard to fathom what could do that. There was no sign of any major new disease outbreak when we left. But I don't want to close the door on this possibility. If we want to rule out disease, we will have to go to the surface. That, of course, could expose all of us if that is what happened. And I don't want to make it sound bleaker that it already is, but we may be all that is left of humanity. We haven't heard from Ararat for years, and I, for one, have no confidence they are still alive."

"I agree," said Morgan. "Whatever we do, we must be extremely careful to protect our people from any possible causative agent.

"John, I asked you to review all of Earth's transmissions to us a few days ago. I don't want to go over all of it now, but was there any discussion of a new disease problem on Earth?"

"No," John Malcolm said. "I reviewed all forty-eight transmissions we received from Brad Johnson since our departure, and he made no mention of any new disease problem or any other major population die-off concern."

"Is there another source of a possible extinction event we should consider?" asked Judy.

"I have been thinking about that," said Laura. "In the broadest sense, we may well be looking at an extinction event, but it will be unlike any that has ever occurred before. Extinction events in the past have involved a broad range of taxonomic groups, sometimes resulting in the extinction of as high as ninety-seven percent of all species extant at the time. Second, we may think of an extinction event as something that happens quickly, but in reality, historic extinction events occurred over thousands of years but merely a blip on the geological calendar. Here, if that is what has happened, it has occurred over a period of only a few years at most. Further, we don't know yet if animal life other than humans have been impacted or if some humans are still surviving. If it was an extinction event, it was caused by something unlike any previous event recorded on Earth."

"How many times has such an event occurred in the past, and what are thought to be the causes of those events?" Tyler Haroldson asked.

"First of all, it depends on how we define an extinction event. Generally, those events where more than fifty percent of all species are thought to have become extinct are considered major events. There are several other lesser events in geologic time which are noticeable in the fossil records. Extinction is a natural part of the evolution of the Earth as it ages. In one sense, we are always involved with an extinction event. It is a sudden rise in the background rate of extinction that leads to what we call an event.

"Several causes have been suggested for major events. The most recent event that led to the extinction of the dinosaurs about sixty-six million years ago is thought to have been caused by a large asteroid impact, particularly if that impact occurred in an ocean. Such a large impact would cause a thermal shock in the ocean, raising temperatures to a high-enough level that large quantities of carbon dioxide would be released into the atmosphere. If enough CO_2 is released rapidly into the atmosphere, it could smother air breathing species. Large amounts of CO_2 injected quickly into the atmosphere can also lead to short-term climate changes. Many species would not have enough time to adapt to rapid changes in the climate and would become extinct.

"Other possible causes include major volcanic activity releasing dust and poisonous gases into the atmosphere. There have been some who thought that the Yellowstone Caldera could erupt as a super volcano. The last major eruption was over six hundred thousand years ago, and yet there is no evidence that eruption caused a major extinction event. Changes in sea levels caused by global cooling or sinking of the ocean floors; changes in the carbon, oxygen, or hydrologic cycles; and bursts of energy from the Sun or a nearby star are theoretically other possible root causes of an extinction event.

"These are all suggested causes of previous extinctions, but I doubt they have any relation to what has happened here. If this is an extinction event, it is something different from anything previously known. The timing and physical evidence we have to date suggests something other than an extinction event."

"I agree," said Phil. "There is no sign of any event so cataclysmal as to lead to any of the causes Laura has described. Other than the lack of any apparent sign of human activity, Earth appears about the same as we left it."

"Is it possible that something occurred that resulted in the extinction of all or most animal life but did not cause dramatic physical damage?" asked Judy. "And what about the plant communities Samuel could see?"

"Theoretically, yes," answered Phil. "Perhaps, a burst of energy from the Sun could interfere with brain activity or other characteristics of animal life. Until we know what species, if any, other than man have been impacted, we shouldn't rule this out as a possibility."

"As to the plant communities, if all or most of the animal life is gone, they will be changing, but not enough time has passed to be able to see those changes from this orbit," said Laura. "Annual plants that depend on animal pollinators that were gone would disappear first, but it could take many years for forests and other perennial plant ecosystems to dramatically change."

"What if all the other animal life is still present?" suggested Tyler.

"Then I think we would be looking for something that man did to himself," answered Laura. "Numerous species have quickly gone extinct but almost always because of human activities. Several bird species in North America have died out after the arrival of Europeans. Even in those cases, however, it took many years for the species to completely disappear."

"Could what has happened be a fulfillment of Biblical prophecy?" asked Christopher Vollbrecht. "I have heard lots of crew members talking about the end times. I'm afraid I don't know enough about the subject to know whether this is a possibility."

"My husband and I have had extensive discussions about this possibility the last few days," Sandra offered. "You all know that Miguel has been spending most of his time the last few years studying Scripture. He believes that what has occurred may well be related to Bible prophecy. But he also cautions that there are many interpretations of Scripture, and only God knows His plans. We all know that man is inherently wicked and evil. In spite of all our efforts to eliminate those traits from this crew, our species' innate character flaws came to light when some abandoned our moral code in order to stay on Ararat. According to the Bible, many years ago, God wiped out most of mankind in a flood. But he saw that Noah was a righteous man and spared him and his family. After the floodwaters receded, God told Noah he would never again destroy all living creatures even though every inclination of man is evil from childhood. The books of Isaiah and Jeremiah are filled with accounts of God's wrath on unrighteous and evil peoples. But the Lord always spared a remnant of those who believed in him. So could this be what has happened? The world was certainly evil when we left. Did God destroy the unrighteous? Are we the remnant?

Was the *Mayflower* our ark? Such a scenario is consistent with the Bible as far as we understand the scriptures. But this still leaves many unanswered questions. Are we really that righteous? Was there no nation or group of people on Earth deserving of God's grace? I don't know the answers to these questions, but I do know that if God's wrath is what has happened and we are the only remnant, then we better try and be faithful to him.

"Another possibility is the so-called *rapture*. In First Thessalonians chapter four verses sixteen and seventeen, Paul writes, 'For the Lord himself will come down from heaven and the dead in Christ will rise first. After that, we who are still alive and are left will be caught up together with them in the clouds to meet the Lord in the air.' This relates to the Gospel of Matthew where Jesus said there will be a return of the Son of Man, and the faithful will be separated from the wicked. There are different interpretations of how the rapture relates to the tribulation described in the book of Revelation. The tribulation is a period of great hardship and suffering prior to the end times. Some biblical scholars believe the rapture will occur before a seven-year period of tribulation. Other scholars think the rapture will happen during the tribulation period and that the severe outpouring of the wrath of God will occur mainly in the second half of the period. Finally, others believe that the rapture occurs at the end of the tribulation period and that the period of tribulation is indeterminate. Under this interpretation, the Earth may have been in the period of tribulation for many years. The history of man certainly shows few, if any, years of worldwide peace and harmony.

"Is the rapture a possible reason for the apparent absence of human life on Earth? I would not begin to think I understand what God's ultimate plan is, but I do have one question about this possibility. If the rapture has occurred, under any of the alternative theories mentioned above the events should be over. The end times have already occurred. If they have, why are we here? We should either be *caught up* with the Lord in heaven, or we should be cast into the eternal burning pit. But we are in neither outcome, at least as far as we can perceive. Could the almighty God have forgotten we were out in space when he brought about his conclusion to the end times? I personally don't think so. Therefore, I believe that if whatever has happened is biblical in nature, then it is a continuation of the visions of the prophets such as Isaiah. But remember, we have no scientific evidence to support that whatever happened was a prophetic event."

"Excellent summary of biblical prophecy, Sandra," Morgan said. "I would only add that some of the possibilities we have discussed such as disease, biological weapon, or natural disaster may be the instrument God allowed to bring his wrath on mankind once again. I agree, however, that your logical argument rules out the end times described in the Bible.

"Does anyone have another possibility we should consider?"

"Well, if we are trying to think of every possibility," Sarah offered, "what about aliens?"

Morgan looked around the table to see if anyone wanted to field that question. Seeing no volunteers, he said, "I thought about that some myself, and once we get into the realm of other world beings, none of our logic will necessarily apply. For example, what was their purpose? Who could possibly know because how do we know what their needs and ambitions might be? If they killed all human life on Earth, how did they do it and why? And where are they now? If they wanted Earth, why aren't they here? Or perhaps they are, and we can't see them. Maybe they are in the sea or underground. On the other hand, we don't have a good alternative explanation. Sometimes when the improbable isn't the answer, the impossible is. So I guess we will keep this one on our list for now. Are there any other suggestions?"

Morgan waited for a few moments, but no one had anything else to suggest. "Okay, let's move on. John, tell us everything that might be the least bit helpful that you gleaned from Brad Johnson's transmissions to us."

"As I said a few minutes ago," began John, "we received a total of forty-eight transmissions from Brad. The last one was received a few weeks before we began deceleration into the Alpha Centauri system. John's transmission was dated July 27, 2073, Earth time, just about one year after we departed. Before we left, I discussed communications issues with Captain Larson and with Brad. The main interest of maintaining contact came from the consortium as they wanted information for possible future missions. I sent rather detailed reports concerning the ship, crew, and our progress. I continued to send these until recently, although not as frequently as I did the first few years. As we originally had no plans to return to Earth, Captain Larson believed that news about Earth would not be beneficial to the crew's morale. Thus, most of Brad's reports were rather brief, providing limited information of the Earth that we might find interesting and updates regarding the consortium and the people we left behind.

"However, I did find a few things in the messages that are worthy of bringing to your attention again. I posted all of John's communications on Purple's bulletin board as they were received, but I doubt the crew paid much attention to them. I don't know whether any of these have any relation to the current situation, but who knows. You may remember that three of the five founding partners of the consortium had died before we left Earth. Only John Chu, who founded the consortium, and Albert Molinari, a billionaire from the pharmaceutical industry, were still alive in 2072. John Chu had always shown the greatest personal interest in our mission and spent much of his time focused on the mission's progress both before and after our departure. Molinari and the other founders were major financial contributors, but their energy was devoted to many other interests. About four months after we departed, we received a communication from Earth that John Chu had died. Brad expressed concern in that communication about the future of his position. Without Chu's influence, he was not sure funding would remain available to keep his facility open. He said there was almost no public interest in the *Mayflower*'s journey. Shortly after the *Mayflower* departed, all major news media quit covering the mission. To the sensational-styled media of the times, our slow progress was simply not worth covering. He did say that Molinari promised that he would keep a minimal staff funded at the base camp, but that was all. Then in a message eight months after we left, Brad said Molinari was ill. Molinari was the youngest of the founding partners, just fifty-one years old in 2072. Brad said he didn't know what was wrong with Molinari, but he was going to a special clinic for treatment.

"Did Brad ever tell you what Molinari was being treated for, or where he was going?" Sandra asked.

"No, he never mentioned him again. But he did say a few weeks later that he was moving north of Dallas to take a new position there. He said he would continue to travel to our base at the former Alliance airport near Fort Worth to download our reports and send us updates when he could. He continued to do that until his last message on July 27, 2073. He never said specifically why most of the consortium's operations were virtually shut down, but I assume with Molinari out of the picture, there was no money. He also said Chu had been selling off or giving away many of the buildings before he died. Brad indicated that he had included his housing unit on the base. I assume that is why he moved. His last message closed with a salutation that he would send another in a couple weeks. There was no indication that anything was an immediate threat to his continued contact with us."

"Did you find anything else in his contacts that might be significant?" Morgan asked.

"About three months after we left, he mentioned that a global initiative was started to address atmospheric pollution. He said it was more of the same political posturing that would be unlikely amount to anything, but a lot of government money had been pledged to the effort. Then a few weeks after Chu died, he mentioned two major volcanic eruptions. One was on an island in Indonesia, and the other was along the mid-Atlantic ridge near Iceland. He said the Indonesian eruption rivaled the Krakatoa eruption of the 1880s. There were many deaths due to the eruption itself and the resulting tsunamis. He said maybe it would actually give the global atmosphere initiative something to think about as there were significant amounts of ash and sulfur dioxide emitted into the sky."

Phil Cavuto asked, "Did he say anything more about the eruptions or the resulting pollutants?"

"Not directly," John answered. After a short pause, he added, "Now that I think about it, he did make an offhand comment shortly before his last transmission that he was glad the air would finally be getting clean again as he was tired of all the poor air quality. As I said before, in accordance with Captain Larson's request, Brad did not provide detailed information about what was happening on Earth. He was our friend, and I know he was disappointed he was not selected to go with us. His communications were always in the form of a conversation between long-distance comrades. He focused mostly on the more personal news and downplayed world events. That's really all I have."

"The volcanic eruptions are worth looking into to see if they might have caused some sort of a calamity," said Phil. "But so far, neither the atmospheric nor the landmass observations we have made give any indication of a global disaster. This is an unlikely explanation, particularly since it appears the plant communities are not impacted."

"Regardless of which scenario, if any, is behind this mystery, we will have to gather more information before we know what happened on Earth, what conditions currently exist, and whether we can safely return to the surface," Morgan said. "Before we discuss how to do that, I want to know what our situation is here on the *Mayflower*. Christopher, what is the mood of the crew now that they know there are no signs of human civilization on Earth?"

"It varies from fear to uncertainty to a sense of despair, depending in large part how old the person is," answered Christopher. "I looked over Melissa's findings when you were making the decision as to what to do after learning the Epsilon Eridani system was marginal for colonization. You may remember she evaluated how the crew would react to a decision to return to Earth. She broke the crew into three groups—adults, juveniles, and young children when we left Earth or were born during the journey. If we fast-forward to today, the same groupings still apply. There are, of course, some individual exceptions, but for the most part, my findings are consistent with Melissa's. The first group, the adults when we left Earth including most of you, was unhappy about the decision to go back home. They assumed Earth would be in worse shape than when they left and that it would be very hard to assimilate. Over the course of the return journey and as they grew older, they gradually began to accept returning to some corner of Earth's society. Now most of this group believes this entire mission has been a failure. They believe that returning to the surface is no longer possible yet have no desire to stay on the *Mayflower* any longer. I see this mood in many of you. We are discussing the situation in a professional way, but the undertone is one of hopelessness."

"As much as I hate to admit it," responded Saundra, "I agree. I'm not sure how much longer I can keep my attitude positive."

"Melissa's second group," continued Christopher, "included those in their twenties at the time of the decision to come back to Earth. Laura and I are in that group. This group wanted the *Mayflower*'s journey to end and looked forward to finding a settled life, even if it was on Earth. Over the last nine years on our return journey, many of those in this group have actually found that settled life here on the *Mayflower*. Most in our group are now married, and many have children. Laura has three, and my second is due soon. We looked forward to a smooth transition to life on Earth. We planned careers that would fit into Earth's society as we understood it. Now we don't know what we will do. I and most of those my age that I talked to are frustrated that what we have been planning for years does not look like it will happen.

"The third group is made up of those who were very young when we left Earth and those born on the *Mayflower*. They haven't known any life other than here on this ship, but for the past nine years, they have been preparing for a new way of living among Earth's masses. They were already very nervous about leaving the *Mayflower* but had accepted it as an inevitable transition they would have to make. Now they don't know what will happen. It depends on their age, but they are generally afraid. Will they die on the surface from something they don't understand? Will we turn around and go somewhere else? Remember, many in this group are the age of the second group when the Ararat decision was made. They want the journey to be over, and they are afraid it's not. In summary, concerns range from defeatism to frustration to fear. None of those attitudes is healthy for our crew."

"I can relate to what you've said about the second group," said Laura. "Bradley and I have been preparing for a quiet family life on Earth for years. It looks like everything is going topsy-turvy. Frustration is a good word to describe my feelings. At the same time, my scientific curiosity is challenging me to find answers to this mystery."

"Your description of the first group fits me pretty well," said Phil Cavuto. "I wasn't sure how a physicist and planetologist would find meaningful work on Earth, so I have worked hard to retrain myself as an energy geologist. It looks like I might have wasted all that effort."

"I also agree," said Melissa. "You hit the nail on the head, Christopher."

"You also touched on something else we need to consider," said Morgan. "If Earth is not habitable, can we go somewhere else? If so, where could we go? Tyler, is the *Mayflower* in good-enough shape to make another long journey?"

Tyler paused for a moment before he responded. "When Randy Edwards did the analysis of hull erosion at Epsilon Eridani, he estimated that the hull would last about nine years under interstellar flight. We used most of those nine years up returning here. I haven't had time to do a space walk since we entered Earth's orbit, but I will do so if you want new measurements. I do have some confirmation of Randy's projections however. When the small rock penetrated the hull two years after we left Epsilon Eridani, Randy and I measured the hull before we patched the hole. There was additional erosion on the exposed skin consistent with his earlier projections. In my opinion, another long flight would be extremely dangerous. Even a return to Epsilon Eridani would have a fifty-fifty chance of a catastrophic failure of our hull."

"Right now, I don't know where we would go other than back to Epsilon Eridani," said Morgan. "The chances of finding a habitable planet at Tau Ceti were less than 10 percent, and it's over twelve light-years from Earth. There are no other stars near Earth with any real chance of having a habitable planet. For now, Earth is our only option. If we have to leave, we will figure out how to deal with the hull-erosion problem. For now, there is no need to risk another space walk."

"What about Mars?" asked Christopher.

"Mars's environment is much harsher that Ararat's," said Morgan. "The consortium looked at Mars early in its planning phase and concluded continued support from Earth would be needed for a colony to survive. That was not the consortium's objective, so it was eliminated early in the planning process. We may have to look at Mars in the future, but now the option of support from Earth no longer looks viable. Another problem with Mars is that we left most of the construction materials on Ararat,"

"Hull erosion is not the only problem we could face if we embark on another long flight," Judy Polachek said. "I think I know why quinoa production is decreasing. We just discussed some of the reasons for extinction events. One of the reasons is relatively rapid changes in systems such as weather, the carbon cycle, or the hydrologic cycle. The *Mayflower* is like a miniplanet with its own cycles. We have tried to collect everything and recycle it to maintain the balance of these cycles and have been pretty successful. But our population has grown since the original five hundred who left Earth. At the time we decided to return to Earth, we had 652 souls on board. Now there are over seven hundred. Add to that the thirty-nine we left on Ararat, and we have a population increase of fifty percent. That increase has tied up a lot of chemicals that were in the various balanced cycles. Also, quinoa production increased during a portion of our flight from Ararat, and we stored a significant amount. Such a temporary increase in a population is often observed when a system is thrown out of balance. I haven't finished identifying the specific element or compound that is causing quinoa production to decrease, but it appears to be one of the trace elements. The quinoa is experiencing an environmental shock equivalent to that of an extinction event but on a much smaller scale."

"Can we do anything about it?" asked Sarah.

"Perhaps. First, we should use the stored quinoa and put it back into the ship's nutrient systems. Second, we could introduce the emergency rations into the cycle. That would offset part of the trace materials bound up in our bodies. But that would leave us without any fallback position if something else goes wrong. Third, we could infuse new material into the system from Earth. That would necessarily expose us to whatever has happened on the surface to get the material, something I know we don't want to do at this point. I'm not going to suggest a population reduction for obvious reasons."

"Is it possible we introduced something harmful into the system from our exploration of Ararat?" asked Samuel. "I know every effort was made to thoroughly clean any suit or other equipment that returned to the *Mayflower* from the surface, but perhaps something got through."

"That is a possibility, but why has it waited so long to manifest itself? Now that you bring up that scenario, we also retrieved the defective control valve from outside the ship. As I recall, it was not isolated when it was brought aboard."

"Good point, Judy," said Morgan. "Nobody thought to do that. I remember Randy said one possibility for the failure of the valve was that it was clogged and then thawed out when it warmed up. Maybe we did introduce something alien into our environment."

"If we did," responded Samuel, "none of our instruments has indicated a foreign substance on the *Mayflower*. As a precaution, I will have our biochemists see if they can find anything. As to keeping our environment in balance, we compensate for oxygen, carbon, and hydrogen changes as the population grows and made further adjustments when we started storing quinoa a few years ago. If Judy can identify a specific element that is throwing quinoa production off, I may be able to find a source here on the *Mayflower* without having to go to the surface. Also we may be able to find what we need in one of the satellites still in orbit."

"I'm working on it," Judy responded. "There are lots of possibilities to sort through. I am hopeful that we will have it narrowed down in a week or so."

"Assuming we cannot find the trace element or other factor responsible for the decline, do you have a sense how long and how fast quinoa production will decline?" asked Morgan.

"As to the how long part, yes. By simply using the stored quinoa, the decline should decrease to less than one percent per month. At that rate, it will be a year or more before we start to see real shortages. As to how far it will decline, I'm just guessing at this point, but without an input of whatever it is that's missing, it could very well go to zero, extinct."

"It appears we are facing a conundrum," said Morgan. "Our ship isn't safe enough to take us anywhere else and may not even be able to sustain us for an indefinite time here in orbit. That leaves the surface of Earth as our only realistic alternative. But how can we go to the surface without exposing the crew to whatever killed off the Earth's population? Yet we have to go to the surface to save the crew. That has to be our focus at this point. We need to find out what happened on Earth whether it's limited to humans or other species are impacted and whether it will kill us if we go to the surface. Until we answer those questions, there is no point in worrying about whether or not the *Mayflower* can make another interstellar flight. Any suggestions?"

"Unless what has happened is beyond our imagination and ability to do anything about, I believe some sort of disease scenario, however improbable it may seem, is the most likely cause," said Sandra. "Therefore, we must proceed with the utmost caution. Any disease that is one hundred percent fatal obviously cannot be allowed to get on the *Mayflower*. But even if it was a disease that killed everyone, it doesn't mean our situation is hopeless. Many of the known diseases are specific to humans, and without a population of humans to maintain a reservoir of the disease, it will disappear. Malaria, for example, is an infectious disease caused by parasitic protozoans. It was still killing millions of people a year when we left Earth, primarily in poor, tropical regions of the planet. But without humans, an essential part of the parasite's life cycle, the disease will not survive. If in fact all humans on Earth are gone, malaria should also be gone. Smallpox and polio, virus diseases that were eradicated years before our journey began, are other examples of diseases that require humans. So if what we are looking for is a disease, we must go forward assuming it is still viable, but it may not be."

"Well, at least that is a glimmer of hope," said Morgan. "John, I want you to send the following message to Ararat— 'People of Ararat, we hope that you are doing well and are receiving this message. We have arrived in orbit around Earth. There is something terribly wrong on the surface. Our observations indicate that all, or at least most, human life is gone. We do not know what has happened, but it does not appear to have been a global war or massive natural disaster. Other than the lack of human activity, our observations show relatively normal conditions. One possibility is a disease that wiped out the entire population. We also have problems with the aging condition of the *Mayflower*. It is unlikely it would survive another interstellar flight. So we may have no option but to stay here. At the same time, quinoa production is declining, and we have not found the cause. We are investigating these problems further, but right now, our future survival is uncertain. By the time you receive this message, you may very well be the only humans left in the universe. The Ararat colony may be humanity's last chance to survive. We will send you further information when we have a better idea of our situation and future status. Once again, we hope that you have adapted to conditions on Ararat and are carrying out the mission we all set out on all those years ago. In the event our future is doomed, we are attaching for you a history of our return journey to Earth.'"

As the meeting broke up and the team returned to their respective work areas, Morgan thought, *Is this the end of our journey? Are we the future of humanity, or are we destined to join all those billions who have died since we left Earth? For my family and friends here on the Mayflower, I trust that we will find a solution to our dilemma. But if we do not and our part of our mission is over, I pray that those on Ararat have survived as a remnant of the human species and that they will achieve the goals we set out for so many years ago.*

"Nels, Nels wake up."

"What is it, Caleb? What time is it anyway?"

"It's about three quarters to the new light," Caleb said excitedly. "You told me to get you up immediately any time the machine came to life. Well, it has. It is making noise, and one of the lights has turned on."

Nels sat up, rubbing the sleep out of his eyes. "Thanks, Caleb. I will be there as soon as I can get my clothes on."

Kayane rolled over in her bed and sat up. "What is going on?" she asked.

"Caleb says the receiver is awake. Somebody is calling us." Nels knew there was only one possible source of that call—the *Mayflower*.

He did a quick calculation in his head. His settlement still used hours, minutes, and seconds to keep track of time but had adapted the shorter Ararat day of twenty-two hours and the shorter sidereal year of 191 Ararat days. It was the year forty-seven on Ararat. So what would that mean to the *Mayflower*? It was about twenty-five Earth years since he had left the *Mayflower*. It should be back to Earth!

"I think they are back, Kayane. The message should come in in about ten minutes. Let's go see how they fared."

He and Kayane quickly pulled their clothes on and headed toward the next room where Caleb slept and the receiver was located. The quick arousal meant Nels did not have time to do his morning exercises, so his limp was more pronounced than usual as he walked the short distance.

Marcus and Susan Clauson heard the commotion from their room on the other side of the settlement and arrived just after Nels and Kayane. "Are we receiving a communication from the *Mayflower*?" Susan asked excitedly.

"I think so," answered Kayane.

"Gosh, it's been a long time. The last time we heard was when they were damaged by a meteorite, right? That was a long time ago. They should be back by now, I think."

"Actually, they should have arrived almost eleven Earth years ago, almost twenty-one Ararat years," said Nels. "That's how long it takes for a message to get from Sol to Epsilon

Eridani. Look, the light has turned green. The communication is arriving."

They read in fascination as the message from the *Mayflower* unwound on the large screen attached to the receiver.

Kayane looked at Nels, stunned as the message ended. "My God, it sounds like everyone may be dead? What could have happened? Are we the only humans left in the universe?"

"I don't know, and we may never find out. But if we are the only humans left alive, then our species is probably doomed. I will head over to the colony at first light and tell them what we just learned."

"What if they still won't work with us, Nels? They still think their way will eventually succeed."

"You and I know it never will. We need to use their transmitting capability to send a message back in case the *Mayflower* is returning to Ararat. They need to know that Ararat is not suitable for humans. I just hope someone is there to receive the message. We should have told them years ago."

ABOUT THE AUTHOR

The author and his wife, Judy, at the headwaters
of the Mississippi River in Minnesota.

After receiving a BS in mathematics from Michigan State University, Conrad served three years in the US Navy as communications officer on the USS Austin LPD-4. After active duty, he returned to MSU for an MS in water resource development. He then spent almost thirty years with the US Fish and Wildlife Service in many different positions around the country. After retiring in 1997, he attended law school and received a JD degree from Arizona State University in 2000. He then had an Arizona law practice focused on employment issues and contract matters for several years before moving to Texas where he worked as a prosecutor in San Marcos until 2013. He then retired again and began serious work on this series of books he had been developing for many years. He currently lives with his wife in Show Low, Arizona. He has three grown children, six grandchildren, and (so far) one great grandson.

CPSIA information can be obtained
at www.ICGtesting.com
Printed in the USA
LVHW101120030423
743308LV00002B/65